CHAPTER ONE

16 Years Ago

Pissing off the Voodoo Spirit of death wasn't in anyone's best interest, but that's exactly what Odette had done. When Baron Samedi visited her dreams last night, he'd made it clear what she had to do: free the soul fragments she'd helped her uncle trap and command the spirits to cross over.

Sending the spirits to the other side would be easy; she'd been able to see and communicate with ghosts since she was little. Freeing them from their *ouangas*, the magical jars that contained them, would require the Baron's assistance. She'd done the proper Voodoo rituals to allow the loa, the Ancestral Spirit, to cross to this realm. Now, all she could do was wait for her dad to take her to her weekly lesson with her uncle.

She rolled onto her back and stared at the ceiling fan, following the path of a single blade as it revolved round and round until her stomach soured and she squeezed her eyes shut.

How was she supposed to know her uncle had been

lying to her about the souls? She was only twelve years old for Spirit's sake, and the man was supposed to be her mentor. A bitter taste crept up the back of her throat, and she swallowed it down.

With his looming presence, dark powers, and heavy hand, Odette had been terrified to cross the man, much less question his morals. Now she had to right the wrong she'd helped him commit.

With a heavy sigh, she glanced at the clock and rolled out of bed. Jerking the earbuds from her ears, she shoved the iPod into her back pocket and closed her bedroom door before padding toward the living room. With any luck, Baron Samedi could make her uncle see the error of his ways, and he'd let his prisoners go willingly. Not that luck had ever been on her side.

The irritation in her father's voice as he shouted into the telephone slowed her pace, and she leaned against the wall in the hallway, peering around the corner, hesitating to enter the living room.

"For the last time, Agnes, she's fine with her uncle. She'd tell me if there was a problem." Her dad let out an irritated grunt. "I don't go to mass, but that doesn't make me any less Catholic…"

He pinched the bridge of his nose and shook his head, the gray strands of his curly salt-and-pepper hair glinting in the sunlight streaming in through the window. "I realize I'm no vodouisant, but I was married to one for ten years. Adelaide was your *Mambo* for Christ's sake. If there's one thing she taught me, it's that Voodoo is a *family* legacy. Mathias is the only family Odette has on her mother's side, and until she objects, he'll be the one to train her."

Odette's heart flopped in her chest like a fish in a flat-bottom boat. No one ever told her she had the option to object. Well, after today, she'd be done with her menacing uncle and his questionable magic. If she had the choice, she'd learn from a Mambo, a Voodoo priestess like her mom had been.

She straightened her spine and strode into the living room as her dad ended the call. He started as he turned to her, a flash of guilt crossing his features before he pulled her into a hug. "How much of that did you hear?"

Odette shrugged from his embrace. "Enough. Agnes wants me learning at the House."

"She was your mom's best friend. She worries about you…and the trouble you've been getting into at school. She says children of Baron Samedi need extra guidance or the loa's carefree ways can keep you from succeeding."

"Please, Dad. I'm fine." Odette rolled her eyes. There was nothing wrong with having a little fun every now and then. "Can we go? I've got an important lesson with Uncle Mathias today."

"Oh yeah?" He grabbed his keys from a hook and ushered her out the door. "What's he teaching you?"

Odette waited until she climbed into the seat and buckled her seatbelt before she answered. "It's a…role reversal today. I'm supposed to be the teacher, with Baron Samedi's help, of course."

"Sounds like fun, sweet pea." He mussed her hair, and she swatted his hand away.

She stuffed her earbuds into her ears and cranked up her favorite Beyoncé album, tapping her thumb on her knee to the rhythm. Fifteen minutes into the drive to the swamp, her dad put a hand on her shoulder. She freed one ear and turned the volume down.

"You're okay with getting lessons from your uncle, right? I mean…your mom never mentioned much about him when she was alive, but he seemed thrilled to take you on as a student when I approached him."

She missed a beat in her reply. "Yeah. He's fine."

Her dad nodded absently as he stared out the windshield. "He doesn't practice any black magic or anything scary, right? Everything is on the up-and-up?"

Odette swallowed and gazed out the window. Spanish moss draped from the cypress branches, giving the swamp a creepy horror movie vibe, and a blue heron swooped from a tree to catch a mouthful of bayou water and crawfish.

She couldn't lie to her father, but if he knew what she'd been tasked to do today, he'd turn the car around and take her straight home. Baron Samedi would never forgive her if she didn't take care of this problem.

Wiping her sweaty palms on her jeans, she turned to him. "I don't know about *everything*, but like Mom always said… 'There's nothing wrong with a little *gris-gris*.'"

Her dad glanced at her, smiling wistfully before focusing on the road. Bringing up her mom and all her words of wisdom was the best way to deflect any unwelcome conversation her dad tried to push on her. Guilt gnawed in her gut for manipulating him, but she couldn't refuse Baron Samedi's demands. She owed the loa her life, after all.

After saying goodbye to her dad, she trudged through the front yard toward the rickety old house. White paint peeled from the wooden slats, and a porch wrapped around the entire structure from front to back. A garden overflowed with herbs, some edible, some poisonous, and she made a wide berth around it before heading up the stairs and around to the back door.

With her hand on the knob, she paused and inhaled

deeply, hoping the fresh air would untie the knot her insides had tangled into. The scents of mud and decaying foliage did nothing to calm her nerves. "I'm ready when you are, Baron. Please make it quick."

A heaviness formed in the air behind her, pressing onto her shoulders as the hum of living energy gave way to the void of death. Baron Samedi was ready too.

As she pushed the door open, a chime made of chicken bones rattled from above, and her uncle shuffled into the room, wiping something that looked a lot like blood from his hands. He kept what was left of his curly, black hair sheered short to the sides of his head, and the yellowish tinge of his bloodshot eyes reminded her of rotten eggs burrowing into his dark-brown, leathery skin.

"'Bout time you got here." The deep creases in his forehead turned to canyons as he frowned at her. "I need heron blood, and I had to send Emile out hunting for one instead of you. Come here." He crooked his finger to call her close as he reached for the belt he kept wound on the shelf.

"I'm not late, and even if I were, it's not my fault. It's not like I can drive myself." She crossed her arms, refusing to budge.

He folded the belt in half, gripping both ends and snapping it. "You listen to me, little one. Talking back'll get you nothin' but a bruised butt. You want that?"

She uncrossed her arms and lowered her gaze. "No, sir." She'd faced the wrath of her uncle and his belt enough times to know better now. This would all be over soon anyway. "Can I please see the *ouangas*?"

His smile revealed three missing teeth. "Later, honey. I have a patient coming in who's agreed to let me store a piece of his soul, so you'll get to work your magic soon enough. Now go on out to the garden and fetch me some sage."

Baron Samedi's presence behind her intensified, giving her the courage to let her own power build. She drew on the energy of the spirit realm, concentrating her magic into her words. "I want to see them now."

Her uncle's eyes widened, and he started toward the other room before shaking his head and swinging the belt toward her, the leathery end slapping across her side with a crack. Sharp pain ricocheted through her ribcage, and she squealed.

"Don't you ever try to use your power against me again. You understand?" He shook the belt toward her. "I got plenty more of these lying around."

With a hard exhale, Odette released control, opening herself up to Baron Samedi. Pressure built in her chest, a burning sensation ripping through her veins as the loa took control of her body. Her spine straightened, and her head turned toward her uncle, but she wasn't making herself move. She tried to run, to turn around and get the hell out of that place, but her will had no effect on her movements. She was like a puppet, Baron Samedi her master.

With long strides, the loa carried her past her uncle, and with strength not her own, she jerked from the man's grasp as he tried to stop her.

"You get back here, girl." He followed after her, and she whirled around to face him.

"Baron Samedi wants to see the *ouangas*. Who are you to stop me, *bokor*?" The Baron made her mouth form the words, and though she fought it, she'd lost all control.

Her uncle's mouth hung open, his arms falling slack at his sides before he ducked his head in a bow. "Baron

Samedi? I had no idea it was you. Please accept my apology."

"Why are you stealing souls that belong to me?" Her body should have been trembling, but her voice was strong and confident, not her own.

"Stealing?" He chuckled. "Naw, I'm not stealing. Most of those people are still alive. I'm just holding onto them while they're sick. I'll give 'em back once they heal."

The Baron used Odette's body to grab her uncle's shirt and twist it in her fist. "You've lied to the girl enough. You're not dealing with her right now, you're talking to a loa." She released her hold, giving him a light shove, and her uncle smoothed his shirt down his chest.

"I'm sorry."

"I'm taking them back." She turned toward the *ouangas* and lifted her hands as an ancient energy buzzed in her veins, growing in intensity until she felt like she would explode. Sweat beaded on her forehead, and her muscles cramped like a Charlie horse had overtaken her entire body. *Please, Baron,* she begged in her mind, *it hurts.*

If she'd had control she'd have crumpled to the floor, her desperate screams piercing through the swamp. Instead, she stood tall, focusing the searing, vibrating energy into her palms and throwing it at the *ouangas.*

The first jar shattered, the pieces flying across the room as the soul trapped inside it was freed, the Baron's magic joining it with the living being to which it belonged.

"No!" Her uncle begged. "Don't take them."

The second *ouanga* shattered, the soul swirling into the air and hovering on the ceiling, confusion furrowing its ghostly brow. Though it had been stolen from a living person, the victim had since died, so the soul had nowhere to go.

It would be Odette's job to cross the dead over to the spirit realm if she survived this possession. The Baron called on more of his power, and her blood felt like it boiled in her veins. It was too much magic for a human to endure. Her muscles screamed for relief. Her steady pulse begged to race in her chest, but the Baron kept her under tight control.

She lifted her hand to free the next soul when her uncle grabbed her shoulders, attempting to tackle her. Baron Samedi's otherworldly strength held her still, and she threw her uncle against the wall, holding him there with the loa's magic.

Jar after jar shattered, the living souls exiting the moment they were freed, the dead collecting in a mass by the corner. Her uncle screamed, angry, hot tears streaming down his cheeks as he struggled against Baron Samedi's hold.

As the last of the *ouangas* broke, the ghost joining the others, the Baron's voice echoed in Odette's mind. *Cross them over and go home, child. I'm proud of you.*

The loa ripped from her body, and she collapsed in a heap on the floor. Her muscles felt like pulverized meat, her nerves raw and exposed as she heaved in breath after breath, the air slicing through her lungs like razor blades.

She scrambled to her feet, doubling over as dizziness threatened to force her to the ground. The mass of ghosts glared at her, their anger palpable in the air. All seven of them drifted toward her, their energy converging into one impenetrable wall of hate.

She stepped backward into her uncle's chest, and he gripped her shoulders, throwing her to the ground. Her head smacked the wood with a clunk, and her vision swam. Dropping to his knees, Mathias clutched her throat, tightening his grip until she couldn't breathe.

"You little bitch," he growled between clenched teeth. "How dare you bring your loa here to steal everything I've worked for?"

Stars glittered in her darkening vision as she clawed at her uncle's hands, but he was too strong, her own strength zapped from the loa's possession. If she couldn't fulfill her duty and cross over the souls, Baron Samedi probably wouldn't accept hers.

"Dad?"

Her uncle loosened his grip as her cousin, Emile, stormed into the room, and Odette gasped for breath.

"Get off her!" Emile tackled his father, freeing Odette from his clutches, and she scrambled to stand, panting.

Mathias focused his anger on his son, wailing on Emile like he'd been the one to free the souls. He landed punch after punch, bloodying his son's face until his eye swelled shut.

"Stop it!" Odette screamed, but the men ignored her. Mathias continued pounding on his son, Emile lying motionless beneath his father's rage.

The ghosts advanced on her again, and she threw up her arms. "Stop!"

The spirits froze, and a euphoric sensation swept through her body, making her tingle from head to toe. "Turn around."

The spirits did as they were told. As *she* told them to do, and her heart sprinted. "Stop Mathias." She pointed to her uncle. "Get him!"

The ghosts converged on Mathias, but their essence passed right through him. Odette opened herself to the spirit realm, channeling the energy of the dead through her body and into the ghosts, making the specters' ethereal forms solid.

A burly ghost grabbed her uncle and yanked him off Emile, while a female spirit punched him in the stomach.

A hysterical laugh bubbled up from Odette's chest. These ghosts were hers to command. No wonder her uncle had been so willing to tutor her; she had a power unlike anything she'd known possible, and he had planned to exploit it.

The ghosts continued their assault, beating her uncle until she screamed at them to stop. The burly spirit dropped Mathias's lifeless body to the ground, his head lolling at an unnatural angle. His neck had been snapped.

Oh, no. No, no, no. She didn't use the ghosts to kill her uncle. That's not what she meant when she told them to get him. This couldn't be happening.

She could fix this. She could use the ghosts to… No. No, she couldn't. No matter how amazing it felt to use her newfound magic, she made a promise to Baron Samedi to cross the spirits over, and that's what she would do.

Raising her hands toward the ghosts, she used her magic one last time and called on Baron Samedi to take the spirits. One by one, they disintegrated into the spirit realm, leaving Odette alone with the man she'd murdered and his bruised and bloodied son.

Tears brimmed in her eyes as she dropped to her knees between them, and Emile rolled to his side and looked at his father. Odette followed his gaze and found Mathias's eyes wide with fear, the light in them gone, and a knot wedged in her throat, blocking her sob.

The room spun. A million thoughts raced through her mind, but she couldn't grab onto one. She'd lost control. First with the Baron using her body and then with her own powers. She'd killed a man. Her own uncle.

Lost in her attempt to form a coherent thought, she didn't notice that Emile had risen until he spoke. "Help me bury him."

Her cousin didn't say another word. He lifted his father's torso, Odette took his feet, and they carried the body to the swamp, laying it next to the water's edge. His expression blank, Emile trudged to the house and returned with a cinder block.

Odette wiped the tears from her cheeks and followed him back up the slope, gripping another cinder block and hauling it to the water. The concrete dug into her palms as she dragged the heavy block through the dirt, and she focused on the physical pain, using the sharp, agonizing sensation to ground her, to keep her from getting lost in the tornado of thoughts in her mind.

With a long piece of rope, Emile tied the cinder to his father's body and shoved it into the swamp. As the corpse descended, a bubble rose from the depths, releasing a cloud of steam as it popped on the surface, and Odette's stomach lurched.

Silently, his face unreadable, Emile returned to the house. She followed him into the living room, where he stood by the wall, staring at the chicken bones hanging over the entrance.

"Emile…" She tried to speak to him a few times, but he clamped his mouth shut and shook his head, refusing to look at her. She sat on the couch, chewing her bottom lip and clutching her hands in her lap until the rumble of an engine signaled her dad's arrival.

Emile slammed his bedroom door, and her lip trembled as she darted onto the porch and scurried around the house to the driveway.

"Everything okay, sweet pea?" Her dad smiled as she climbed into the car and slammed the door.

"Fine." She stared out the window as the rickety old shack and all the horrors it contained faded from view.

Odette waited until her dad drove her home and they were safely inside the house before she opened the flood-gates. She told him everything, vowing never to use her magic again.

"Please, Daddy, can we move away? I never want to see this place again." She was done with Voodoo, done with Baron Samedi, and done with New Orleans.

CHAPTER TWO

PRESENT DAY

The sense of foreboding tightening Odette Allemand's throat didn't mean anything. The sinking feeling in her stomach was merely anticipation, and the fact that her heart hadn't beat this fast since the time she'd come face-to-face with an opossum she'd thought was a poltergeist proved this house was worth every penny she'd be paying for the next thirty years. Who wouldn't be excited to own a historic Creole home like this?

Heat clung to her skin, baking her in the summer sun as she peered at her prized purchase. The salmon color of the exterior would be changing soon enough, but the pristine white front porch looked exactly as it would have in its glory days.

Pausing on the second step, she inhaled the sweet scent of the bougainvillea blooming in her new front yard. The familiar perfume stirred nostalgia in her soul, and a feeling of finally being home mixed with the anticipatory emotions swirling through her chest. She had this situation completely under control.

She climbed the next two steps and stood on the front porch. The moving box tucked under her right arm dug into her hip, so she shifted it to her left side and fished the key from her purse.

An oval window of cut glass in the center of the front door provided a distorted view into the darkened foyer. Rays of sunlight spilled across the wooden floor, giving the entrance a warm and welcoming vibe, but she hesitated to step inside.

The nineteenth-century mansion wouldn't have had a door like this in its original condition, and though she intended to restore the home to the grandeur of the 1800s, it wouldn't hurt to make a few modernizations. Maybe the light would help clear out the darkness that followed her around like a storm cloud waiting for the perfect lightning strike to unleash its fury.

"You gonna stand outside all day or are you going inside?" Natasha, a Voodoo priestess and Odette's closest friend, laughed as she ascended the steps, breaking whatever trance Odette had succumbed to.

Pressing her hand to her heart, she spun around. "Sweet Spirits, Mambo, don't do that. You scared me to death."

"You look plenty alive to me." One corner of Natasha's mouth tugged into a teasing grin, and she crossed her arms over her burnt-orange blouse. A matching orange scarf encircled her head, and her dark-brown hair sprouted out from the center of the fabric in tufts, like a potted plant. "You still haven't figured out the meaning, have you?"

Odette let out her breath and forced herself to open the door. "It's a beautiful Creole mansion that I've admired since I was a little girl. There is no other meaning."

"Mm-hmm. You know you can't lie to your Mambo. What's wrong?" Natasha followed her into the foyer.

If you only knew. Gripping the box in both hands, she carried it to the kitchen and set it on the counter. She'd hired a contractor to do the renovations, and she hadn't felt a hint of this ominous dread when she'd opened the house for him last week. But now she was moving in, and that made her more nervous than she cared to admit.

"Nothing's wrong. Once I do a smudging to clear out the old energy and get my altar set up, I'm sure it will feel like home."

Natasha leaned a hip against the counter. "There's something else."

Could the Voodoo priestess sense her emotions in her energy, or was her body language that obvious? Whichever it was, discussing it was pointless. She'd bought this place, and she intended to stay. Straightening her spine, Odette put her hands on her hips. "I'm not thrilled about having to move in before the renovations have even started. Karma should be biting my old landlord in the butt any day now."

"And sending that kind of energy out into the world will bring it right back to you."

Odette crossed her arms. "I'm not the one who promised my tenant an extension on her lease and then changed her mind at the last minute. That's no way to do business, and I'm lucky I have a place to live."

"You can call it luck, or you can admit fate might have plans that required you to move in sooner. That maybe you don't have as much control as you think you do. Everything happens for a reason, and *everything* has meaning. Even this old house. My guess is that it's related to a past life."

She clenched her teeth and took a bundle of sage from her box. Staring at the herbs, Odette whispered, "I would rather not know," before flicking her gaze to her Mambo, pleading with her eyes. Natasha had guided her through several past-life regressions, trying to help her overcome her fears in her present life, and she'd learned more than she needed to know.

Her past couldn't help her with the present, anyway. Her current issues stemmed from this life alone, and she wasn't about to divulge the reasons why. To anyone.

"It will help you understand—"

"I understand enough to know I can't go through that again. Maybe I did live here in a past life, but you know that life ended in tragedy. I don't need to experience it again." She *couldn't* do it again. Reliving the horrific murders of her former selves had left her emotionally drained and physically ill for days afterward. She glanced at her watch. "Would you mind doing the blessing now, so I can smudge and have this place clean when my furniture arrives?"

"Always on a schedule." Natasha gave her a knowing look—one that said Odette would eventually give in and do what the Ancestral Spirits guided her to do, but Odette never gave in. Not anymore.

Closing her eyes, Natasha took a few deep breaths, her body swaying slightly from side to side as she whispered a prayer in Haitian Creole. With a long exhale, she opened her eyes. "I thought you said there weren't no ghosts here."

"I've been here several times since I bought the place. No one has made contact." Not that she'd tried very hard to find any. All old homes held residual spirit energy. Odette could see it if she wanted to, but if she left herself open to the spirit realm twenty-four-seven, she'd never have a moment to herself.

Ghosts were everywhere, all the time—especially in New Orleans—and if they didn't feel the need to contact her, she'd let them be. So long as they weren't malevolent. The bad ones *always* made themselves known. No searching required.

"Did you command the ghosts to reveal themselves? You know some of them can hide."

Her fingers curled into tight fists, her nails biting into her palms. "And you know I will *never* command the dead."

It was the same discussion over and over. Natasha would say she wouldn't have been blessed with the powers if she shouldn't use them. Odette's retort would state the power in question was firmly planted on the black side of magic and she refused to dabble in the dark arts. Her friend would call Odette's ability to command the dead gray and follow up with, "There's nothing wrong with a little *gris-gris*," like her mother used to say.

Natasha opened her mouth as if to continue the argument, but she let out a long sigh and grasped Odette's hand instead. "Open your senses and feel. Someone's here." The priestess closed her eyes again and shook her head. "He's a strong one too; took me some searching to find him, but he's here. Can you sense him now?"

Odette closed her eyes and took a deep, centering breath. Allowing her walls to fall away, she opened her mind and reached out to the energy in the house. The same bumpy, vibrating charge, left behind by the countless families who'd called this place home, hummed around her. The sensation swirled through the house, creating a rough cacophony of energy grating against her senses like sandpaper.

She pushed through the bramble, opening herself even more, but all she felt was the static leftovers of those who lived here before. Natasha squeezed her hand, reminding her to focus, and she gave one more push.

There, in the corner of the kitchen, she felt him. A spirit unlike any she'd encountered before…and she'd encountered plenty. Even when she'd turned away from Voodoo and refused her connection with Baron Samedi, the loa of the dead, Odette could never get away from ghosts. This was the first time in as long as she could remember that a specter had been able to hide itself from her when she'd reached out.

"Will you please show yourself to me?" She opened her eyes, ready to see at least a faint outline of the ghost, but nothing manifested in the spot where she felt him. "Who are you?"

Her chest tightened, and she gasped as a feeling of overwhelming love expanded in her core. The sensation grew, her heart aching at the intensity of the emotion.

"Are you okay?" Natasha released her hand and wrapped her arm around Odette's shoulders.

"He's making me feel his emotions. How is he doing that?" No run-of-the-mill ghost could affect her this way. In her relations with the spirit realm, she always stayed in control.

"What do you feel?"

She sucked in a trembling breath as tears welled in her eyes. "Adoration. He loved someone deeply. And happiness. So much joy."

"I told you he's a strong one. If he has no ill intent, the

blessing of the home won't get rid of him. We'll have to cross him over ourselves."

The happiness and love swirling in her heart converged, slamming into her like a knife twisting in her back. Gripping the countertop, she pressed a hand to her chest. "Betrayal. Unrelenting sadness." The tears of joy brimming in her eyes cascaded down her cheeks in trails of sorrow. "Will you please stop," she whispered, and the ghost released his hold. The emotions dissipated as quickly as they had formed.

She straightened and wiped the tears from her cheeks, grabbing her bundle of sage. "I'm okay. The ghost can stay." Forcing a spirit to cross over…one who wasn't ready to leave…required Odette's magic. The mere thought of opening herself up to that much power made her stomach turn. She rummaged through her box, moving aside the items for her altar, and found a lighter. "Can we begin?"

Natasha's brow furrowed. "Are you sure you want him to stay? You're not an empath, so if he can send you his emotions like that, he can cause you a world of trouble." She nodded to the box. "You've got everything to set up your altar right there. Maybe we should call on Baron Samedi for help."

"No." Her *met tet*, the main loa that guided her, hadn't completely forgiven her for turning her back on him—and the entire religion—when she was young. "I don't want to bother the Baron with this. I didn't sense any hostility from the ghost. It'll be fine." She'd save calling on her guardian Voodoo Spirit for the big things.

Anyway, there had to be a reason the ghost lingered. If she could figure it out, talk to him and get him to cross over on his own, maybe she'd get back into Baron Samedi's good graces. Talking to a ghost, she could handle. That ability was built into her soul and didn't require calling on any dark magic from the spirit realm.

Odette toyed with the purple and black braided bracelet adorning her wrist. Wearing the colors was an act of honoring Baron Samedi, something she should have been doing her entire life. "I'll open the windows if you'll continue the blessing."

"Stubborn as ever, just like your momma was." Natasha closed her eyes and resumed her Haitian prayer.

A familiar pang of longing tightened Odette's chest. Natasha couldn't have been older than fifteen when Odette's mom died, but from the way she talked about her, she'd idolized her.

Pushing the thoughts from her mind, she scurried around the house, opening all the windows—upstairs and down. Cleansing a home required positive energy, and dwelling on the fact that her mom had died saving her life was anything but.

Back in the kitchen, Odette struck the lighter, setting the end of the sage bundle ablaze and then blowing out the flames. She walked the perimeter of her house, fanning the smoke to the four corners and waving it around the windows and doors. "Negative energy be gone. Only peace and love may remain in my home."

The ghost followed her as she and Natasha cleansed each room. She could feel its presence as a solid form, almost as if a living person stood behind her, but when she turned to look, nothing was there. She'd coax him out eventually—no commands necessary. Her ability to communicate with the dead had intensified when she'd returned to her Voodoo roots.

Unfortunately, as her magic strengthened, the black-ness grew in her soul. She had powers no living person should have, and if she lost control of herself, even for a minute, like before… No, she would never let that happen again.

They closed the windows, and Natasha shut the front door, ending the cleansing. "That should do it." She hugged her. "You sure you can handle that ghost?"

"I think I need to." Whomever the dead man had been in life, Odette couldn't ignore the emotions he'd sent to her. Maybe this house called to her because the ghost called to her.

"Then you must." The Mambo picked up her bag. "Some of us are meeting at Rusty's tonight for dancing and drinks. You should come."

"Thanks, but I'm sure I'll be exhausted from unpacking. The movers will be here soon." She followed Natasha onto the porch, avoiding eye contact.

"How much you gonna unpack when the renovations start tomorrow? Come have a little fun."

"I'll pass." When vodouisants, magical beings who practiced Voodoo, got together for dancing and drinks, the epic party lasted into the early morning. Odette had things to do. Responsible things, like getting to work on time and making sure her company ran in tip-top shape.

Natasha chuckled. "If Baron Samedi hadn't told me he was your *met tet* himself, I wouldn't believe it. What child of the Baron doesn't like to let loose?"

Most vodouisants reflected the personalities of their *met tets*, their deep connections with their guardian loa affecting every aspect of their lives. Known for his antics, his love of sex, rum, and cigars, and his gyrating dance moves, Baron Samedi's personality was the exact opposite of Odette's.

"People go to bars to meet other people, which is

exactly what I'm trying to avoid. Falling in love will end with a horrific murder that I'd rather not experience in this life if I don't have to. It's happened enough in my past lives." She shivered at the memories. After her fourth past-life regression revealed the same gruesome ending, she'd resolved to spend her life alone. It was her only chance at making it past forty.

Natasha gave her a sympathetic smile. "Some people go out to spend time with their friends. If anyone hits on you, I'll shoo him away."

She sighed. "There's also the *other* reason."

"Letting loose and having a little fun ain't gonna turn you evil—not that you have an ounce of evil in your soul, whether you believe it or not. Your powers are strong because you can handle them. Your *met tet* has faith you won't use them for nothing but good. You should too."

She forced a smile. "Maybe next time."

"Between my hair salon and running the Voodoo shop, I don't get out much, so I'll hold you to it." Natasha nodded. "Next time it is."

"I said maybe." Odette waved as Natasha descended the steps and sashayed up the path toward the sidewalk.

Stepping inside, she closed the door, and with a deep, cleansing breath, she opened her senses once more. The blessing the Mambo had placed on the home rid the air of the rough, grating energy, replacing it with soft warmth… a clean slate. Well, except for the ghost hovering in the corner.

Odette put her hands on her hips and stared at the area where she sensed him. "I'm willing to listen whenever you're ready to talk."

As she shuffled to the kitchen, that same over-whelming feeling of utter adoration expanded in her chest, making tears brim in her eyes. Whomever this guy loved in life was one lucky lady, but if Odette didn't put up some barriers now, he might figure out a way to take advantage of her.

She picked up the extinguished sage and waved it in his direction. "Will you please stop that. Right now." The sensation dissipated, rolling away from her and into the invisible entity. "Let's get one thing straight. I don't want you to force your feelings on me, understand? I'm not an empath. I don't deal with other people's emotional baggage. If you want to communicate with me, you're going to have to figure out another way. Like with words."

Grabbing her box from the counter, she carried it into the living room and set it on the floor. She smiled at the grand mantle on the enormous wood-burning fireplace. The dark-wood ledge stretched across the entire front of the brick hearth and wrapped around the sides to meet the doorframes on either side. The first time she'd stepped foot inside the house, the mantle had called to her—the perfect place to set up the altar honoring the loa who walked with her.

She glanced at her watch and quickened her pace. The movers would arrive within the hour.

Pulling a deep-purple scarf from the box, she shook it with a flourish and draped it across the front of the mantle. Then she hung the Baron's *vévé*, the spiritual symbol to represent the loa, on the wall behind it. Composed of a cemetery cross, which represented the crossroads, and two coffins, the hand-stitched *vévé* had been a gift from Natasha after Odette's initiation into the Mambo's House of worship.

She continued setting up the items to represent and honor her guardian Spirit: a human skull replica with a top hat and dark glasses, purple and white candles, a small bottle of rum, and a fine Cuban cigar. A string of silver and black Mardi Gras beads completed the altar, and she stepped back to admire her creation. "That's a beautiful testament to my servitude, don't you think, Baron?"

A heaviness in the air formed behind her right shoulder, and a woodsy scent, both familiar and foreign, crept into her senses. She turned, and though she couldn't yet see him, the presence of her resident ghost was unmistakable. "I'm not scared of you. Why don't you show yourself to me?"

The presence drifted closer, until the empty energy of the entity reached her skin. She sensed in her mind an arm reaching toward her, and the sensation of fingers gliding down her cheek raised goose bumps on her arms. For a dead guy, he sure was warm.

Her heart thrummed, and she swallowed the dryness from her mouth. "Who are you?"

A deep, musical voice danced through her head. "Have you forgotten me?"

CHAPTER THREE

JAMES MALVEAUX SCANNED THE CROWD, SEARCHING for the woman of his dreams, but the likelihood of finding someone in a dress that looked like it came straight from the set of *Gone with the Wind* in a crowded nightclub was nil...even in New Orleans.

The DJ played a mix of modern music, the heavy bass line masking the melody so that it sounded more like he stood inside a giant heart beating an irregular rhythm. Bodies gyrated on the dance floor, moving in time to the vibrating tempo, and the scents of alcohol, sweat, perfume, and Axe body spray swirled through the air.

His friends Noah and Cade had wandered off to hit on women, and James would have normally been right in the middle of it, but that damn dream had him so confused he didn't know his head from his tail. The mystery woman was all he'd thought about since the dreams started three weeks ago. Every time he managed to get her off his mind, his wolf would throw her back into his thoughts front and center...as if he'd already claimed her...but how could he claim someone he'd never met?

And that dress… He rubbed at the scruff on his chin. He hadn't planned on attending any costume balls in the foreseeable future, but plans could change.

Leaning an elbow on the bar, he tossed back a double-shot of whiskey and focused on the warmth trailing down to his stomach. He needed to get out of his head and into the moment. Or at least dull the thoughts with a little libation. Unfortunately, it took three times as many drinks to get a werewolf buzzed. His body processed the alcohol at lightning speed, so the buzz—if he managed to get one—wouldn't last half an hour.

"You okay?" The bartender, Nikki, a witch from the local coven, leaned toward him, her shoulder-length earrings swishing as she tilted her head. "You've usually found a date by now." She grinned and popped the top on an Abita beer, sliding it to the man next to him.

He chewed the inside of his cheek. He *should* have found a date by now. "Give me a rum and Coke. Make it a triple."

"Who is she?" Ice clinked in the glass as she filled it.

"Who?"

"The woman who broke your heart." She held up a bottle of Captain Morgan. "The usual?"

James huffed. His heart couldn't be broken when he'd never been in love. He'd never allowed himself to even come close to that emotion. He glanced at the rack of liquor behind her and focused on a bottle with a purple label. A skeleton wearing a tuxedo jacket and a top hat stared back at him. "Is the rum with the dead guy on it any good?"

She shrugged. "The Baron? I like it. The distillery is here in New Orleans. Been around since the late eighties, I think. It almost went under a few years ago, until the owner sent his daughter in to whip it into shape." She poured in three shots and topped it with a splash of Coke before sliding it to him.

Gripping the drink, he focused on the chill seeping through the glass. Beads of condensation formed on the surface, and he wiped them away with his thumb. "You know a lot about your liquor."

"I'm a bartender. It's my job."

He took a sip and swished the concoction around in his mouth. Warm, earthy tones greeted his taste buds, with an undercurrent of cinnamon and some other exotic spices he couldn't place. The Coke added a touch of sweetness to the robust aroma of the rum. He closed his eyes to savor the flavor and took another sip.

Nikki chuckled. "Good, huh?"

He opened his eyes. "I've found my new favorite drink. You said it's called The Baron?"

She held up the bottle. If O'Malley's didn't stock it, he'd have to convince the pack's headquarters to start. Where had this delicacy been all his life? "The woman who runs it now...do you know her name?"

"She's a vodouisant, and everyone calls her the Baroness. She comes from money, and she runs a tight ship." She leaned in closer. "I've heard rumors that some kind of black magic was involved. Baron Samedi is the Voodoo god of death, after all. I don't know much about Voodoo, but why would you dedicate your business to death? Sounds dangerous to me."

He took another sip of his drink. "Sounds like my kind of woman."

Nikki arched an eyebrow. "No offense, but a woman like that wouldn't bat an eye at a werewolf construction worker. You wouldn't have much to offer someone who's made a deal with the devil."

He straightened his spine. "I've got plenty to offer. Werewolves are known for our stamina."

She snorted. "Was that supposed to be a reference to your prowess in the bedroom? If so, you'll have to forgive me. The only wiener I'm interested in is the kind that's smothered in creole mustard and comes on a bun." She returned the rum bottle to the rack and nodded at something behind him. "Speaking of vodouisants. There's the Queen herself."

James turned to find Natasha, the Mambo of the biggest New Orleans House of Voodoo, waltzing through the door, followed by six other vodouisants.

"I bet she'd know who the Baroness is," Nikki said.

James downed the rest of his drink and slid off his seat. His head spun as the buzz he'd been so desperate for finally fogged his senses. His interest in the distillery owner dissolved as he strode toward Natasha. He had another question for the Mambo.

He waited until she finished saying hello to a woman near the bar before offering his hand to shake. "Hi, Natasha. I'm James Malveaux. It's nice to finally meet you."

She accepted his outstretched hand and paused as his magical signature registered on her skin. "Werewolf?"

He nodded. "I need your help."

"You've visited my readers at the temple a few times. I remember seeing your name on the books. Did they not answer your questions?"

He raked a hand through his hair and tried to collect his muddled thoughts. "They did. Kinda. Not really, but I've been having these dreams…"

"Why don't you stop by the temple tomorrow around seven, and I'll read your cards?"

His heart sank. "Yeah. Okay, I will." He blew out a breath and shoved his hands in his pockets, kicking a flattened plastic cup toward a trash can.

Natasha sighed and motioned for him to follow her. She disappeared into the crowd, and he stumbled around the patrons, catching up to her as she went out the back door.

Two wrought-iron tables occupied the small, grassy area of the courtyard, and a cobblestone path led to a separate building that housed a storage area for the club and the restrooms. A thin layer of wispy, white clouds stretched across the crescent moon, and pale stars twinkled in the midnight sky.

The humid, summer air clung to his skin, and the vibrating bass from the club muffled, giving his ears a reprieve from the incessant noise as he strode deeper into the courtyard.

Natasha settled into one of the metal chairs and gestured for James to take the other one. As he lowered into the seat, she chuckled. "Your eyes match your shirt."

He glanced at his pale-blue button up. "I've been told I look good in blue."

"My Spirit Guides approve."

"Spirit Guides?"

She nodded. "They're the reason I'm out here, about to give you a reading, instead of having drinks with my friends."

Thank goodness for Spirit Guides, then. "What else did they tell you?"

"That I should talk to you. What have you seen my readers about?"

He swallowed and glanced up as two women, walking arm-in-arm, disappeared into the restroom. Talking to a vodouisant in the privacy of a reading room at the temple had been hard enough, but to spill his guts out here in the open? He wiped his sweaty palms on his jeans.

"You don't have to be embarrassed; I won't tell a soul. We take our readings seriously."

He ran a hand down his face. How could he explain this without sounding like a complete wuss? "I'm having these dreams about a woman, and…" Heat crept into his cheeks, but he couldn't tell if it was embarrassment or the alcohol. He blew out a breath and looked into the Mambo's eyes. "I feel like I love her. My wolf does anyway. It feels like he's claimed her."

She arched an eyebrow. "*Claimed* her?"

"It's a werewolf thing. My wolf wants me to take this woman as my mate. He's telling me she's my fate-bound… my soulmate. But I've never met her. I don't even know if she exists." Saying it out loud made it sound more ridiculous than it already was. His wolf *couldn't* claim a woman he'd never met. It wasn't possible.

"Mm-hmm." Though her tone sounded doubtful, with her blank expression, the woman was impossible to read.

"Anyway, all the readings have said the same thing. That I have to *break the cycle*, but I don't know what the cycle is. I just want to know who this woman is. My wolf won't rest until I find her."

Natasha held his gaze for what felt like an eternity. His buddies inside must have been looking for him by now, but he *had* to hear whatever the priestess had to say.

He'd been perfectly happy living his life as a bachelor, seeing a woman a time or two and then ending it before any emotions had time to bloom. He'd been counting on his wolf to let him know when it was time to settle down. Mating with anyone but his fate-bound was out of the question. If fate didn't have a specific mate in mind for him, he'd rather stay single for the rest of his life. He'd seen what could happen to a werewolf who mated with someone fate didn't choose. His dad was a broken man because of it.

Natasha inhaled deeply and swayed slightly, almost as if she were slipping into a trance. Then, she straightened her spine. "Let me see your hands."

Reaching across the table, he placed his hands palm up in hers. Her magical energy pricked at his skin as she gazed at the place where his right pinkie finger should have been.

"I thought werewolves were fast healers."

He fought the instinct to jerk his hand away. He'd been asked that question so many times, he'd lost count. *Most* werewolves were fast healers. "We can't regrow limbs."

"You couldn't reattach it?"

If his body worked like a normal werewolf's, then yeah, he could have. "It got caught in a cement mixer. There wasn't much left to reattach."

She frowned. "This makes sense. My guides told me a piece of you was missing, and here it is."

He ground his teeth, trying to quell his frustration. His buzz was already wearing off, and he needed answers. "What's the cycle people have been talking about, and who is the woman from my dreams?"

With a sigh, Natasha reached into her purse and pulled out a deck of tarot cards. She shuffled them and then offered the stack to him. "Mix them up, and I'll do a quick card reading. Don't expect much though. The alcohol you've drunk is mucking up the waters."

He shuffled the cards and handed them back to her. "I didn't drink that much."

"You've had enough." She turned over three cards and narrowed her eyes at them. "You are stuck in a cycle that needs to be broken. Not just for your sake. There are others involved."

His heart raced. "What's the cycle?"

"It's unclear." She turned over a few more cards. "Your dreams are trying to tell you something."

No kidding. "Who is the woman?"

She turned over another card and frowned. "Also unclear."

"Damn it." He fisted his hands and slammed them on the table.

Natasha arched an eyebrow at him. "If the Spirits say it isn't time for you to know, then it's not time."

"I'm sorry." He opened his fists and folded his hands on the table. Being an ass to a priestess wouldn't get him anywhere.

"I'm sensing an unrest."

He'd never felt more restless in his life.

Placing two more cards face up, she shook her head. "This is bigger than you."

She turned over another card, and his heart sank. The most recognizable card in the tarot deck stared up at him, and he could barely force the word through his tightening throat. "Death."

Sympathy softened her eyes. "In tarot, the death card rarely means literal death. It's the end of one cycle and the start of something new. Whatever cycle you're stuck in, you gotta end it soon."

"But you can't tell me what the cycle is? What I need to do to stop it?"

She stacked the cards and returned them to her purse. "The Spirits ain't sharing that information with me. It could be something you're supposed to discover on your own, or it could involve another person, and you'll have to end it together." She rose to her feet. "Or it could be the alcohol. The waters around you are murky. Come see me when you're sober, and we'll try again."

"Thank you."

She bowed and shuffled into the club. With his elbows on the table, he held his head in his hands. That wasn't what he'd wanted to hear. And the fact that the Mambo, the most powerful vodouisant in New Orleans, couldn't give him any new information didn't make him feel any better about his problem.

Natasha was right when she'd said a piece of him was missing, but it wasn't his finger like she thought. He'd always felt that way, even before he'd lost it in a construction accident. A piece of him was missing from somewhere deep in his soul. He'd never felt whole, and he blamed it on his mother. If she'd been around more, maybe he wouldn't be so opposed to love and his wolf wouldn't have claimed an imaginary mate.

His mom had cheated on his dad more times than he could count. Probably a lot more than James was aware of, since it started when he was a kid. There was no guarantee that a werewolf would find a fate-bound, so many chose to mate with whomever their human side fell in love with, rather than waiting to see if their wolves would bond with anyone. His dad mated with the first woman he fell for, and look how that worked out for him.

James shook his head. A fate-bound mate would never cheat, and he wouldn't settle for anything less.

Of course, his mom being human didn't help his circumstances either. He was already slow to heal because he only had his father's magic running through his veins. Maybe his human side made him incapable of finding his fate-bound too.

"There you are, man. I was starting to think you jetted on us." Noah, a second-born were with auburn hair and dark-brown eyes, sauntered into the courtyard. "He's out here," he called over his shoulder to Cade. With a flick of his wrist, Noah dragged the chair through the grass and plopped into it.

James glanced through the doorway, but luckily no one had seen his friend's display. "Are you drunk? Don't use your power where people can see."

Noah grinned. "I checked. No one saw." Second-born werewolves lacked the ability to shift, but most of them had some sort of psychic power. Telekinesis was a rare talent for a were, and Noah's cocky attitude about it grated on James's nerves.

"It's not parlor magic; it's a unique werewolf gift. Don't flaunt it like it's cheap."

"When did you become a grumpy old fart?" Noah crossed his arms.

When indeed?

"Cade's holding down the fort in there. We met a group of three, and they're up for leaving the club. We need you."

A quick glance inside revealed Cade standing near the doorway, a mug of beer in one hand, his other arm wrapped around the waist of a tall blonde. Cade's own blond hair had that mussed, just-got-out-of-bed look, but

James knew better. He'd seen the amount of hair products his friend used to make himself look thrown together.

James held in a groan. With his buzz gone, he wasn't in the mood to play wingman. "You can handle two, can't you?"

Noah narrowed his eyes. "What's wrong with you? You—"

"Hold on." James inhaled deeply, and the distinct scent of rotting garbage and death assaulted his senses. "You smell that?"

Noah sniffed. "Is that...demon?"

He rose to his feet. "Sure smells like it. Get Cade."

James crept toward the back of the courtyard and glanced at his friends. When Cade didn't respond to Noah's shout, Noah flicked his fingers, making Cade spill his beer down the front of his shirt.

"Goddammit." Cade stormed out of the club, but he stopped short, his nostrils flaring. "Why didn't you tell me we were going hunting tonight?"

They flanked James on either side and slinked out of the courtyard and into the alley between two clubs. A two-foot-tall dark mass darted behind a dumpster, and James ran toward it. The fiend leaped into the trash container, and a rancid wad of rotting meat flew out, slapping James in the face. He wiped the slimy substance from his cheek and stood on his toes to peer inside the dumpster.

An array of garbage and empty beer bottles hurled from the container, and James sidestepped around the spray.

"What the hell?" Noah used his telekinesis to slam the dumpster lid shut and held it closed as the tiny demon knocked against it, trying to escape. "What is it?"

James shook his head. "Some kind of lower-level

demon. I'd guess it answers to a bigger master, but this is the only one I can sense." He scanned the alley, finding it empty.

"What's the plan?" Cade asked.

"Check the alley entrance. When we're clear, shout. Then Noah will release the lid, and I'll shift and take it out."

"You sure, man?" Cade made his way to end of the alley. "Shifting in the city is against the rules."

"When have I ever cared about rules?"

"Inside, when I…" Noah laughed. "All right, maybe you're not such an old fart after all."

"Clear," Cade shouted.

James tensed, calling his wolf to the surface. He looked at Noah. "On three."

Noah nodded. The demon thrashed inside the bin, denting the side of the container from the inside.

"Three," James shouted.

Noah released the lid, and the fiend sprang from the dumpster. James leaped toward it, shifting in mid-air as the creature bounced off a wall and clamped its razor-like teeth onto his front leg.

James held in a grunt as the demon's teeth met bone, and he bit into its neck, ripping it from his leg and tossing it across the alley.

"Make it fast," Cade said between clenched teeth. "Group of tourists heading this way."

Advancing on the fiend, James swiped a massive paw across its chest, piercing its heart with a claw, and the demon exploded into a cloud of ash. As James shifted to human form, he shoved his hands in his pockets and coolly strolled toward the sidewalk as the group of women came into view. They glanced at the men in the alley and quickened their pace, linking arms as they hurried past.

"That was fun. I told you I'd be a good demon hunter." Noah's grin slipped into a scowl as he nodded at James's arm. "Oh, man. It got you."

Blood oozed from the puncture wounds, trailing down to his wrist, and one of the fiend's teeth had torn a two-inch gash near his elbow. The bite stung, but the bleeding had slowed. He'd heal. Eventually.

Cade sauntered closer, reaching for James's arm. "Do you need medical attention? We could call Alexis…"

He jerked away. "I don't need medical attention, dammit, and I definitely don't need a healer. I'll be fine."

"Are you sure?" Noah cut his gaze between James and Cade. "If I had a gash like that, I'd need stitches."

"You're second-born; I'm not." His voice came out in a growl, and Noah flinched. James might as well have been second-born too, at the rate this wound was healing, but he'd be damned if he'd let his packmates fuss over a little demon bite.

Noah gritted his teeth, crossing his arms over his chest. "Thanks for the reminder, Captain Obvious."

"I…" James let out a slow breath. His old man had warned him not to join the demon hunting team. Hell, his dad wouldn't even let James hunt gators with his friends when he was a kid. *The pack is only as strong as its weakest member,* he'd say. *Never let them know that's you.* But James wasn't a lone wolf. He belonged in the pack, and he refused to be the weakest link.

"Look, it's healing." He held up his arm. The small punctures had already closed, and the gash was beginning to seal. "Let's get out of this alley before someone calls the cops. I'm going to text Luke, and we'll meet him at O'Malley's."

"We don't have to report it to the alpha right now, do we?" Disappointment was evident in Noah's voice. "It's barely past midnight, and if you cleaned up the blood, we could…"

"There could be more out there." James jerked his head toward his Chevy, indicating his friends should follow. "This is what demon hunters do. You want to be on the team, don't you?"

Noah gazed wistfully at the club. "Yeah. Let's go."

They trudged up the sidewalk to James's truck, and he found an old paint rag in the back seat to wipe up the blood. It killed him that his friends saw his weakness like that. If they'd have been in the swamp, he could've stayed in wolf form until the wound closed—and he'd have healed much faster—sparing himself from their sympathy.

He more than made up for his…limitation…with his faster-than-normal shifting speed and his keen demon-hunting abilities. Cade and especially Noah…he outranked them for God's sake; pity was the last thing he needed from the pack. From anyone.

CHAPTER FOUR

ODETTE GROANED IN HER SLEEP AND ROLLED OVER. As a spectator in her dream, she stood on the side of the road, watching the same event she'd been forced to relive in her mind countless times since it happened in real life.

A little girl with shiny black ringlets and freckles across her nose played with a bright-purple ball in the front yard, while her beautiful momma pulled weeds in the flower bed. Odette remembered the scene as if it happened yesterday. The sun warming her light umber skin. The sweet fragrance of bougainvillea drifting through the summer air.

As the girl tossed the ball into the air, she spotted a little boy with blood running down his face across the road. The ball bounced on the grass and rolled into the street, and a car zipped past, catching it beneath a tire and flattening it. Too young to recognize the difference between the living and the dead, the girl called to the boy, *"Are you okay?"* and he met her gaze with fearful eyes.

"He's a ghost," Odette tried to say to the girl in her dream, but her mouth wouldn't form words. The girl stepped off the curb to help him, and her momma yelled, *"Be careful, child."*

The girl turned to see her momma running to her, her face contorted with fear. She pushed her, and the girl tumbled, rolling across the street and smacking her head on the pavement.

Odette's heart raced in her dream. A truck rounding the corner slammed into the girl's momma, the tires rolling over her neck, crushing her. The sound of crunching bone and tearing flesh was so real and loud it echoed in her head like razorblades ripping through her skull.

She wanted to scream. To run to the woman and do something…anything to save her. But there was no saving this woman, even if her feet weren't stuck to the ground in the dream. Odette couldn't save her then, and now she'd been buried for twenty years.

She looked at the eight-year-old version of herself, and her heart wrenched. Young Odette scrambled to her feet, screaming, and threw herself onto her momma's lifeless body.

"No, Momma! You can't leave me!" The little girl sobbed and lifted her gaze to her momma's spirit hovering near her body. The ghost drifted higher, and young Odette sobbed, *"You have to stay with me always."*

Her momma's ghost jerked, obeying the command, and drifted toward her daughter. *"You have to let me go, child. It's my time."*

"No!" Odette said in unison with the younger version of herself, and she covered her mouth.

"You're going to stay with me always," the girl repeated. *"Baron Samedi will bring you back."*

Sirens sounded in the distance, and a crowd gathered

around the girl and her momma's body. A neighbor rested her hand on young Odette's shoulder. *"Your momma is gone, sweetheart. Why don't you come with me, and we'll call your daddy?"*

"No!" Young Odette shrugged away from her touch and stood, blood—her momma's and her own—dripping down her face and covering her dress, making her look as if she belonged in a Stephen King movie. *"She's going to come back to life. Baron Samedi's going to bring her back."*

The neighbors glanced at each other uncomfortably. *"Her body is ruined,"* one of them said. *"If you brought her back now, she'd be a zombie. Is that what you want?"*

"She won't be a zombie! Baron Samedi can bring her back whole like he did me."

"Nobody brought you back to life," another neighbor said.

The paramedics and the police arrived and ushered the on-lookers to the sidewalk.

Tears rolled down the little girl's cheeks, and her hands trembled. *"I died when I was born, and Momma did a ritual for Baron Samedi to bring me back, and he did."*

"Hush, child," her momma's ghost said.

The neighbors whispered to each other, and a para-medic guided young Odette to the back of an ambulance. Another pair of EMTs loaded her momma's body onto a stretcher and covered her head with a sheet.

"Don't take her!" the girl screamed. *"She's coming back to life, just like I did!"*

Odette woke with a gasp, sitting up in bed and clutching her sweat-drenched sheets. Tears streamed down her cheeks, and she pressed a hand to her chest, trying to slow her frantic heart.

A presence gathered in her bedroom, a solid form

taking shape in the atmosphere. Sympathy warmed her chest, and the calming presence moved closer, stopping at the edge of the bed.

"While I appreciate the support, I asked you not to push your feelings on me." She swung her legs over the side of the bed.

The calm dissipated, allowing her to feel the grating, raw emotions her dream left behind. She rolled her neck, stretching the tightness from her muscles. That dream always left her with a headache.

Rising to her feet, she padded across the wood floor and headed for the shower. The entity followed her to the bathroom door, and she paused in the threshold without turning around. "I would appreciate it if you didn't come into the bathroom. Will you please give me some privacy?" She closed the door, and thankfully, the ghost respected her request.

Avoiding the mirror, she stripped and showered quickly. The contractor would be there soon, and she didn't want to keep the alpha werewolf waiting. He seemed like a nice enough guy, but magical beings that strong should never be tested. She emerged from the bathroom thirty minutes later dressed in a black pencil skirt with a matching blazer, and ready for work.

The ghost followed her to the kitchen, hovering in the corner as she brewed her coffee and ate a container of strawberry yogurt. "I wish you would show yourself to me." She looked in the direction where she felt the presence. "It's not fair that you can see me, but I can't see you."

A deep, masculine voice drifted to her ears. "Have you really forgotten me?"

She shivered as goose bumps rose on her neck. "Maybe

I would remember if you let me see you. Or at least tell me your name."

The air in the room grew cold, which was typical when a spirit was trying to manifest. The goose bumps on her arms turned to pin-pricks, and the air around her seemed to thicken. An image wavered before her, the air shimmering like heat coming off a blacktop in the summer.

"Keep trying. I'm starting to see something." A pang of guilt flashed in her chest as she watched the ghost struggle to appear. She could easily give him the power he needed, her own body acting as a conduit, allowing the energy of the spirit world to pass through her and into the specter. Letting go and supplying the power would be easy. Shutting it off was another issue altogether, and she'd learned the hard way not to start something she couldn't stop. Give a ghost too much power, and the consequences would be dire.

After a few more pained minutes, the form solidified, and a man stood before her wearing a dark-gray suit with a vest and pocket watch. He was handsome, with fair skin, a strong jaw, and bright-blue eyes, but his clothing and the style of his light-brown hair were reminiscent of the early 1800s. Definitely not someone she knew when he was alive.

"That's better. Can you tell me your name?" She waited as the ghost opened his mouth a few times to speak, closing it again when no sound would form. "That's okay; becoming visible zapped your energy, which is normal. You probably haven't shown yourself to anyone in a long time, have you?"

The man shook his head.

"Are you stuck here?"

His brow furrowed, and he looked at his surroundings

with a confused expression. Lifting his shoulders, he turned his palms up as if to say he didn't know.

"That's okay. We'll figure it out together. Most people won't be able to hear you speak, but I can. Direct your energy to your voice so you can tell me your name."

The spirit stiffened, his eyes widening as his mouth opened. "My name is Nicolas. How did you do that? You told me to speak, and I felt...compelled to." He drifted toward her, stopping a few inches in front of her.

Taking a step back, she swallowed the bile from the back of her throat. She'd accidentally given him a command. That was worse than giving him energy.

Nicolas smiled. "It's wonderful to speak to you again, *mon cher*."

Cher? Who did this guy think she was? "Listen, Nicolas. I'm glad you're talking now, but I have some men on their way over."

He tilted his head.

"Construction workers. I'm having the home restored to its original state, and I would appreciate it if you left them alone. Will you please make yourself scarce when they're around, so they don't get scared?" Not that she thought werewolves would be scared of ghosts, but there could be humans on the team.

The ghost's smile returned, and he reached a hand toward her. Curling a strand of hair around his finger, he slid the back of his hand down her cheek as he released the lock. "You look different."

Her breath caught at his tender touch, the warmth of his non-existent skin making her shiver. She had so many questions for the ghost, but with the contractor about to arrive, she didn't have time to deal with him now.

Clearing her voice, she took a few more steps away.

"Right. Well, we all change. I have to get some work done, so if you don't mind, maybe we can talk some more this evening when I get home?"

The ghost opened his mouth, but he could only emit a tiny squeak, like air releasing from a balloon. His form faded, the energy he'd expended to say those few words taking its toll. Confusion clouded his eyes, and he dissipated.

Odette reached out with her senses, but he'd gone wherever it was that Earth-bound ghosts went, leaving her alone. Settling at the kitchen table, she fired up her laptop and logged into her work e-mail in an effort to make a dent in her inbox while she waited for her contractor to arrive.

As James sauntered through the door into O'Malley's Pub, a curtain of crisp air blasted his skin. Shaded lights hanging from exposed beams cast a smoky glow over the bar, even though no one had been allowed to smoke indoors in the last ten years.

He slid onto a barstool as Amber, the alpha's sister, poured him a cup of black coffee. Clutching the mug in both hands, he inhaled the rich aroma and took a sip. "Are you picking up on anything new? Any more little monsters for me to chase?" After he'd reported the incident to Luke last night, they'd patrolled the city for hours and found nothing.

Her brow furrowed. "The feeling is muddy, but I think you're going to be fighting more evil soon. There's…" She shook her head. "Something is going to happen, but I don't know what."

"I'll be ready." He winked, and she gave him a curious look, tilting her head. He didn't dare ask the next question dancing on his tongue.

As a second-born were, Amber had the ability of empathic premonitions. She felt things about the future, but she rarely picked up on details. She'd already told James she sensed change in his future...of the romantic type... but it seemed that change would be his wolf trying to claim a dream woman he'd never meet. And if the modern-day Voodoo Queen of New Orleans couldn't help him solve his problem, he was up shit creek without a paddle.

Amber opened the coffee maker and put in a fresh filter. "Luke's not in yet. Do you want breakfast while you wait?"

"Nah. I'm good."

A high-pitched giggle emanated from the sidewalk outside and turned into a squeal of delight as the door opened. Emma, a seven-year-old were with dark hair and hazel eyes, darted inside, and her mom, Bekah, sighed as she followed her.

Emma scrambled onto a barstool, but the joy on her face transformed into a scowl as she glared at Amber. "Where's Uncle Chase?"

"That's rude, Emma." Bekah stood behind her daughter. "You should say hello first."

The girl rolled her eyes. "Hi."

Amber laughed. "Hi, Emma. Chase had to help Rain in the bakery this morning. He'll be in later."

"Sorry, kiddo." Bekah took Emma's hand. "Maybe we can see him this afternoon."

Yanking her hand from her mom's grasp, Emma crossed her arms. "We'll wait."

"No, we won't. You have to go to school."

The girl's shoulders slumped. "Please, Mom. I haven't seen Uncle Chase in a week."

"We've all been busy." Bekah tried to tug her off the stool, but Emma gripped the edge of the bar.

"I'm not leaving until I see Uncle Chase."

"Hey now." James sauntered toward her and sank onto a stool. "Don't you know what happens to kids who don't listen to their moms?"

Emma cut him a sideways glance and pouted. "They get in trouble."

"Worse than trouble. The Rougarou knows when kids are misbehaving, and he'll wake up from his deep sleep in the swamp to come and *get you*." He tickled her ribs as he said the last words, and she squealed.

"I'm not afraid of the Rougarou." She grinned.

James crossed his arms. "No? Why not?"

"Because *you're* the Rougarou." She tried to tickle him back, but her fingers caught his arm instead.

He chuckled. "I'm not the werewolf boogeyman. Do I have red eyes and fangs?"

Her smile faded. "No."

"You've seen me shift. Do I have a wolf's head on a man's body, or am I a full wolf?"

Her little brow furrowed. "You're a full wolf."

"I don't sleep in the swamp either. So how could one of your packmates be the Rougarou?"

Her eyes widened, and she slid to her feet. "I'm ready to go to school, Mommy."

Bekah held back a laugh as she waved goodbye and led Emma out the door.

Amber shook her head, fighting her smile. "You

shouldn't scare her with made-up stories about a werewolf boogeyman."

"Why not? My dad scared me with it when I was a kid. It's a rite of passage." He picked up his mug and drank the rest of his coffee as Luke sauntered through the door.

At six-foot-four, Luke stood two inches taller than James—the biggest wolf in the pack, like an alpha should be. His light-brown hair was tied back in a band, and he carried a tablet computer beneath his arm.

James chuckled. "I can't believe I beat the alpha to work."

Luke fought a grin. "I was…distracted this morning." And by the gleam in his eyes, his mate had something to do with the distraction.

Longing tightened James's chest, adding another layer of unwanted emotion to his inner battle with his wolf over a woman he'd never met, who might not even exist.

Sliding onto a stool, Luke tapped the screen of his tablet. "I wanted you to go to the new site with me on Esplanade today. The owner wants to restore the house to its original state."

"Those are my favorite."

Luke nodded. "Mine too. But we're running behind on the Ursulines project, so I need you there to pick up the slack."

Damn. He'd much rather work on a restoration than the modernization they were doing to the building on Ursulines.

"Mmm…" Amber tapped a finger against her lips. "I feel like James needs to go to Esplanade."

Luke arched an eyebrow. "Details?"

"I feel like both good and bad things will happen if he

goes." Her brow scrunched. "But there will be a disaster if he doesn't."

Luke paused, cutting his gaze between his sister and James. Then, he typed on his tablet screen and nodded. "I sent you the details. Read through it before you get there, and have her walk you through the house to confirm everything she wants done."

"Got it, boss." A drip of adrenaline rolled through James's veins…just enough to clear his head and straighten his spine. He'd get to work on his favorite kind of project, and there was the possibility of impending doom. His day kept getting better.

The alpha looked at his sister. "Does this feeling have anything to do with the change you've been predicting for him…female-wise?"

"Possibly." She refilled James's cup. "But I'm feeling good and bad things, so be careful."

Luke squared his gaze on James. "No sleeping with the client unless you plan to take her as your mate."

James choked on his coffee, spewing it across the bar. "I've never slept with a client."

With his hand on the bar, Luke paused, narrowing his eyes before rising to his full height. "Something tells me this time might be different."

CHAPTER FIVE

JAMES PARKED ON THE CURB IN FRONT OF A SALMON-
colored two-story mansion on Esplanade. Four steps led
up to a wrap-around front porch, and a dark-wood door
framed an oval cut-glass window. White columns held up
the second-story gallery, where two doors on either end of
the house were painted white.

The colors were wrong. The doors were wrong.
Shaking his head, he pulled up the file Luke had sent him.
The corners of his lips tugged into a smile as he scanned
the document. Everything the owner had requested accu-
rately portrayed what it would have looked like in its nineteenth-century prime.

He chuckled. This particular house had always been
his favorite. Since he was a teen, his dream had been to
own the place, but he didn't even know the property had
been for sale. Not that he could have afforded the two-
million-dollar price tag attached to it. Being in charge of
the renovation would have to suffice.

Scrolling to the top of the document, he glimpsed the
owner's name. Odette Allemand. *Hmm.* He'd known an

Odette once, a long time ago. He hadn't seen her since seventh grade when she'd moved away, and she'd hardly spoken to him...to anyone...in junior high. A strange flush of excitement rolled through his veins. How many Odette Allemands could there be?

He slid out of the truck and tucked his phone into his pocket. Slamming the door, he paced up the walk and climbed the front steps, wiping his palms on his jeans.

He knocked and held his breath. The sound of heels clicking on the wooden floor emanated from inside, and a tall silhouette appeared in the glass oval.

She opened the door halfway and gave him a once-over with her gaze before speaking. "Can I help you?"

His throat thickened, making it hard to force out an answer. This was the same Odette from his childhood, but she'd grown into a stunningly beautiful woman. She wore a black skirt that stopped two inches above her knees and a tailored black blazer with a purple silk shirt beneath. Her black hair hung in ringlets down to her shoulders, framing her delicate face, and the same sprinkling of freckles across her nose that had made his heart race in junior high accented her light umber skin. Her dark eyes narrowed as she waited for him to answer.

He cleared his throat. "Odette?"

"Yes?"

"I'm James. We had a few classes together in school. I..." *Damn it.* His heart raced, and his palms were still sweating. He never got nervous around women, but that was exactly what this unwelcome emotion felt like.

She gripped the door handle, probably ready to slam it in his face if he didn't get his act together. "What can I do for you, James?" Her brows lifted, and she pressed her lips together, her expression indifferent.

She didn't remember him. Or if she did, she didn't care. The sting of rejection brought him out of the past, reminding him why he had come here. "I'm with Mason Remodeling. Luke had to attend to an emergency at another site, so he sent me to finalize the details with you this morning."

She glanced at his truck on the curb, squinting as if trying to read the magnetic sign on the side. Seemingly satisfied, she opened the door fully. "Welcome. Come on in."

He stepped through the threshold, and she closed the door. The size of the floorboards indicated the wood was original to the house. The previous owner had kept it in excellent condition, though it shined more than it would have in the nineteenth century. A modern, chrome light fixture hung in the foyer, but the switch was off, allowing the morning sunlight cascading in through the windows to light the room.

"I was hoping you could show me the place, so we can go over any last-minute changes you might want to make."

She blinked at him, her gaze sweeping down the length of his body before meeting his eyes. "I don't want to make any changes. I want this house as close to the original as possible. All of the paint and wallpaper selections are based on that." She glanced over his shoulder with a curious expression.

He turned to see what she was looking at, but an empty room was all that lay behind him. He raked a hand through his hair. "Do you mind if I have a look around myself, then? So I can make sure everything Luke wrote up is clear?"

She glanced behind him again and gave her head a tiny shake. Confliction sparked in her eyes before she let out a sigh and relaxed her posture. "I suppose I have a few minutes to show you around before I leave for work. Are you starting today?" She turned and headed for the kitchen. "This way."

He followed, allowing his gaze to focus on her swaying hips for a moment. An image of the woman from his dreams flashed behind his eyes, like it had been doing every time he'd seen someone who piqued his interest for the past three weeks. But this time, the picture of whom his wolf wanted didn't kill his libido instantly.

Instead, a confusing mix of attraction and longing drew his wolf to the surface, and if he didn't know any better, he'd say it felt an awful lot like his wolf was considering Odette a possible mate. His chest warmed at the idea, his mouth curving into an involuntary grin.

Whoa. Put the brakes on, man. He wouldn't consider anyone a potential mate until his wolf told him it was ordained by fate, and there was far too much confusion swirling through his mind. Fate didn't get confused, and werewolves only claimed one fate-bound mate.

He hadn't been laid in over a month. That's all it was. Feeling sexual attraction to anyone but his dream woman had taken him off-guard. And sexual attraction was all this was. It was all it would ever be.

James wiped the thoughts from his mind and focused on the architecture. The modern kitchen had an island and stainless-steel appliances. Granite countertops reflected the recessed lighting, and the cabinets had chrome handles and glass fronts.

"I realize some of the amenities of this home didn't exist in the early eighteen hundreds." She reached for the sink and opened the tap. "But I would like to hang on to the modern luxuries of indoor plumbing and air conditioning."

"I can't blame you." He looked at the notes Luke had written. They'd be changing out the cabinetry and lighting, but the appliances and all the plumbing would remain intact.

She led him through a few more empty rooms downstairs, and his breath caught when he spotted the altar she'd set up on the fireplace. A skull with a top hat and lots of black and purple items occupied most of the space. He stepped toward it to have a closer look, but she cleared her throat and motioned toward another room.

James had learned a little about Voodoo over the years, but the religion, and the people who practiced it, remained shrouded in mystery. She obviously wasn't open to questions, so he followed her into the next room. A queen-sized bed sat against the far wall, and half a dozen moving boxes were scattered about the space.

"All this room needs is a coat of paint, so I'm using it as my bedroom until the renovations are done and I can finish moving in." She held his gaze with another curious expression before strutting toward the door.

The back of her hand brushed his on her way out, and her magical signature tingled across his skin, sending a jolt straight to his heart. *Get it together, man.* Just because his wolf didn't revolt at the thought of being with this woman, it didn't mean anything. That strange stirring in his soul was not his beast attempting to claim a second person. It wasn't possible. Anyway, she was a client, so she was off limits.

Unless he planned to make her his mate.

He shook himself, stopping the ridiculous thought before it could wriggle any further into his mind. If he slept with her, the feelings of attraction would dissolve, and he'd turn tail and run like he always did. Until he figured out how to break whatever cycle he was stuck in, and either find the dream woman or convince his wolf she didn't exist, he was screwed.

Odette showed him the upstairs, and he glanced at Luke's notes. Everything was crystal-clear as he'd expected from the alpha. They returned to the room with the altar, and she turned to him. "Any questions? I need to get to work."

"You don't remember me, do you?"

Her expression softened, but as she parted her lips to answer, something slammed into his chest, knocking him off his feet. The air *whooshed* from his lungs as his back smacked into the hardwood floor, and he skidded across the room. The side of his head slammed into the brick fireplace, and the room spun before everything went dark.

"James!" Odette raced toward him. "Nicolas, stop it! Get out of him." Reaching with her mind, she grabbed hold of the ghost invading James's body and ripped him out, throwing the entity across the room. She dropped to her knees next to James. Placing her hand on his chest, she relaxed at the gentle up and down motion of his breaths. The bloody gash on his forehead was already healing, and she rushed to the kitchen, grabbed a clean dish towel, and returned to his side.

She gently wiped the blood from his face and marveled at the way he healed. Anyone else would need stitches and weeks of recovery to mend a wound that deep, but his body took care of itself, the fibers of his skin slowly reconnecting in front of her eyes. Blood oozed from the partially-healed cut, and she dabbed the cloth on his brow to keep it from running into his eye.

Dark lashes fringed his closed lids, and the stubble peppering his jaw gave him a rugged, handsome appearance. His wavy, dark-brown hair was sheared short on the sides and long enough on top to have that messy, care-free look. He was cute in junior high; time had made him downright sexy. His head rolled to the side, and she pulled him into her lap, cradling his shoulders with her hands.

Lifting her gaze to Nicolas, she glared at the ghost. "You will never do that again, do you understand? You will leave him alone."

The spectral figure stiffened as her command took hold of his consciousness.

She cringed as her magic flared in her veins. A magic no living being should hold. Taking a deep breath, she got herself under control. "Why did you do that to him?"

Nicolas began to fade.

"Answer me." Another flush of magic raced through her veins, and she tried to ignore how good it felt.

His figure grew opaque, and his eyes widened. "My home."

The last thing she needed was a territorial ghost attacking the men who came over. Her house would be full of them for the next few weeks until the renovation was done. "This is *my* home now. You can't attack people like that because you're jealous. You are not allowed to do that to anyone again."

Nicolas's brow furrowed, and he disappeared.

James's eyes fluttered open, and she wiped another trail of blood from his forehead. Glancing at her briefly, he lowered his gaze. "Thanks." He reached for the towel, his fingers brushing hers, and his magic seeped into her skin.

Her stomach fluttered at his touch. *Uh-oh.* That was not a good sign. "Are you okay?" She glanced at his hand and bit back her next question. If she recalled correctly, he'd had all ten fingers as a kid, but how he'd lost one was none of her business.

"I'm good." He tried to push to a sitting position, but he clutched his head and lowered back into her lap. "Give me a minute." He gazed up at her. "What happened?"

"That was my resident ghost. He seemed harmless before, so I'm not sure why he did that to you."

He sat up, gripping the towel in his lap, avoiding eye contact as if he were embarrassed. The bleeding on his head stopped, a thin crust of scab sealing the wound. "What did he do?"

"He jumped you." She caught his gaze, and the intense blue of his eyes made her breath hitch. Forcing herself to look away, she shifted to her knees and smoothed her skirt down her thighs. "He was trying to get inside you, but you don't have to worry about him anymore. He won't bother you again."

He gingerly pressed his fingers to his head and winced. Something between a grunt and a chuckle resonated in his chest, and he rose to his feet and offered her a hand up. "How do you know he won't?"

She took his hand and rose to her feet, slipping from his warm grasp as soon as she was steady. "Because I told him not to."

"The dead do what you say?"

She wrapped her arms around herself. "I've always been able to communicate with the dead. To see and hear them." That wasn't a lie. Hopefully, he wouldn't notice she'd avoided the question.

"I see." He looked at the blood on the towel, and a strange expression crossed over his face. Was it disappointment? Disgust? She didn't know him well enough to tell yet.

Yet. As if she planned to get to know him at all. "Here, let me take that for you." She reached for the towel, but he jerked it away.

"That's okay." He shoved it into his pocket. "I'll take it home and wash it and bring it back to you tomorrow."

She started to argue, but he was a werewolf. They had rules about their blood. "I wasn't planning to use it for a spell."

"I didn't think you were, but…" He shrugged.

"I understand." She lowered her gaze, trying to avoid his mesmerizing eyes. She could get lost in them if she looked too long. "I do remember you." She'd recognized him the moment he'd introduced himself, and an undeniable spark had flared in her soul. A fire she'd been trying to extinguish since he stepped foot inside her home. She refused to fall for a man in this life…but James was one hell of a man. Tall, muscular, hotter than hellfire. Sweet Spirits, it was happening.

A tiny voice in the back of her mind whispered, *he's the one,* but she silenced it.

"What do you remember?" He smiled, and her heart melted. Warning bells went off in her mind. She needed to end this conversation now. Tell him she was late for work and walk out the door before the heat building in her core turned into an inferno.

But her feet felt glued to the floor. "After my mom died, when I came back to school, you were the only kid in class who didn't call me…zombie girl." She held his gaze, refusing to allow the memory to consume her. The ravings of a bloodied little girl in the middle of the street had turned into rumors that spread like a prairie fire with a tailwind. Her dad eventually stomped out the blaze, but not before the kids at school overheard their parents' gossip.

"You looked plenty alive to me. You still do." He stepped toward her, and she instinctively took a step back. "Although, when you disappeared in seventh grade, I did wonder… Where have you been all these years?"

"We moved to Alabama. My dad bought a company there, and he needed to be closer to it." She did not need to get into the real reason they'd moved. That was a memory she'd rather forget.

He angled his body toward her, and though his feet didn't move, the distance between them seemed to shrink. "No one knew what happened to you. One day you were at school, and then you were gone."

She laughed dryly. "And I'm sure people spread all kinds of rumors, right? The devil took me back to hell?"

"I've never been one for rumors." He shrugged. "Is it true, though? What happened to you when you were a baby?"

She chewed the inside of her cheek and glanced at her altar. She really should get to work, and that would be the perfect reason to excuse herself from this conversation. But something about being near this man made her want to be closer. The warning bells sounding in her head turned to full-blown sirens, but she felt compelled to tell him the truth. At least a little of it. "I did die when I was born, yes. But my mom didn't make a deal with the devil to bring me back; she prayed to Baron Samedi." She nodded at her altar. "He's the loa of death, and he's in charge of the cross-roads…whom he takes to the spirit realm and who gets another chance at life."

James clutched his hands behind his back and stepped toward the altar. "I've heard of this guy."

She moved next to him, close enough to invade his personal space, but not nearly as close as the fire inside her urged her to be. When he didn't step away, the flames grew hotter. "He's not evil or a demon or anything else people claim. He granted my mom's wish, and he spared my life."

He leaned in closer to the altar, examining the offerings she'd laid on it. "He's the rum god, right? He makes good rum." He grinned and winked.

She laughed. "He's not a god, and he doesn't make rum." Taking a small bottle from the mantle, she ran a finger across the label. "I make the rum to honor him. My parents opened the distillery as an offering to Baron Samedi in exchange for my life. Now that I'm back in New Orleans, I'm running it."

He blinked. "You're the Baroness?"

Returning the bottle to the altar, she ground her teeth. "Only people who don't know any better call me that. Baron Samedi crowned me when he gave me my life back, but I'm not his wife."

"Crowned you?"

"He's my *met tet*. Sort of like a guardian angel. He's the main loa who walks with me, and he gave me my abilities to communicate with the dead."

"Fascinating." He looked at her, an expression of awe softening his handsome features.

Her pulse quickened. The self-preservation instinct caused most people to back away the moment she mentioned her guardian angel was death himself, which was why she rarely mentioned it. "You're not afraid of me now that you know I'm crowned by death?"

He chuckled. "I've never been afraid of death."

She held his gaze a little longer, and the spark she'd been failing miserably at extinguishing grew hot enough to consume her. If the suspicion gnawing her gut was true, he needed to be very afraid.

She'd done everything she could to avoid this. Ever since she figured out her horrific life cycles, she'd steered clear of men to prevent the possibility of falling in love. She needed to squelch the desire burning in her core and get away from this man before her feelings could form into anything more than attraction.

"Right, well, I have to get to work. Is there anything else you need from me?"

He opened his mouth as if to say something, but he closed it again. Sweeping his gaze across the room, he shoved his hands into his pockets. "You're sure your ghost friend won't be an issue?"

She couldn't hide her grin. "So, you are scared of something?"

"I'm not scared, but I'd rather not wake up on the floor again."

"He won't try to jump you." A sense of unease settled in her stomach. Nicolas was strong, and controlling him had been way too easy.

He nodded. "The rest of the crew should be here any minute, and we'll get started. I'll always be the first one here and the last to leave, so I'll lock up if you aren't home. No worries."

"I'm not worried." Not about the renovation, anyway. "Thank you, James."

"My pleasure." His smile could have lit a city block. And the way his eyes crinkled with the curve of his lips had her mouth watering.

Not good, Odette. Walk away now.

She turned on her heel and strode to the kitchen. Shoving her laptop into her bag, she swung it over her shoulder and headed out the door without looking back. So she was attracted to a sexy werewolf. Who wouldn't be? Just because she'd felt a little something for a man for the first time in more than a year, it didn't mean he would be the one to doom her to death. Everything would be fine.

CHAPTER SIX

ROLLING HIS NECK TO STRETCH OUT THE SORENESS, James shuffled into the living room. He'd spent all day in the house prepping it for the retexturing of the walls and painting, and his shoulders ached from hunching over to tape off the baseboards.

As Odette had promised, the ghost didn't mess with him again, but he couldn't shake the feeling that something was watching him, following him through the house as he worked.

The crew had done their best to steer clear of this room. His men had taken one look at Odette's altar to death, and they'd found any excuse they could to work somewhere else. He couldn't blame them. Voodoo was a mysterious religion, and people on the outside...werewolves included...often misunderstood it. Once she'd explained her reasoning for having the altar, though, it made sense.

James wiped his hands on the towel he'd been carrying all day and peered at the smear of blood on the fabric. After staying wadded up in his pocket, the stain was probably set. He owed Odette a new towel. He wouldn't mind taking her to dinner for the trouble too. Getting to know her.

He scratched his head. His wolf had been dead set on claiming a woman he'd never met, but the moment he'd laid eyes on Odette, his beast started having second thoughts.

Normally, any inkling of wanting to know a woman on a deeper level stopped him in his tracks, warning him it was time to move on. If his wolf wasn't on board, he wasn't wasting his time. But as this train of emotion blew its whistle, preparing to depart the station, the beast seemed to have one foot on the train and the rest on the platform. *Make up your mind, buddy.*

Luke would have his ass if he made a move on her without approval from his wolf. Not that she would be receptive to his advances if he tried. Up until that ghost slammed into him, knocking him out, she'd lived up to the rumors he'd heard about the Baroness. Stiff. Proper. All business.

It was a shell though, and he'd witnessed it crack when she'd cradled his head in her lap. She had a soft and tender side, and it intrigued him.

"I have to admit, I was expecting a shit hole." Noah sauntered into the living room, pulling James from his thoughts. "But this place is nice. We'll probably finish ahead of schedule."

"Yeah." James scanned the room, but he couldn't remember why he'd wandered in here.

Odette didn't want anything done to the fireplace, and he could see why. The previous owners had kept it in...or restored it to...its original grandeur. A dark wood mantle lined the exposed brick of the hearth, and with winter lasting all of two or three weeks in the South, the inside was as pristine as if it had never been used.

"That's creepy." Noah reached a hand toward the altar, and the skull and top hat flew into his palm. "It's not real is it?" He turned the skull, and the hat slipped off.

James caught it before it hit the floor. "Put that back, dumbass. It's a religious altar." When Noah didn't move to return the item, James yanked it from his hands and gingerly set it back in place. "Would you go into a Catholic person's house and take their crucifix from the wall?"

"I guess not." Noah leaned in to examine the artifacts. "Is she a devil worshipper?"

"She's a vodouisant, and she has psychic medium abilities. She can talk to the dead, so she honors the Voodoo loa of death."

Noah curled his lip. "Like I said. Creepy."

"She's not creepy. She's…never mind." There was no use in trying to explain it. Odette had close ties with death. Hell, she'd been dead at one time. Most people would find that disturbing, but James had grown up around death. It was part of life.

"At least she has good taste in liquor." Noah reached for the bottle of rum on the altar.

James slapped his hand. "Don't touch that. It's an offering for the loa."

"Not like the dude's ever going to drink it." He rubbed his hand and cut his gaze between the bottle and the skull. "Is that the same guy?"

"Yeah."

"So she's offering The Baron rum to Baron Samedi. Kinda cliché, isn't it?" Noah laughed.

James ground his teeth. His friend's clowning attitude

usually didn't bother him, but when Noah's jokes were directed at Odette, they struck a chord. "She owns the distillery. The whole operation is an offering to the Spirit."

Noah lifted his eyebrows. "Wait. We're working for the Baroness?" He let out a disbelieving huff. "No room for mistakes then, I guess."

"You know her?"

"One of my old man's drinking buddies works there. I've heard stories. She's all business. Dresses like she's on her way to a funeral. Never smiles." He crossed his arms. "They don't even have company picnics or Christmas parties or anything. They go in, get the job done, and go home. Have to save the socializing for their own time."

James furrowed his brow. His friends knew more about Odette than he did—he hadn't even known she was back in town, and that bothered him more than it should have.

Noah grinned. "I recognize that look."

James tried for a neutral expression. "What look? I don't have a look."

"You've got the hots for the client."

"No, I don't."

Noah slapped him on the shoulder. "Whatever you say, man. Better not let Luke know. He'll have you reassigned faster than a topless woman gathers beads at Mardi Gras."

James narrowed his eyes. "I don't have the hots for Odette."

"Then why are you still here? The crew left half an hour ago."

If he were honest with himself, he'd admit he was hoping Odette would come home from work before he left. That she'd show up and invite him to stay for dinner.

Then one thing might lead to another, and… *Damn it.* She was a client. He couldn't think of her that way. "Why are *you* still here?"

"I came in to see if you needed any help patrolling tonight. You're on the first shift, right?"

Crap. After his run-in with the ghost and his strange feelings for Odette, he'd forgotten about his demon-patrol duties. Those little minions rarely showed up alone. "Yeah. Let me lock up, and I'll meet you outside."

Noah paused. "You don't think she's responsible for summoning them, do you?" He nodded to the altar. "I mean…"

"No." He shook his head. "We were friends in school. I know her; she's not like that." At least, he didn't think she was. Really, he didn't know the woman at all. Being acquaintances in grade school didn't count as much of a relationship, and based on the rumors he'd heard about her, she wasn't the sad, scared little girl he remembered. His judgment was based on a feeling he had about her, but unless his wolf put all four paws on the train, it would be leaving the station empty.

"If she is responsible, we'll find out soon enough." James jerked his head toward the exit. "Let's go patrol, and we can hit the club after." With his wolf finally allowing him to notice another woman, maybe he could satiate his desires with someone other than Odette and forget all about his feelings for his client. That would prove his attraction to her was nothing more than the shallow desire of a man for a beautiful woman.

Shoving her key into the ignition, Odette leaned her head

against the headrest and closed her eyes. The cool leather seat pressed into the backs of her legs, and the air freshener stuck to the vent filled the car with the subtle scent of lavender.

Her secretary had fielded her calls, sending through the important ones, while Odette spent most of the workday locked in her office. She'd meditated, but it didn't clear her mind. She'd hyper-focused on the marketing proposal for the upcoming line of white rums, but it didn't distract her from the sinking feeling of dread hollowing out her stomach.

Her prayers to the Baron hadn't been answered yet. Her *met tet* would know if James was the one who'd doom her to a horrific death, but Baron Samedi was either too busy to provide insight, or the question was too big for a simple prayer.

She ran her hand along the soft leather of the console and reached for the key again. Turning it, she started the car, the engine purring to life as she gripped the steering wheel and eased on the gas, exiting the parking garage. Driving along Tchoupitoulas Street, she took in the majestic view of the Mississippi River until she turned onto Poydras and headed into the Central Business District.

Breathing deeply, she tried to keep herself calm as she made a right and headed into the French Quarter to Mambo Voodoo, Natasha's store that doubled as both a tourist shop and a temple. She parked on the curb and walked two blocks to reach the quiet shop. The woody, sweet scents of sandalwood and lotus greeted her as she opened the door, and the tension in her muscles eased. Something about this place always felt like coming home.

"Evening, Cybil." She nodded to the vodouisant manning the cash register.

Cybil tucked a strand of deep-blue hair behind her ear. "Hi, Odette. Natasha's in the back, waiting for you."

She glanced at her watch. The emergency appointment she'd made with her Mambo was set for fifteen minutes ago, but she'd been so distracted that she'd left the office later than planned.

As she stepped through the first threshold, she swept her gaze across the plethora of altars lining the walls, and even more tension slipped from her shoulders. *Vévés* sewn into colorful cloths adorned the spaces set up to honor the loa. Various offerings from tourists and vodouisants alike lay about the altars: keys for Papa Legba, perfume bottles for Erzulie Freda, silver for Damballah, and of course rum and tobacco for Baron Samedi.

She stopped in front of her *met tet's* altar and pulled a cigarette from her purse. Though she'd never smoked one herself, she always carried them to make offerings to the loa. "I could really use some help, Baron." She laid the cigarette next to the skull and closed her eyes, opening her senses in hopes of receiving a message.

But the Baron seemed to be ignoring her. She sighed and shuffled to the back room.

Pushing aside the beaded curtain hanging in the doorway, she found Natasha sitting at her reading table, shuffling a deck of tarot cards. "Sorry I'm late."

"I expected you would be. Sit." The priestess set the cards on the table and folded her hands. "What's so important, child?"

Odette settled in the chair across from her and swallowed the thickness from her throat. She'd had all day to mull over the fact that James might be the one, but saying it out loud, and possibly getting confirmation, had her stomach tied in knots. "I met someone today."

"Oh?" Natasha arched an eyebrow. "Any someone or *the* someone?"

She let out a heavy breath. "I think it might be him. I hope it's not, but there's…something. I feel connected to him somehow, and I shouldn't. I hardly know him; he works for my contractor." She wrapped her arms around herself, clutching her elbows.

"It could be your libido talking. A capable man, who's good with his hands, working on your house. Who wouldn't find that attractive? You've been denying yourself any fun at all for years. Maybe you need to let loose. See where it goes."

"No." She straightened. "I feel this in my bones. Our destinies…our souls are entwined somehow, and if it's because…" Closing her eyes for a long blink, she took a slow breath. "Please, will you do a reading for me? If it's him, I have to make it stop."

"If it's him, I don't think you can." Pursing her lips, the Mambo gave her a sympathetic look. "All right. Let's see if the Spirits will shed any light on it. What's his name?" She slid the stack of cards toward Odette.

"James." The edges of the weathered cards had smoothed from years of use, and a tingle of magic seeped into Odette's fingers as she shuffled them. "James Malveaux."

Natasha reached for the cards but paused, her hand hovering over the center of the table. "The werewolf?"

"Yes. I hired the alpha's construction crew to do the renovations." She slid the deck to the Mambo.

Natasha pressed her lips together and drummed her fingers on the cards.

"What aren't you telling me?" The hollow sensation in her stomach expanded, taking in half her chest.

"Did he mention his readings?"

And there went the rest of her chest, sinking into oblivion. "No. Why? What have you read for him?" Werewolves rarely let their issues leak outside the pack. If James had come to a House of Voodoo for help, it must have been his last resort.

The priestess picked up the cards. "Let's focus on you right now." She turned over the cards, laying out ten in a Celtic cross spread, scrunching her brow, and lightly humming with each addition to the shape.

Tapping a finger on the top card of the deck, Natasha hesitated to turn it over. Odette gripped the sides of her chair, tensing as she waited for her to finish. The look on the priestess's face and her reluctance to display the final card made Odette want to explode with anticipation. This was bad. She could feel it.

Natasha peeked at the final card and locked eyes with Odette. "Remember this card has many meanings, especially for you."

A brick settled in Odette's stomach. She didn't need to look at the card to know what it was, but as she lowered her gaze to the table, a skeleton stared back at her. "Death." Lacing her fingers together, she rested her head on her hands.

"Change." Natasha's voice was firm. "Sit still and give me a minute." The priestess closed her eyes and breathed deeply, swaying from side to side. The energy in the room shifted as she made contact with her Spirit Guides.

Odette held her breath, the hairs on her arms standing on end as the vibration in the air increased. She shivered, and the hollow sensation consumed the rest of her body.

She knew the answer as confidently as if it had been ingrained in her soul since birth.

James was the one. The man she was fated to fall in love with and in whose arms she was doomed to die.

Natasha opened her eyes and smiled sadly.

"I knew it." Odette clenched her trembling hands into fists. "I knew it before I came here. I've known since the moment he knocked on my door, but I was hoping…"

"You hoped I'd tell you otherwise."

Her shoulders slumped as the weight of the realization pressed down on her. "And now, there's no hope. I'm going to die a horrific death, and I'm taking him with me. I wonder what it will be this time? A knife to the chest? A slit throat? I don't think I've been fully beheaded yet. I suppose I have that to look forward to."

"You hush your mouth." Natasha rose to her feet and shuffled around the table. "There's always hope." She tapped the death tarot. "It's inverted, which means you're resistant to the change that needs to happen."

"Of course I'm resistant to being murdered."

"My guides tell me your death isn't the change this means. And James… I've felt an unrest in the air ever since I talked to him. What I learned in his reading makes sense now."

"How so?"

"I kept hearing that he's stuck in a cycle that has to be broken. I thought it had something to do with his past, and it does. Not his past in this lifetime though. He's stuck in the same cycle as you, and the two of you have to break it together."

Odette leaned her elbows on the table and dropped her head in her hands. "We haven't been able to break the cycle in how many lifetimes? Why would we be able to stop it now?"

Natasha shuffled to a counter against the wall and lit a white candle in honor of her guides. "Because you're meant to."

"How do you know?" She leaned back in her chair, dragging her hands down her face. "Did a Spirit tell you that?"

"Why did you move here?"

She shrugged. "It's my home. I missed it."

"You moved away when you were twelve years old. Why come back sixteen years later? Did you really miss it? Or did the Baron call you home?"

She sank in her chair. "You know the Baron called me. His distillery was about to go bankrupt, and I had to turn it around. It was part of the deal."

"That was your momma's deal."

"And I'm honoring it." She sat up straight. "I owe Baron Samedi my life."

"Do you think he would have called you back here if it was gonna cut that life short? He gave you a gift, and he's not gonna see it wasted. You're here for a reason, and that reason is to break this cycle. You're a powerful vodouisant in this life, and James is a werewolf. I think the stars have finally aligned for you, and you can end it."

"I'm not powerful anymore."

"You could be. We need to do another past life regression to see if we can figure out why you're holding back. You'll need to use all the power you have to stop this cycle. We can focus on the house this time. See if—"

"No." Odette shot to her feet. She didn't need to delve into any more past lives to know why her own powers terrified her. That incident occurred in *this* lifetime, and no one could ever know what really happened. Not even her Mambo. "The house is… I think I was drawn to it because of the ghost there. He knows me, and he seems to think I should remember him. I probably talked to him when I was a kid. Before I learned to block them out, I saw ghosts everywhere I went. I probably walked by that house with my mom a lot and saw him then. I'm sure that's all it is."

Natasha arched an eyebrow. "You don't think it's possible you lived in that house in a past life?"

"If I did live there…if I knew the ghost when he was alive…it was the early eighteen hundreds, and I do *not* want to relive that. No more regressions."

Natasha eyed her skeptically. She needed to pull herself together before the Mambo figured out that she already knew the reason she held her powers back. Straightening her spine, she held her chin high. "I'll figure something out. If the Baron called me here to meet James and end this cycle, then that's what I'll do…once I figure out how to tell James."

"I suggest you do some digging into your ghost. I have a feeling he's gonna play a role whether you want him to or not."

"I'm one step ahead of you. He told me his name, and I have one of my interns researching his connection to the house. She'll call me as soon as she has some information."

Natasha nodded. "You ain't alone in this, you know? Whatever the Baron tells you, whatever you have to do, I'm here. The whole House will help you."

"Thank you." She couldn't get the entire House involved, though. It may have been her fate to die a gruesome death life after life, but she wouldn't pull anyone else down with her. "What if I made an offering to Erzulie

Dantor? She can keep me from falling in love, right? That's what she does. Protects women scorned by their lovers."

Natasha laughed. "You're welcome to try, but you haven't been scorned, and James seems like a good man. I don't think she can help you."

"It's worth a try. If I don't fall in love, I won't be vulnerable."

The Mambo shook her head. "I'm going home. Call me if you need me."

Odette strode into the altar room with new purpose. She wouldn't allow herself to fall in love with James. It was as simple as that. She bought a blood-red rose from the gift shop and laid it on Erzulie Dantor's altar. Clasping her hands over her heart, she closed her eyes and offered her prayer to the loa. "Please, Erzulie Dantor, I'm begging you. Guard my heart. Keep me strong. This man will be the death of me if I fall in love."

CHAPTER SEVEN

"Ms. Allemand?" The intern hesitated in the doorway, clutching a folder to her chest. Her too-long bangs fell across her eyes, and she nervously jerked her head, brushing the blonde locks aside. "I have the information you asked me to find."

Odette held up a finger and finished typing the last sentence of her e-mail with her other hand. *It's about time.* She'd given the job to Kathryn, her most promising intern, because she thought she'd be the fastest. But the research had taken her two days to complete.

Peppering the ghost with questions hadn't helped either. The more she'd talked to Nicolas, the more confused he'd become, until he'd stopped communicating altogether. Sadly, he didn't know he was dead until she'd told him.

Kathryn shrank into the hallway and picked at her fingernails. Odette would have to give the girl a lesson in projecting confidence. Too many sharks lurked in the waters of life, waiting to prey on the weak.

"What do you have for me?" She closed her computer

and folded her hands on her desk, giving the intern her full attention, and ignoring the way her heart rate kicked up in anticipation.

Kathryn shuffled through the doorway, sweeping her gaze across the lavender walls before focusing on the mini altar next to Odette's desk. The skulls she used were made of plaster, but word on the company's rumor mill said they belonged to human sacrifice victims. She'd grown accustomed to people fearing her, so she let them believe the rumors.

The intern shivered. "Um…I'm sorry it took so long."

This lack of self-confidence would never do. She'd be doing the girl a disservice if she didn't correct her behavior. "Did I ask for an apology?"

"No, ma'am." Kathryn tightened her grip on the folder, creasing the edge.

"Do I look the slightest bit upset with you?"

She hesitated. "No, ma'am. I'm sorry."

"Don't apologize unless there's a need for it. It makes you seem weak. There are people in this world who prey on weakness. Never allow yourself to be taken advantage of."

"Yes, ma'am. I'm sorry. I mean…" Rather than having her confidence lifted, the poor girl was crumbling.

Odette softened her tone. "Sit down and tell me what you found."

Kathryn nodded and sank into a deep-purple velvet chair across from the desk. "The records are so old they haven't digitized them yet. I had to search through property records and newspapers on microfiche."

"And what did you discover?"

"I found one Nicolas associated with the address you gave me. Nicolas Dubois was a French immigrant and the original owner of the property. He built the house that's there now in 1820."

That partially explained why the ghost was attached to the house, but it didn't account for why the man expected Odette to remember him nor why he didn't cross over when he died. Odette scribbled the name onto a Post-it Note. "Was there any more information on Mr. Dubois?"

Kathryn fought a smile. "Oh, yeah. He was murdered in that house. In his own bedroom."

Odette straightened her spine. Here was the reason his ghost lingered. "Details?"

Opening the folder, Kathryn pulled out a sheet of paper and passed it to Odette. "I found this in the newspaper. His brother, Antoine, had come to visit him one night, and he found him in his bed, decapitated and stabbed in the heart."

Odette cringed. No wonder the poor ghost was stuck. A murder like that would cause anyone to have trouble crossing over. She glanced at the newspaper clipping, but she couldn't bring herself to read the words. "Do they know who did it?"

"Antoine also found Nicolas's house servant, Serafine, in the room. She was hysterical and covered in blood. She came after Antoine with the knife, so he pulled out his own blade and slit her throat."

"I see." A sickening feeling pooled in her stomach. Did the ghost remember any of this? She'd attempted to get more information from him over the past two days, but the poor man had been too confused to answer. Now she understood why. "Thank you for the information, Kathryn. That will be all."

Kathryn scooted to the edge of the chair. "There's more, if you're interested."

She raised her eyebrows. "Oh?"

"It's speculation, passed down by word of mouth, but when the librarian saw whom I was researching, she said there's another story to go along with the newspaper. Rumor has it that Mr. Dubois had taken Serafine as his mistress. She fell in love with him, and when she realized he would have to marry someone else, she murdered him. If she couldn't have him, no one could."

"She loved him." A chill crept through her veins. Was it possible that Nicolas expected her to remember him because *she* was Serafine? No, it wasn't. In her past lives, Odette had always been the one to die first. She died in her lover's arms, at the hands...or claws...of a monster, not a man. And James was to be her lover in this life. A living, breathing man, not a ghost.

Warmth spiraled up her spine at the thought of him. James wouldn't be alive and tempting her if his ghost were haunting her house. Maybe Odette had been another servant for Nicolas. Or perhaps the other woman he'd intended to marry. Who knew?

Armed with the new information, hopefully she could help the ghost to cross over and be done with him. Then, she could focus on the other, much bigger problem.

"Love makes you do crazy things." Kathryn's voice pulled her from her thoughts.

"Is there anything else?"

The intern dropped her gaze for a moment and bit her bottom lip. "I have a question." She briefly looked into Odette's eyes before shifting her gaze to the small purple and black altar. "People say you can talk to ghosts. Is that why you had me research this guy? Did you see his ghost? Is this your house?"

Odette rose and strode around her desk, standing in front of the intern.

Kathryn scrambled to her feet. "I'm sorry. It's none of my business."

Motioning toward the door, Odette paced toward it and gripped the knob. "I appreciate your curiosity, and you're correct, it's none of your business. Thank you for the information. That will be all."

"Yes, ma'am." Kathryn scurried out the door, and Odette closed it behind her.

She turned to her altar and stared at the *vévé* embroidered on the purple flag. Nicolas's mistress had murdered him. She'd been brought to justice…if one could call death justice…so that wasn't the reason his ghost lingered. If he'd been sleeping when she stabbed him, he might not know who killed him.

Maybe that was all he needed—to know the truth about his death—to be able to pass on. She ran her fingers across the soft, purple cloth representing her *met tet*. "Will you take him once he knows the truth?"

Grabbing her purse from her desk drawer, she strode from her office to the parking garage. Excitement tingled in her limbs as she pressed the button on her key fob, and the car chirped. She could finally help the distressed ghost find peace.

———

James parked on the curb and killed the engine, kneading the steering wheel as he stared at the half-painted mansion. The light-blue Odette had chosen for the exterior fit the Creole style as if it had been blue all along.

After spending a few days working inside, he was more than impressed with the structure.

With the crew running ahead of schedule, they'd be finished with the job in two more weeks. James wouldn't be finished with Odette, though. Since he'd met her, his dreams had changed, the sultry vodouisant flitting in and out in place of the nameless woman who'd occupied his mind for too long.

He couldn't bring himself to so much as flirt with another woman—he'd tried…several times—but now it was the image of Odette flashing in his mind that stopped him. He *had* to see her again.

Raking a hand through his hair, he let out his breath in a huff. Leaving his toolbelt in her kitchen was a thinly-veiled excuse to return to her house this evening—he wouldn't need it until morning—but it was all he had.

His wolf had been set on him finding the mystery woman from his dreams, but now the beast didn't know what he wanted. His friends who'd found their fate-bounds made it sound so easy. From the moment they'd met their future mates, they'd…*known*…even if they'd refused to see it at first.

James didn't know. He had too much human blood running through his veins, and his wolf was confused as hell because of it. The beast realized he couldn't claim both women, but that's exactly what it seemed like he was trying to do.

Maybe everything James felt for Odette had come from his human side, and his half-blood nature was what confounded his wolf. "Damn it." The only way to solve this mystery was to spend some time with the woman. He slid from the truck and slammed the door.

82   CARRIE PULKINEN

The scent of the bougainvillea blooming in the flower beds reminded him of the ones his mom had planted at their own house when he was a kid—that two-year stretch when she'd actually stuck around—and the sweet perfume added to the anxiety churning in his core. He climbed the porch steps and knocked, and a curvy silhouette appeared in the window.

Odette opened the door, and his wolf sprang to attention. She wore a black T-shirt and yoga pants that hugged her curves, flaring slightly at the bottom. She was barefoot, and her purple-painted toenails caused his stomach to tighten, heat pooling in his groin as if he'd gotten a glimpse of way more than her toes. He cleared his throat and forced his gaze to her eyes. "Hi."

She tilted her head. "James. I wasn't expecting you. Is there a problem?" Her own gaze swept the length of him, the corners of her lips tugging upward briefly before she flattened them.

"I think I left my toolbelt inside. Do you mind if I come in and look for it?"

"It's in the kitchen. I can get it for you." She regarded him, narrowing her eyes. Damn it, she saw right through his sad attempt at an excuse to see her, and now she'd probably leave him on the porch and get the belt herself. He should have hidden it.

Opening the door wider, she stepped to the side. "Would you like to come in?" She sounded liked she wasn't sure she should have asked, but he wouldn't waste the opportunity.

"I'd love to." He strode through the door before she could change her mind.

Following her into the kitchen, he made himself take in the surroundings...looking at anything but her tempting curves as her hips swayed. "The job's coming along nicely. At this rate, we'll finish ahead of schedule."

She stopped at the kitchen counter and turned to face him. "That's good to know. Do you want something to drink?"

Holy hell, she'd offered him a drink. That meant she was interested. Did he want her to be interested? His wolf sure seemed to. *Say something, dumbass.* He grabbed his toolbelt and set it on the edge of the counter. "Yeah." *Yeah? That's all you've got, Casanova?*

She held his gaze, the moment stretching into what should have become awkwardness, but it didn't. Looking into her dark-brown eyes, he almost felt as if he were glimpsing her soul. His wolf was restless, a feeling stirring in his own soul that he'd never felt before, and he couldn't blame the primal sensation on his human side.

She didn't move as he took a step toward her; she merely inclined her chin, daring him to come closer. A strange energy charged between them, as if the poles of their soul magnets lined up perfectly, drawing them together.

Her gaze cut to the right, and she furrowed her brow. "Please, not now, Nicolas."

James turned his head in the direction she looked, but he saw nothing. "Your ghost?"

"I've been trying to talk to him all evening, and *now* he decides to make an appearance. He hasn't bothered you, has he?" She glided to the opposite side of the counter.

With the safety of the stationary object between them, the moment they'd shared...or almost shared...dissolved. "No, but I think he follows me. I feel like I'm being watched the whole time I'm here, but I'm sure it's my imagination."

"He probably is following you." She took a glass from a cabinet. "He's confused. I think he knows he's dead now, but I'm not sure he comprehends much else."

"That's sad. Can't you help him?"

She stiffened. "I'm trying. You mentioned you like rum, didn't you?" Grabbing a bottle from a shelf, she didn't wait for his response. "We're releasing a new line of white rum this year. Do you want an advance tasting?"

He grinned. "Hell yeah, I do."

Her lips curved into an almost-smile as she poured a sample into the glass and swirled it. "Give it a taste. If you like it, I'll mix a drink for you."

Taking the glass, he sniffed the liquid. For a white liquor, it had a rich, earthy aroma, almost like a spiced rum. He took a sip, and the smooth liqiud glided down his throat like warm honey. "That's amazing. What's in it?"

"That's a secret." She retrieved the glass and mixed more rum with Coke and ice. Then, she grabbed a flavored sparkling water from the fridge and motioned to the table.

He sank into a chair and clutched his glass. "You don't like the rum?"

"I don't drink alcohol."

He laughed, expecting her to at least crack a grin, but she didn't. "You own a rum distillery, and you don't drink alcohol?"

"Alcohol lowers inhibitions and can make you vulnerable. I prefer to keep my wits about me."

"You're quite the contradiction, aren't you?"

"You have no idea."

He sipped his drink, looking at her over the rim of

the glass, and she returned his gaze. She had a presence about her, commanding, confident, in charge, but the undercurrent of her magic...of her connection to death...flowed through the energy around her as if she held a key to the gateway of the underworld and could send souls through it at her will. No wonder she intimidated people.

"I remember seeing you in the cemetery when we were kids."

She arched an eyebrow. "You frequented the cemetery?"

"My dad is the caretaker. He took me with him on the weekends when he did the landscape and repaired the tombs. You would come with your mom and leave offerings at the entry. I figured you were visiting a relative, but you were honoring your Baron, weren't you? It's appropriate to leave offerings for him at cemetery gates."

"Someone's done his research."

"I was curious." He chuckled. "My dad always grumbled after you left because he'd have to clean it up. He didn't mind so much when you left the bottles of rum, though."

A genuine smile curved her lips, brightening her eyes, and she laughed. "I bet not." As she relaxed, her magical aura strengthened, buzzing with energy.

Her smile drew him in. Hell, everything about her called to him. *To his wolf.* This was more than a human-level attraction, and he wanted to get to know her. To know Odette and not the Baroness everyone was afraid of.

She sucked in a breath as if she'd realized her guard had slipped, her eyes widening briefly. The smile faded as she sipped her sparkling water and stared off into the distance.

Leaning forward, he rested an arm on the table. "You don't have to do that with me."

"Do what?"

"Hold back. You can be yourself. I'm not afraid of you."

She leaned toward the table, resting her fingertips on the edge. "Maybe you should be. I am a child of death."

He chuckled. "I grew up with death; it doesn't scare me. Neither does your guardian Spirit. I don't know what powers you have, but if you can send me to my grave with your magic, you'd have done it by now if you wanted to."

"Hmm…" She slid her hand forward until her forearm rested on the table.

Placing his hand on hers, he traced his thumb across her soft skin. Her magic seeped into him, sending a jolt straight to his heart. She lowered her gaze to where they touched and drew in a shuddering breath.

"We have rules about dating clients, but after this job is done, would you mind if I asked you out to dinner?"

She lifted her gaze to his eyes, parting her lips to answer. Her jaw trembled for a moment before she clamped her mouth shut and slid her hand from his grasp. "That's not a good idea. It would never work for us."

"Yeah. I guess you're right." He tossed back the rest of his drink and crossed his arms. The first time both he and his wolf had ever felt an inkling of attraction to someone, and she rejected him cold. Who was he kidding? This spark was turning into a full-blown fire. But the bartender was right. A werewolf construction worker had nothing to offer a woman like Odette. Hell, he wasn't even a full werewolf. She deserved someone whole. He gestured to the room. "You can afford to buy a mansion like this, while all I can hope to do is repair it for you."

"No, James. It's not that at all. It's…" She let out a hard breath, and her brow scrunched, confliction tightening her eyes. "If we got together, it wouldn't end well. It never does." Rising, she took his glass and dumped the ice into the sink.

Damn it. He wasn't proud of his reputation with women, but Odette was different… She'd commanded his wolf's attention, and she needed to know *he* could be different too. He strode around the counter. "Who says it has to end?"

"James…" She shook her head and faced him. In her bare feet, she stood four inches shorter than him, and he had to fight the urge to reach for her. The way she looked at him. How her body drifted toward him as he inched a little closer. She felt *something* for him.

"I'll admit I don't have the best track record when it comes to dating, but a man can change when he finds the right woman." He clamped his mouth shut. Those words had come straight from his wolf. It would have been nice if they'd registered in his brain before they'd spilled from his lips, but every one of them had been truth.

Her eyes searched his, and she swallowed. "What makes you think I'm the right woman? Or is that what you say to all the girls?" One corner of her mouth tugged into a grin, making his heart race.

The truth seemed to be working so far. Why not go all in? "I've never said that to anyone. Honestly, I've never been this interested in someone. You're different."

"I'm *very* different, but you've known that since second grade."

"You make me *feel* different." Should he tell her about the dreams? About how his wolf was slowly letting go of the stranger he'd never met because of Odette? He wanted to know more than her body; he wanted to know her mind and her soul.

No. That was too much and way too soon. He was still trying to come to terms with what his wolf was telling him himself.

When he didn't elaborate further, Odette sighed and stepped away from him. "There's a lot you don't know about me. You and I...as tempting as it is, I wouldn't survive the ending. Let's keep it in the friend-zone, okay?"

"Yeah. Okay, I understand. I should get home; I have to work in the morning." He had a couple of weeks to help her change her mind. He grabbed his tool belt from the counter when a pair of glowing red orbs flashed across the window. *What the hell?* "Do you have pets?"

"No." She followed his gaze. "What did you see?"

He strode to the window and peered out the glass, but he couldn't see a damn thing in the dark backyard. "Eyes."

"It could have been an opossum. I seem to attract those." She rested a hand on his shoulder as she looked out the window, her touch sending a flush of warmth through his veins.

An intense urge to protect her grew in his core, and his wolf demanded that he investigate. "The silhouette was too big for an opossum, and the eyes looked red."

She dropped her arm to her side and whispered, "Demon."

"Stay inside. I'll go out the back and check it out."

Following him to the door, she touched his elbow. "Be careful."

He chuckled. "Werewolves were made to hunt demons. I'll be fine."

The porch steps creaked as he descended, and he skirted around a ladder, narrowly missing a stack of paint cans. Adrenaline spiked in his veins, though he wasn't sure if the thrill was for the hunt or for protecting the woman standing in the doorway.

He waved an arm at her and whispered, "Go inside," but she didn't budge. She crossed her arms and leaned against the jamb as if fear didn't exist in her vocabulary.

Though a privacy fence surrounded the yard, he stayed in human form as he scanned the bushes for the fiend. A grunt sounded to his right, and he jerked his head to the side in time to see the squat, black figure barreling toward him. It latched onto his shoulder, sinking its razor-like teeth into his arm.

"Goddammit!" James spun, trying to throw the little shit to the ground, but it hung on with a death grip.

"James!" Odette ran toward him.

"Go back inside. I'm fine." If the damn thing would let go for a second, he could shift and vanquish the bastard. He didn't want to end up with a tooth embedded in his bone if he shifted with it attached to his shoulder.

"You're not fine." Odette grabbed a paintbrush from the ladder and jabbed the wooden handle into the demon's back. With a squeal, the fiend let go and lunged at Odette. She stumbled, tripping over a loose brick and falling to her back.

"I don't think so." James shifted, clamping his jaws on the fiend's leg before it could attack. He yanked it away from her, releasing his hold to bite into its neck. As the demon fell limp in his maw, James dropped it and swiped a claw across its chest, piercing its heart. The minion eroded into a pile of ash.

Odette stood, dusting off her backside, as James returned to human form. She peered at the ash and then looked at him, tilting her head as she studied him. "I've never seen a werewolf shift before. I didn't know you could change form so quickly. Or that your clothes stayed intact."

"The magic absorbs them when I shift. Let's get you inside." With his hand on the small of her back, he guided her through the door. A demon tried to attack her in her own backyard, and she was more concerned about how he shifted. Was the woman afraid of anything? With death as her guardian, he supposed she wasn't.

He locked the door and led her to the kitchen. Turning around, he found her smiling at him. "I'm one of the faster shifters. It's why I hunt demons. I was made for it. You, though…unless you can control creatures from hell like you can control ghosts?"

Her smile faded as she lowered her gaze. "I don't control ghosts, and I have no power over demons."

"You could have been hurt."

"So could you. You're bleeding." She flashed a challenging stare.

He huffed and wiped the wound on his shirt. He didn't need yet another person questioning his strength, especially not her. "I'm going back out to see if there are any more. Please stay inside this time."

"Okay. I will."

Exiting through the back door, James searched the entire property, front yard and back, but he didn't find a sign of any more demons. Like the first one they'd encountered a few days ago, it seemed to be alone. He hung around the yard a bit longer, giving his arm time to heal, before heading up the porch steps.

When he came back in, Odette stood in front of her altar, her eyes closed, and she whispered something too quietly for him to understand. A prayer, maybe? The thought that she could have summoned the thing flashed through his mind, but he dismissed it immediately. Noah had planted that thought, and James didn't buy it for a second.

He stood beside her, and she opened her eyes. "No more, I guess?"

"He was alone, like the other one."

"Other one?"

"We found a demon outside Rusty's a few days ago. This is the second one the pack has come across. Have you encountered anything like it before?"

She shook her head. "What kind of demon is it?"

"It's an imp. Minion to something much bigger and nastier, but I don't know what. With the sightings so sporadic, my guess is whatever is summoning them hasn't fully manifested itself yet. I'll have to check in with the alpha and see if he's found anything."

"There have been two so far, and you've been the one to find them both?"

"Yeah."

Odette nodded, and the first hint of fear finally sparked in her eyes. "I'll talk to my Mambo too. She might be able to ask the Spirits what's going on." Glancing at her watch, she frowned. "I'll call her in the morning. It's getting late. You better go talk to your alpha."

He hesitated. That was his cue to leave, but if any more demons showed up here… "I don't want to leave you unprotected. I can stay the night. I'll sleep on the floor."

She arched an eyebrow. "Are you doubting my powers?"

"No. I don't know what kind of power you have, but you said you can't control demons."

"No evil can get inside this house. Natasha helped me

cleanse it, and we put a charm on it. I'm safe. I promise not to go outside until morning."

"Are you sure? I don't mind staying."

"I appreciate your chivalry, but I can take care of myself. Go home, James."

"All right. I'll be here first thing in the morning." Pulling a business card from his wallet, he handed it to her. "My cell number is on there. Call me if you need anything."

"Thank you." She opened the front door and stood to the side, a silent command for him to leave.

He shuffled down the walk to his truck and grumbled as he climbed inside. She may have been safe, but he'd have a wolf watching her house until morning to be safer.

CHAPTER EIGHT

ODETTE LAY IN BED, STARING AT THE CEILING, TRYING to cool the inferno the werewolf had lit in her soul. Her plan to stay away from James, thus ignoring the growing emotions and avoiding the inevitable had failed, like she knew it would. The short time she'd spent with him this evening had sealed her fate. He was her soulmate. Of that she was sure. How she would escape the horrific death awaiting her, she had no clue.

Squeezing her eyes shut, she focused on the image of his handsome features. Dark hair, sky-blue eyes, and from what she could tell with his clothes on, a sexy, muscular body. Oh, to get his clothes off…

Sitting with him, talking to him, looking at him had been a tedious exercise in restraint when all she'd wanted to do was wrap her arms around him and kiss him. But Odette was the queen of restraint. She'd been holding back since she was twelve years old. Losing control was not an option.

Something about James made her want to let her guard down though. It had slipped a little this evening, and her power had intensified briefly. He'd felt it too. The curious look in his eyes as he'd leaned toward her told her he sensed her power, but he could never know what she was capable of. What she'd done before she learned control.

She'd made an offering to Baron Samedi before climbing into bed, all but begging him to visit her in her dreams and give her guidance. If this was the life when she and her soulmate would break the cycle, like Natasha suggested, she'd need all the help she could get.

Focusing on her feet, Odette relaxed each muscle in her body, working her way up to the top of her head as liquid warmth flowed through her limbs. Relaxing even more, she imagined herself floating in a starless night sky until she drifted into a deep sleep.

But Baron Samedi didn't visit her.

As her sleep sank into a dream state, she found James waiting for her in her bed. Dream James wore a light-blue shirt that matched his eyes and dark jeans that hung low on his hips. He rose as she entered the room, and she went to him willingly, allowing him to take her in his arms, giving in to the temptation she'd resisted in life.

He undressed her, and though his calloused hands were rough against her skin, the sensation of his touch was like nothing she'd felt before.

She rolled to her side and hugged a pillow, the ecstasy he gave her in her dream bringing her halfway to consciousness, to a state of awareness that she was in a dream, but she willed herself to stay in the world her subconscious mind had created a little longer.

The dream was so life-like she could have stayed there forever, letting go of her inhibitions, surrendering control like she could never do when awake. In her mind, she lay on her back, looking up into his loving eyes.

As she gazed at him, her vision blurred. His face transformed into another familiar man. Nicolas. Alive and breathing in her dream, he smiled as the pressure of his body on hers held her immobile.

Her stomach fluttered, but the shock of finding another man in her bed didn't send her reeling. Dreams were weird like that. Willing herself to consciousness, she pushed the image from her mind and focused her senses on her surroundings. The feel of the soft cotton sheets against her skin. The soft breeze caressing her cheeks from the ceiling fan whirring above. The presence of a man…

She pried her lids open to find the ghost of Nicolas hovering on the bed as if he lay next to her. Warmth radiated from his form, though he had no body to produce it. She expected to recoil from his close proximity—the dead seemed to draw the life from her whenever they manifested—but Nicolas's presence had an almost comforting effect. She turned toward him. "What are you doing?"

Nicolas smiled and twirled a lock of her hair around his finger. "I've missed you, my sweet Serafine."

"What the…" The woman who murdered him? Sitting up, she clutched the blankets to her chest. "Will you please get out of my bed? This is my private space."

His brow furrowed, confusion clouding his eyes as he faded from the room. Why the hell would he call the murderer his *sweet* Serafine? He couldn't know his mistress was the one who killed him. Odette's assumption had been right. He didn't know the truth about his death, and that was why he was stuck there.

Her stomach sank. She would have to tell him. Explain exactly what happened to him so he could let go.

Swinging her legs over the side of the bed, she grabbed her phone from the nightstand and stared at the blank screen. First, she'd have to convince the ghost she wasn't Serafine. Who knew how he'd react to the news of his murder? And if he thought Odette had killed him, he might lash out. Then she'd have to command him to cross over. She shivered.

Running her finger over the screen to wake up her phone, she glanced at the time. Five a.m. No point in going back to sleep now. She texted Natasha to call her as soon as she woke up and made her way to the shower.

When she emerged from the steamy bathroom twenty minutes later, the message light on her phone was blinking. Tugging the towel tighter around her chest, she retrieved the device and returned her Mambo's call. "I've got a problem. Several."

Dishes clanked in the background, followed by the sound of a refrigerator door opening and closing. "I'm listening."

"Where do I start?" Odette sank onto the edge of her bed. "My offering to Erzulie Dantor didn't work. I saw James last night...then I dreamed about him." A shiver ran up her spine at the memory of her dream.

"I didn't figure she'd be much help in your case." Her smile was evident in her voice. "He's a good man."

"I know, and he wanted to ask me out, but I told him it wouldn't end well."

The muffled sound of liquid pouring into a glass filled the silence, and more shuffling ensued before the fridge door opened and closed again. "And what did he say to that?"

"He said that maybe it didn't have to end." A dozen butterfly wings flitted against her abdomen. Under normal circumstances, his words would have thrilled her. "He doesn't have a clue."

"If you're going to be with him, you have to tell him. Did you ask him about his readings? I think he'll understand."

"No, I was too busy trying not to like him. I was hoping if I could avoid falling for him, the monster wouldn't come for us. If we can keep our distance and not start a relationship, maybe we can keep our lives too." She inhaled deeply and blew out a hard breath. "But there was a demon in my backyard last night. James called it an imp. I mean, the monster that's always killed me before is bigger than a man. This one was two feet tall, but…"

All sounds of movement on Natasha's end of the line stopped. The Mambo didn't speak for a moment, and the silence grew heavy and foreboding.

"Are you familiar with imps? He said they're lower-level demons who get summoned by something bigger and nastier." And her fated murderer was both of those. She'd never encountered imps in her past-life regressions, but the moment James had mentioned what summoned them, the first inklings of terror had clawed through her mind.

"He knows what he's talking about. Was it just the one?"

"There was one other, a few days ago. He said he killed it outside Rusty's." Her heart sank. "This is it, isn't it? The beginning of the end?"

"We don't know that. It's possible he has enemies, and the imps are targeting him. It could have nothing to do with you."

The Mambo had a point. James was the common denominator here, not her. Then again, all her friends were at Rusty's the night he killed it. Odette could have been there too. "Or it could have been sent to kill me. I've met my soulmate. Maybe I don't have to fall in love with him to trigger the curse. Maybe it's already happening."

"Where are you?"

"I'm at home."

"Stay there. Work from home today; you're safe inside. I'll prepare a ceremony for this evening, and I'll pick you up at six. We'll contact the Spirits and see if they can guide us."

She rubbed her forehead, closing her eyes for a long blink. "I've been asking for guidance since the moment James walked into my life, but my prayers have gone unanswered."

"You know why. Unless you're ready to let go and embrace your gift, you'll continue to be left to go it alone."

"My powers are not a gift." She bit her tongue to stop herself from continuing. The argument would get her nowhere.

Natasha clucked her tongue. "Don't let the Baron hear you say that. And don't worry. If we gather enough vodouisants, the Spirits are bound to show up."

"I'll see you tonight. Thanks." She pressed end and slid the phone onto her nightstand. Working from home wasn't an issue. She was the boss, after all. But being home all day meant she'd be spending all day with James.

Her stomach fluttered at the thought of seeing him again, and she groaned. She wasn't ready for her life to end.

James parked in front of Odette's house and slid out of his truck. A spark of excitement tingled in his chest at the sight of her car sitting in the driveway, but his anticipation of seeing her again crumbled into worry as he tucked a basket of kitchen towels under his arm and paced up the walk.

He'd watched her house himself most of the night, until Cade showed up insisting the alpha had ordered James to get some sleep. Though he hadn't caught so much as a whiff of demon, his wolf had protested leaving her the whole way home and most of the night.

The few hours of sleep he'd managed were plagued with confusing dreams. His mystery woman appeared as usual, making his heart swell with what he wanted to call love, though he had no experience with the romantic side of the emotion. His heart didn't normally react to women at all, leaving the swelling to his dick instead.

But the mystery woman hadn't stayed in his dream for long. As soon as he'd taken her hand, she'd morphed into Odette, and damn it if the L-word feelings hadn't intensified when he'd looked into her dark-brown eyes.

Now, the sun peeked from behind the mansions on Millionaire's Row, casting the sky in shades of deep pink and orange. The bougainvillea mixed with the scents of fresh paint and sawdust, and he inhaled deeply, letting the familiar aromas calm his nerves.

A werewolf manual laborer had no chance with a woman as polished and professional as Odette Allemand, but his wolf sure seemed to think he did. He glanced at his right hand. Hell, he wasn't even a whole werewolf. He'd spent his entire life trying to hide his slow healing and prove his worth to the pack. Now he was setting himself up to have to prove himself to a woman too. He exhaled a curse and rang the bell.

A tiny smile lighted on Odette's mouth as she opened

the door, and she didn't try to hide it this time. Screw it all; he needed to get a taste of those lips.

"You could've let yourself in. You have a key." She stepped aside for him to enter, and he shuffled into the foyer, a smile tugging at his own lips as he took in her outfit. She was barefoot again, and her dark-blue skinny jeans emphasized the length of her legs. Her black silk shirt flowed over her hips, and with the top two buttons undone, it revealed just enough skin to make him yearn to see more.

"This is the first time I've seen you in a color other than black or purple." He gestured to her jeans.

"I'm working from home today." She paused in front of him, holding his gaze as if trying to gauge his reaction.

He arched a brow, his heart rate kicking up at the thought of spending the entire day with her. "Everything okay?"

"Natasha, my Mambo, thinks it's best if I stay home until we figure out where the demon came from." She nodded to the basket under his arm. "What's that?"

"Oh." He clutched it with both hands and held it out to her. "I couldn't get the blood stain out of that towel, so I bought you new ones."

Her smile widened as she took the basket and ran a hand over the lavender cloth. "It was one towel. You didn't have to buy me an entire set."

Heat crept up his neck, and he shoved his hands into his pockets. *Get over yourself, man.* "Consider it a house-warming gift. I thought they'd look good in your kitchen when it's finished."

"Thank you." She lifted her gaze to meet his, and the corners of her eyes tightened in uncertainty for a moment before she straightened her spine. "Do you have time for a cup of coffee before you get started?"

He glanced at his watch. The crew would arrive in fifteen minutes, and he liked to do a sweep of the property before they began work. But he couldn't refuse Odette. He'd make time. "I've got a few minutes to spare."

"Good." She motioned for him to follow her to the kitchen, one of two rooms that had furniture. "Have a seat. I just made a fresh pot."

She'd set up a workstation at the breakfast table, her laptop and notepad occupying one of the spots. James sank into the opposite chair and watched as she took two mugs from the cabinet and filled them with coffee. She had the posture of a ballerina, and she moved as gracefully as if she'd spent years in a dance studio. The woman was alluring, and that was putting it lightly.

She smiled as she glided to the table and set the mugs down. "Do you need cream or sugar?"

"Black is fine." He sipped the coffee, and his admiration of her intensified. Bold and robust, the rich aroma of the coffee went well with her personality. Any woman who took her coffee this strong was a keeper. *Wait.* It was way too soon for thoughts like that. He cleared his throat. "Were you ever a dancer? Ballet or anything?"

She sat next to him. "No. I don't dance. Not even at our ceremonies. Why do you ask?"

"You're built like a dancer. Graceful." He took another sip, eyeing her over the rim of the mug.

Arching an eyebrow, she inclined her chin. "Is that your way of hinting that you like my body?"

He nearly choked on his coffee. A trail of the warm liquid rolled down his chin, and he wiped it with the back of his hand. Setting the mug down, he squared his shoulders.

"Who says I like graceful women? Maybe I'd prefer a klutz." With a grin, he took a successful sip from his cup, silently congratulating himself for grabbing control of the conversation before she could turn him into a babbling idiot.

"That's a shame." She traced her finger around the rim of her mug. "I seem to have a thing for men who are good at restoring things. Bringing life back to something nearly lost to time."

He opened his mouth to respond as she held his gaze, but the words didn't come. Something had changed between last night and this morning, and whatever it was, James wasn't about to complain. He also wasn't letting her have the upper hand.

He swept his gaze across the room, doing his best to act like her comment didn't faze him. "I've admired this house since I was a kid, and I've always wondered what it would look like on the inside. Restoring it is a dream come true." He locked eyes with her. "What do you dream about, Odette?"

A blush spread across her cheeks, and she cleared her voice. "Natasha told me I should ask you about your readings. She said you've been into the temple a few times, and she expected to see you again soon."

Heat crept into his ears as he ground his teeth. He had planned to make another appointment, until he met Odette. "So much for her readings being private. What else did she tell you?"

"Nothing." She held up her hands in a show of innocence. "She didn't tell me anything about your reading; she said I should ask you about it. With the ghost here showing so much interest in you, and then the demon last night…I guess she thought it might be related."

He let out a slow breath, quelling his frustration. What would Odette think about his dream woman and the fact that she herself was now battling for control of his wolf? He'd rather not know. "The ghost hasn't bothered me since the first time. Why do you think he's showing interest in me?"

"Because he's been present since you got here this morning. I think I upset him earlier, and he hasn't shown himself...until you knocked on the door. He's been watching you ever since."

He cut his gaze to the left, following her line of sight, but he couldn't see the ghost. "What's he doing?"

"Staring at you. He looks confused but also...interested." She focused on the empty space in the corner. "Why are you looking at James like that? Do you know him too?" Her shoulders drooped as she picked up her mug. "He disappeared again. Every time I start asking him questions, he vanishes."

"That's weird. Maybe he doesn't want you to know."

She narrowed her eyes and shook her head. "Maybe, but...does the name Serafine sound familiar to you?"

The syllables flowed in his ears like music. Was it the name or the way Odette said it? His chest tightened, and he wracked his brain for the memory that skittered around the edges of his mind. "I feel like it should, but it doesn't ring a bell. It's a pretty name, though. Why?"

She chewed her bottom lip and drummed her manicured nails on the table. "Nicolas, the ghost, mentioned the name. I thought maybe she was someone famous...or infamous...in New Orleans that I hadn't heard of."

"It's possible." The sound of an engine rumbled from outside, followed by doors slamming and the clanking of equipment. "That's my team. I better get to work. Thank you for the coffee."

He rose, but she caught his hand. "What were you looking for in your readings?"

A low growl rumbled in his chest, so quiet she couldn't have heard it, and he lowered himself into the seat. The imploring look in her eyes drew the words from his mouth before he could think twice about telling her. "My wolf is restless. It's time for me to settle down, but…"

She leaned toward him. "But?"

He couldn't tell her about the dreams; they were crazy. *He* was going crazy for having them. "I haven't had good luck in the love department, so I was looking for guidance." *Smooth move, Romeo.* Why didn't he tell her about his broken wolf too? That would really impress her. *Get it together, man.*

He looked into her eyes. "But things have changed since I met you."

She started to speak, but the front door swung open and boots thudded on the wooden floor. "Hey, James. Can we get started?"

Damn you, Noah. "Yeah. We're good to go." He stood and carried his mug to the sink. "That's my cue. We'll try not to make too much noise inside, but I can't make any guarantees."

"Of course." She fumbled for something next to her computer and lifted it in the air. "I've got headphones, so…no worries."

"Good deal. I'll be around if you need me." He turned on his heel and strode out of the kitchen.

Sweet Spirits, that was not what she'd expected to hear. The headphones slipped from her trembling hand as she sank lower in her chair. Things had changed since he'd met her. If he thought meeting her meant his luck in love was getting better, he was in for a rude awakening.

He'd be better off single for the rest of his life than to fall in love with Odette and deal with the tragedy her love would bring.

Natasha wasn't convinced the imps were a sign of things to come, so maybe there was still a chance. Maybe she could convince him she wasn't the one he was looking for. If they never fell in love, maybe...

A clank sounded in the foyer, and she leaned to the side to see James setting up a ladder beneath the chrome light fixture. Two other men held either side of a refurbished nineteenth-century crystal chandelier and waited as he removed the fixture from the ceiling.

As he reached his arms overhead, his dark-blue T-shirt lifted above his waistline, revealing smooth skin and a hint of the delicious V disappearing into his pants.

She bit her lip. How could she convince him she wasn't the one when her insides melted from simply looking at the man?

He caught her gaze and grinned. "The new one's going to look so much better. You've got good taste."

She couldn't help but return the smile. "Thanks."

The rest of the morning crawled by. She couldn't focus on her work when the sexiest werewolf she'd ever laid eyes on kept coming into view. If she didn't know any better, she'd think he was purposely working on little things close to the kitchen so he could steal glances of her the way she'd been doing him.

Nicolas followed him around too. Could the ghost be

jealous of the time James was spending with her? With the way Nicolas had looked at her this morning, it made sense. She'd have to find a way to convince him she wasn't his former mistress, but she'd hold off on that conversation until after the ceremony tonight. The loa may have been ignoring Odette, but they wouldn't ignore the whole House.

When James moved to work upstairs, taking the temptation with him, Odette finally focused on her job. She plowed through her inbox, reviewing reports and crunching numbers until her eyes stung. She'd instructed her assistant to call if any emergencies arose at work, but her phone had remained silent all day. Her company ran like a well-oiled machine, both the office end and the distillery.

Why couldn't running companies be her gift? She didn't mind her simple psychic medium powers. Having the ability to see and speak to the dead meant she'd never been afraid of ghosts, even as a child, but she could do without the other magic Baron Samedi had granted her when he'd brought her back to life.

Boots thudded on the staircase, pulling her from her thoughts, and she glanced at the clock. Five p.m. The afternoon had flown by.

"Y'all go ahead." James's deep voice drifted in from the foyer. "I'm going to walk the property with the client to make sure she's happy with the progress."

"I bet you'll make sure she's *real* happy." That voice came from the younger man with auburn hair that she'd heard James call Noah.

Leaning off the edge of her chair so she could see the men, she caught a glimpse of James punching Noah on the shoulder. "Watch yourself," James said.

Noah chuckled. "Sorry, man. Have fun." The men left, and James shuffled into the kitchen.

Odette fought the grin tugging at her lips and folded her hands on the table. "All done for the day?"

"Do you want to do a walk-through? Make sure everything meets your expectations?"

"I've done my own walk-through every day, and I saw you working today. You're exceeding my expectations." In every way imaginable.

He held her gaze with his smoldering blue eyes and cocked his head slightly. "I live about fifteen minutes away. If I run home and take a quick shower, could I come back and take you out to dinner?"

An image of James, naked and dripping wet, formed in her mind, chasing all rational thought from her head. Her body acted before her brain could process a response, and she rose from the table, gliding toward him.

She could have dinner with James…and dessert. Preferably his delectable body covered in chocolate. If she was going to let go and give in to passion, he was the man to do it with. He was supposed to be her soulmate after all. She could trust him, couldn't she? "I thought you had rules against dating clients?"

"It's more of a suggestion, really. I've never been much of a rule-follower."

She couldn't help herself. She drifted a little closer and rested her hand on his shoulder. His muscles were firm, his skin warm beneath his shirt. "As tempting as your offer is, I have to be at the temple in an hour. We're having a ceremony."

"That's cool. Maybe another time." He patted her hand on his shoulder and stepped away. "I'll be back in the morning." He strode to the foyer.

"James…" She followed him to the front door. "You don't take rejection well, do you?"

He stopped and faced her, his eyes narrowing. "I'm not used to being rejected."

"I'm not rejecting *you*. I'm simply not available tonight." She looked into his eyes, willing him to take the hint and ask about another time.

He pressed his mouth into a thin line and lifted his chin. "I see."

Damn it, he didn't take the bait.

She bit her bottom lip. With her poise and the general spooky aura surrounding her, most people backed down instantly when she pressed them. James was the first person not afraid to push back, and that made him all the more intriguing.

She moved closer, placing her hand on his shoulder again. "Will you be watching my house tonight or are you assigning the job to someone else?"

His brow furrowed. "I…How did you know?"

"I could feel your presence, and I saw you across the street. When I woke up around three a.m. someone else was there. I guess you're working in shifts?"

He inhaled deeply, holding her gaze, silently reminding her she couldn't scare him away. "I'm not a stalker. With the demon on your property…we hunt in shifts all night anyway, and I was worried one might try again."

"And the fact that it's *my* house had nothing to do with it?" She inched a little closer until she could feel the heat radiating from his skin.

"This is a high-paying job. Luke would have my ass if something happened to you and you couldn't pay." His gaze flowed between her eyes and her lips.

"Is that the real reason?"

He rested a hand on her hip. "I think you know the real reason. I—"

Tugging him closer, she pressed her lips to his. He stiffened at first, but as she slid her arms around his shoulders, his body relaxed, conforming to hers as if he were made to fit in her embrace.

His lips were soft, his body firm, and as he wrapped his arms around her waist, a growl rumbled up from deep in his chest. She opened for him, brushing her tongue against his, reveling in the way their magic mixed and tingled across her skin.

With a deep, shuddering breath, she pulled away, cupping his face in her hands before stepping back and dropping her arms to her sides. "Natasha is picking me up in a few minutes, so you'd better get going."

He opened his mouth, but he didn't speak.

"She drives a silver Toyota Camry, if you're planning to follow us to the temple. Sometimes these ceremonies last into the early morning, so if you want to send someone to follow me back home, I can't give you an exact time."

"We'll have eyes on you all night. Don't worry."

With Natasha's magic and her own, she wasn't the slightest bit afraid of a little imp. But she couldn't deny that she found James's protective nature appealing. "I won't." She placed a soft kiss on his cheek. "Bye, James."

CHAPTER NINE

ODETTE HELD A BAG OF CORNMEAL IN ONE HAND, the fingers of her free hand lightly tracing the bow of her lips as she replayed the kiss in her mind for the fifteenth time. How could her skin *still* be tingling from his touch?

She shouldn't have kissed him. With the imp showing up at her house, she was all but convinced her demise had begun, but if she could keep her hands to herself and her lips off the sexy werewolf, maybe she could spare him from their horrid fate.

Tell him it was a mistake. That it would never happen again. Shut it down before it began. She could call his boss and ask for a different foreman to finish her house so she wouldn't have to see him anymore. It was the only way to keep James safe.

Then again, with the way he'd reacted to her advances this evening, they'd both boarded a bullet train headed straight for death.

"You bite that lip any harder, and we're going to have a blood offering for Papa Legba." Natasha took the bag from her hand and set it on a table in the corner.

Odette blinked, releasing her bottom lip from the clutch of her teeth and sweeping her gaze across the room. In the ten minutes she'd been internalizing, six vodouisants had entered the room with offerings for the various loa who may or may not grace them with their presence during the ceremony.

Natasha had drawn the *vévé* for Papa Legba, the loa of the crossroads, in cornmeal on the floor. The intricate cross with swirls and stars embellishing each of the corners would act as the gateway, Papa Legba the gatekeeper, allowing the other loa to enter the ritual.

"You've outdone yourself this time, Mambo." Odette gestured to the *vévé*.

Natasha smiled proudly. "My artistic skills are improving."

Pulling a bottle of premium rum from her bag, Odette placed it on the offering table. "I'm sure he's abandoned me, but in case the Baron decides to make an appearance."

"Who abandoned who?" The priestess arched an eyebrow.

"Is anyone else coming?" She didn't need to run down that rabbit hole again. Odette and Baron Samedi had abandoned each other, and she refused to argue about the topic further. It didn't matter who strayed first.

Pressing her lips together, Natasha narrowed her eyes, giving her that *you know I'm right* look. Maybe she was right; maybe she wasn't. The point of this ceremony was to find out where the imps came from, and they didn't need the loa of death to figure that out. Demons didn't die.

"Are we waiting on anyone else?" Natasha scanned the crowd, and when no one spoke up, she lit a black candle and knelt in front of her freshly-drawn *vévé*.

Jackson and Tyrell, two priests-in-training picked up

their drums and beat out a melodic rhythm, while Rasheda, Amy, and Darlene, three of the women dressed in all white, began swaying to the cadence. Her voice low, Natasha hummed, slowly increasing her volume as the hum turned from a mumble into a full-blown chant.

Odette recognized few words of the Haitian Creole prayer the priestess recited to the rhythm of the drums, but the message was as clear as if she'd said the chant in English. The Mambo was calling on Papa Legba to open the gates and allow the loa through to deliver their messages.

As the drumbeat changed, the energy in the room shifted, a buzzing, living electricity dancing through the air, making goose bumps prick on Odette's arms. Darlene spun, taking a bottle of Bacardi from the table and pouring a few drops on the *vévé* as an offering to the loa of the crossroads.

The cadence changed again, and Rasheda and Amy joined Darlene in a dance to honor the Spirits. The pull of energy had Odette leaning toward the dancers, her body betraying her as it swayed in time with the drums. Fisting her hands, she focused on the bite of her nails into her palms, keeping herself firmly grounded in the here and now. Giving in to the rhythm would mean relinquishing control, opening herself up to ritual possession, and *that* was something she'd never do again.

The room buzzed, the vibration increasing as Papa Legba opened the gates, giving the loa permission to visit the Earthly realm. Odette whispered her thanks along with the other vodouisants, and Rasheda placed a coconut on the *vévé*.

"This is intense." Chelsea, a new initiate, wrung her

hands as she stepped next to her. "How long have you been a vodouisant?"

Odette unclenched her jaw and glanced at the girl. With her red hair styled into a pixie cut, torn jeans, and Adidas shoes, she didn't look a day over eighteen. "All my life." She tried for a smile, but the corners of her mouth merely twitched.

"Then, why aren't you dancing? I can't wait for my *lavé tet* so I can join in."

Odette focused on her Mambo. "I never dance."

"There's demons after our girl." Natasha sashayed toward her. "Will someone tell us where they came from? Is it her curse?" She stood between Odette and the initiate, carefully eyeing the drummers and dancers for signs of possession.

The atmosphere thickened, the drum cadence quickening, welcoming whatever loa was about to make its presence known. Darlene stiffened, her eyes going wide for a second before they closed and she collapsed into Rasheda's arms.

As she held her breath, Odette clenched her fists tighter, the sensation of her nails cutting into her palms the only thing keeping her in place. The visitor could be any one of the hundreds of loa, and he or she may not even be there to answer her questions. Voodoo Spirits thought for themselves, and they didn't always cooperate.

It was foolish to hope her own *met tet* would arrive to help her. Baron Samedi hadn't shown himself at a ritual Odette attended since the day she turned her back on Voodoo. Even now he rarely visited her in her dreams.

She let out her breath as Darlene regained her footing, righting herself and taking on a posture not her own. Her head held high, she pointed to the perfume and flowers on the table, and Rasheda and Amy draped her in a pink shawl, the color of Erzulie Freda, the loa of love.

"This is the last thing I need," Odette muttered under her breath. If the loa was there to talk about her love life, the demon was most definitely after her. The cycle had begun.

Darlene's gaze locked on Odette, but her smile wasn't her own. She slinked toward her, batting her lashes at Jackson as he softened the beat of his drum. Stopping two feet in front of her, Erzulie Freda smiled sweetly, shaking her head and making a *tsk* sound as she smoothed a strand of Odette's hair back into place. "You found a good one, but you need to work on your presentation if you want to keep him."

She fought the urge to slap Darlene's hand away. This wasn't Darlene; it was Erzulie Freda. "My appearance doesn't seem that important when I'm about to be joining the Baron in the land of the dead."

Resting her hands on her hips, Freda tilted her head and offered a small smile. "The Baron doesn't want you to join him yet."

"I don't think I have a choice."

Freda wrapped an arm around Odette's shoulders and led her away from the others. "What's your beau's name, child?"

"James." She straightened, furrowing her brow as the realization hit. She hadn't hesitated. Didn't argue that he wasn't her boyfriend like she'd expected to. That kiss seemed to have sealed the deal, sealing her fate—and his—along with it.

Closing her eyes, the loa smiled softly, nodding as if

receiving messages from the spirit world. "He's a good one. You're lucky."

Odette scoffed. "Until we both end up dead."

Freda stopped and turned to face her. "Maybe you have three more days with him, or maybe you have fifty years. However long you have left, don't you want to make the most of it?"

Odette crossed her arms but quickly dropped them to her sides to avoid showing disrespect to the Ancestral Spirit. "I…" Of course she wanted to make the most of it, but how could she when demons lurked outside her door? "The demon that James killed… It was after me, wasn't it?"

The loa sighed, shaking her head like a disappointed mother. "You were hoping to see your *met tet* tonight?"

"I don't mean to offend, but I already know James is my soulmate. Baron Samedi could help me fight this thing that's coming for me. Whether or not I give in to temptation with James is irrelevant. The cycle has already started."

"The Baron isn't pleased with the way you've been living your life. All work. No fun. Refusing the gifts he blessed you with."

Odette cast her gaze to the floor. "I know."

Freda grinned. "You could start by pleasing that beau of yours." Her husky voice sounded nothing like Darlene's higher-pitched tone. "Let him please you, too, if you know what I mean. Your *met tet* knows that sex and death are part of life. How long has it been for you, child?"

"I really don't want to talk about this."

The loa lifted her chin. "You don't want to talk about your love life with Erzulie Freda? I guess I shouldn't have bothered coming." She turned toward the others who continued the ceremony, dancing and drumming to honor the Spirits.

"Wait." Odette touched her elbow and then let her hand fall to her side. "I mean no disrespect. It's been...a long time."

"How long?"

Not since her past-life regressions with Natasha revealed what would happen when she finally fell in love. "A few years."

Freda let out a low whistle. "That's too long. And with that scrumptious werewolf in your house all day, how do you resist?"

"It hasn't been easy, but I have to. If I give in and bring him into this, he'll die too."

"He's already in it. Like you said, the cycle has started, and he's part of it whether you enjoy him or not."

Enjoy him. She could think of dozens of ways to enjoy James. Her lips curved into an involuntary smile, so she covered her mouth with her fingers.

"Mm-hmm. You haven't completely strayed from your *met tet.* He'd be proud of the thoughts that are probably dancing through your mind right now."

Boy, would he. Odette cleared her throat. "Message received. Thank you, Erzulie Freda."

The loa straightened the shawl on her shoulders, running her fingers over the silk. "I have another message for you."

She sucked in a breath. "From the Baron?"

Ignoring her question, Freda sank into a chair, her playful smile slipping into a frown. "There are things you don't know...things you can't know until the puzzle is solved." She folded her hands in her lap as tears collected on her lower lids.

No. The loa's shift in mood meant her time here was done. Odette wanted to scream. To shake the woman and beg her to answer her questions, but it was no use. Erzulie Freda's possessions always ended in sadness.

"James can help. The two of you have to solve the puzzle so you can break the cycle and have a lifetime of love." Her shoulders shook with her sob. "If you don't, you'll both die, and your love will die too." Lifting her gaze to Odette's, she pleaded with her eyes. "Love is precious. Please don't let it die this time."

Odette's throat thickened, the sight of the loa in tears making her own eyes sting. "I'll do my best."

With a deep, shuddering breath, Freda closed her eyes and slumped in the chair. When she came to, Darlene blinked, her gaze darting about the room. She lifted the shawl from her shoulders and folded it in her lap. "Erzulie Freda?"

Odette nodded. Her friend wouldn't remember a word of the conversation they'd had. Her consciousness had slipped aside for the loa to take control.

Darlene wiped the tears from her cheeks. "Did you find out what you needed to know?"

"A little." Not nearly enough. Solve the puzzle. What puzzle did she mean?

"Are you banging the Baroness yet?" Cade took a swig of beer and nodded toward the window. "Or is it a coincidence you chose a bar across from the House of Voodoo?"

James narrowed his eyes. "Don't be a dick." He set his

empty glass on the bar. "Her name is Odette. Show a little respect."

Cade raised his eyebrows and looked at Noah, who shook his head, chuckling under his breath. James ignored his friends and let his gaze drift across Dumaine Street to the dark-green wooden door covering the entrance to the Voodoo temple. The front third of the establishment acted as a store where practitioners and tourists alike could buy dolls, potions, herbs, and *gris-gris* bags to help with whatever ailed their bodies or souls.

He'd had his cards read several times in the curtained-off corner booths, and he'd glimpsed the middle section of the store, where the altars to the various Spirits were erected in the temple area. He'd never given the area much thought, but now that he'd seen Odette's own altar in her home, curiosity had him itching to go inside.

The green door was locked, no doubt, though. Odette and the other vodouisants were in the back third of the temple, doing whatever it was that Voodoo practitioners did when they summoned their gods.

Cade chugged the rest of his beer and slammed the bottle on the bar. "What the hell's wrong with you, man? You're about as fun as a canker sore lately. Don't tell me you're pining over the Baron—over Odette."

"Pining? Hell no." He wasn't pining. He wanted to make the woman his, but his damn wolf was insane.

Odette wanted him. That kiss she'd planted on him earlier in the evening was all the confirmation he'd needed, but her back and forth behavior raised his hackles. Why did they need to perform a ritual to find out where the imps had come from? The werewolves dealt with the demons in the Quarter; it was the natural way of things. The vodouisants had never gotten involved before.

He cracked his knuckles. "She knows something… She's hiding something from me."

Noah swiveled in his seat. "You starting to think she's summoning them?"

"No, but I think she knows who is. She's protecting someone, and I need to find out who."

CHAPTER TEN

AN ODD MIX OF EXCITEMENT AND DREAD BUBBLED IN Odette's stomach, fizzing up to her chest where it expanded into an anxious sensation that made her want to crawl back into bed and hide under the covers.

She'd steeled herself to pull James aside as soon as he arrived that morning, tell him about the curse and their impending deaths to get it over with, but he'd come in with the rest of the crew, forgoing his usual early arrival.

When she'd asked why he was late, he'd mumbled something about being on the phone with the warehouse, given her an inquisitive look, as if he were about to ask a question, and then his team stomped in with their arms full of cabinet doors, and she hadn't spoken to him since.

She drummed her nails on the folding table she'd set up in the altar room and stared at her watch, counting the seconds until the crew would leave and she could get James alone. She had so much to tell him, but she had no clue where to begin. How could she tell him that because she was falling for him, they'd both be dead within a few weeks? Or days?

"Kitchen cabinets are done if you want to come have a look." James stood in the doorway wiping his hands on a rag. He half-smiled, but it didn't ease the tightness in his jaw. Whatever his problem was, he needed to get over it. They didn't have time for bruised egos.

He stuffed the rag into his pocket. "They're beautiful."

She rose from her seat and strutted toward him, allowing her power to pool in her core. As her aura tingled with energy, Nicolas, attracted to the magic, appeared behind James, growing more solid as he fed off the energy from the spirit realm passing through Odette. She reined it in, keeping the magic to herself, and lightly touched James's shoulder as she passed. "They better be. That's what I'm paying you for."

He should have felt the void of death as she touched him. The cold emptiness should have made him shiver. That little trick was normally enough to make any grown man cower, and it was the most she ever did with the power the Baron had erroneously gifted her—a tiny boost to remind people she wasn't one to mess with.

But James simply chuckled, catching her hand before she could walk away. "I'm not afraid of you, so if you're trying to get rid of me after last night…"

She squeezed his hand before pulling from his grasp. "I'm not trying to get rid of you. Just having a little fun."

"Is that what you call it?" He closed the distance between them, and taking her hand again, he held it between both of his. "We need to talk."

His magic buzzed on her skin, shimmying up her arm and sparking in her heart. She swallowed the thickness from her throat and gazed into his deep, blue eyes. "I know." He had no idea. "After the crew leaves, okay?"

"Yeah."

He led her into the kitchen, and her breath caught when she saw the transformation. Dark mahogany with elegant scrollwork etched into the trim, the new cabinets deepened the room, giving it an antique yet stylish ambiance. She brought her fingers to her lips as she admired the woodwork.

"Told you they're beautiful." James stood so close his breath tickled her ear. "Classic." He rested a hand on her shoulder. "They're as close to the original cabinetry that we could find. Well, original to the first kitchen that was actually inside the house."

"They're perfect. Thank you." She leaned into him, the warmth of his firm chest against her back making her wish the crew was already gone.

The clank of tools sounded from the foyer, and Noah cleared his throat as he sauntered into the kitchen. James stepped back, taking his warmth with him, and Odette wrapped her arms around herself to rub at the goose bumps on her arms.

"Crew's heading out. You sticking around?" Noah's gazed flicked between James and Odette.

James nodded. "I need to get a few signatures on the paperwork. I'll meet up with you later."

Noah fought a smile and dipped his head at Odette. "Have a good evening, ma'am."

The moment the door clicked shut, James turned to her. "What did you find out at the ceremony?"

"Oh, um…not much, really. I was hoping Baron Samedi would show up, but it seems he's still mad at me." She backed against the counter, gripping the edge. She should say it. Tell him he's her soulmate and they're both going to die because of it. He could handle the truth, couldn't he?

He narrowed his eyes. "Nothing about the imps? You said your loa might be able to tell you where they came from."

Pressing her lips into a hard line, she gripped the counter tighter. If she told him now, he might turn tail and run. That wouldn't help anyone. Death would find him anyway, right after it claimed her.

He stepped toward her and rested his hand on the counter behind her. "Who are you protecting?"

Both of us. "No one. I…" She exhaled a sharp breath. "There are some things you need to know, but it's complicated." Gazing into his eyes, it took every ounce of her willpower not to lean in and kiss him. If he didn't realize they were soulmates yet, he might not believe her. Erzulie Freda said they had to work together if she wanted a chance to break the cycle. She couldn't risk scaring him off. "The loa that spoke to me said there's a puzzle that needs to be solved and you have to help me solve it."

He frowned. "A puzzle?"

"Yes, but she didn't say what, and it's hard to explain." Releasing her grip on the counter, she straightened and brushed a hand down his arm. "I'm free tonight, if you're still interested in having dinner with me. It's going to take a while to explain it all."

He glanced at her fingers where they rested against his and took a deep breath, his gaze roaming from her eyes to her lips and back again. "Now you're asking me out?"

It was either that or push him to the floor and climb on top of him. A date seemed like the more sensible option…for now. "I like you, James. I'd like to get to know you better. Let you get to know me."

Holding her gaze, he purposely hesitated in his reply,

drawing it out, trying to get the upper hand. That wouldn't do.

She cocked an eyebrow and slid away from him. "But if your ego is still bruised, then never mind." Pulling her phone from her pocket, she tapped the screen. "I'll have my dinner delivered. Please lock up on your way out."

He yanked the phone from her hand. "Ordering dinner from Instagram? I didn't realize they offered that feature."

Damn it, she should have clicked the Uber Eats app. "I was checking my notifications first."

Stepping toward her, he cupped her cheek in his hand, angling her face toward his. He drifted closer, his nose brushing hers, the warmth of his breath caressing her lips. "I'm going to run home and shower. I'll be back to pick you up in thirty minutes." He paused, his lips an inch from hers, his grin crinkling the corners of his eyes.

Sweet Spirits, if he didn't kiss her, she was going to explode.

His thumb grazed her cheek as he stepped back and dropped his hand. "Stay inside until I get here." With a wink, he turned and strode from the room.

She didn't remember to breathe until the sound of the lock on the front door pulled her from her trance. That man didn't just make her body burn; he lit her soul on fire.

James watched Odette from the corner of his eye as he pretended to be absorbed in the music. A five-piece band sat on a small raised platform in the corner of The Apothecary, a popular hangout for locals and tourists alike to hear live music with a flair only found in New Orleans. Tonight, the music ranged from big band to jazz to the musician's original tunes, and Odette's elusive smile had almost become a permanent fixture throughout the evening.

They'd started with dinner at Chez Jacques. The Tour of New Orleans had included jambalaya, shrimp creole, and a hearty serving of seafood gumbo, and he'd savored every bite of it. Odette's shrimp and grits had smelled divine, and she'd polished off the entire bowl, plus half the loaf of French bread. He admired a woman who wasn't afraid to eat. The more time he spent with her, the more comfortable she became, and the fact he'd helped to put the smile that most people rarely witnessed on her lips made his pulse pound a little harder.

Sitting in this old pharmacy-turned-bar, with the jazz music playing and the rum flowing, was the perfect ending to their first date. Well, with any luck the date wouldn't end until tomorrow morning, but he was still working on that.

He slid his arm across the back of her seat, letting his hand rest on her shoulder. She glanced at him, biting her lower lip and leaning into his side. Damn, this felt right. The evening. The company. The restlessness that had been stirring in his soul had settled, contentment expanding in its place. He kissed the top of her head, and she let out a quiet sigh.

Mine.

The idea shook him to his very core. He could actually spend forever with this woman. He hadn't known her long, but he felt it in his bones. In his soul. Closing his eyes for a long blink, he sat with it, letting it resonate, waiting for his wolf to tell him otherwise. His beast didn't argue.

He couldn't fight his smile. It had finally happened. He'd found his fate-bound.

No sooner had the thought entered his mind when an image of the dream woman flashed behind his eyes.

Also mine.

He held in a groan. Damn his wolf. The *man* had made up his mind. He wanted Odette, but he sure as hell wouldn't take her as his mate unless his wolf was one hundred percent in agreement that she was the *only* one for him.

It would take some convincing, but he was up for the challenge. Hell, he planned on enjoying every minute of it.

The band played a slow, sultry tune, and several couples took to the small dance floor to sway to the rhythm. He grasped Odette's hand and rose to his feet. "Let's dance."

"Oh." Her eyes tightened, and she didn't move from her seat. "I don't dance." Tugging from his grasp, she clutched her hands on the table.

He sank into his chair and covered her hands with his. "What do you mean you don't dance? We live in the Big Easy. The birthplace of Jazz. Everyone dances here."

"I don't." She looked into his eyes, challenging him to argue.

He pried her hands apart and took one in each of his, lowering them to his lap as he scooted closer. "Can I ask why not?"

"Dancing, and music in general, have a hypnotic effect on people. When you surrender to the music...to the rhythm...you are, in a sense, relinquishing control. It takes you to another place."

Which was one of the things he loved about music. A simple tune could transport a person back in time, into a memory he hadn't thought about in ages. "What's wrong with that?"

She squared her shoulders. "I prefer to stay in control of myself. I don't want to relinquish power to anyone or anything. It's safer that way."

He furrowed his brow. "Safer? Did something happen?"

Her eyes widened. "No, I..."

"Prefer to keep your wits about you?" He grinned, trying to lighten the mood. Whatever the reason for her need to be in constant control, she'd share it with him when she was ready. They had all the time in the world to get to know each other.

Her posture relaxed. "Exactly."

"Do you want to get out of here? Go for a walk or something?"

"I don't think it's safe wandering the streets at night with a bunch of imps on the loose, do you? No one has been injured yet, but I'd rather not be the first."

"Good point."

"We could go to my place." She squeezed his hands. "I'd like to talk to you some more." The sly curve of her lips and the way she trailed her fingers along his thighs as she released his hands said she wanted to do more than talk.

"I like the way you think."

The moment she closed the front door, James swept Odette into his arms and pressed his lips to hers. They did need to talk, like she'd said. He should press her for more information about the imps; he had no doubt she knew more than she let on. At that moment, though, all he could think about was how perfectly she fit into his arms and how soft her skin felt beneath his fingers.

She snaked her hands behind his neck, leaning into him, parting her lips and slipping out her tongue to tangle with his. A growl rumbled from his chest, and he fought the overwhelming urge to lift her from the ground and carry her to the bedroom. No wonder his friends who'd found their fate-bounds were so happy. If their relationship kept going at this pace, his wolf would have to put all four legs on the train and enjoy the ride.

As if on cue, an ache expanded in his chest. A longing for the woman he'd never met. Damn it, this had to stop.

Odette must have sensed the shift in his energy because she let out a soft sigh and pulled away. "We have an audience." She nodded to her left.

James followed her gaze, but the house stood empty. "Nicolas?"

"Mm-hmm. Maybe we should get that talk out of the way." She laced her fingers through his and led him down the hall.

They passed the empty living room, and he glanced through an open doorway at another room devoid of furniture. The one other space in the house that she'd furnished was her bedroom…

Holy hell. What kind of talking did she think was going to happen in there? He could barely keep his hands off her as it was.

"Don't get any ideas." She grinned. "I have a love seat

in the bedroom. I thought we'd be more comfortable there than at the kitchen table."

A small television sat on a dresser, and the pale-blue love seat faced it at an angle. A cream-colored duvet covered the bed, and the faint scent of lavender greeted him as he entered the room. She sat on the sofa, curling one leg beneath her, and patted the space next to her.

"I bet you can't wait until the renovation is done. It'll be nice to not be confined to two rooms." He sank onto the cushion and turned to face her, his knee resting against hers.

She glanced at where their legs touched and placed an elbow on the back of the couch. "There's no rush. I kinda like having you around."

His stomach fluttered, a thousand butterflies taking flight and landing in his chest. "I like being around."

She smiled. "There's a reason for that."

He leaned toward her. "I'm positive it's you."

Her lips parted as if she were going to speak, but instead, she narrowed her eyes and chewed her bottom lip. Lowering her gaze, she picked at a loose thread on the cushion.

"Hey." He reached for her, trailing his fingers down her cheek before gently lifting her chin. "What's wrong?"

"This is going to sound crazy. I'm not even sure where to begin."

He dropped his hand to his lap and leaned against the back cushion. "Why don't you start with the imps. You know where they came from, don't you? Who summoned them?"

She sat up straighter and regarded him, studied him as if she were weighing her words. With a deep inhale, she relaxed her shoulders, a sad smile playing on her lips. "The demons are from my past, but I don't know exactly who summoned them."

"You don't know *exactly?*" He relaxed his fist on the back of the couch and traced his finger across the fabric. "Whatever happened in your past, I don't care. If you know where the demons are coming from, the werewolves can take out their boss and keep anyone from getting hurt. Just tell me."

"They're from your past too. That's what I wanted to talk to you about." Her eyes tightened.

"I've never seen those things before." He shook his head, her accusation taking him aback. How could she charge him, a werewolf, the natural-born enemy of demons, of summoning the imps? "I had nothing to do with them showing up."

"I'm not accusing you. Hear me out, okay?" She sighed and took both his hands in hers. "Do you believe in reincarnation?"

He shrugged, her touch taking the edge off his nerves. "Sure. But demons can't die, so they can't be reincarnated, if that's what you're getting at. When we vanquish them, they go back to their hellish dimension until someone summons them again."

She shook her head. "Do you believe in soulmates? That two people can be meant for each other because their destinies are entwined? Because they've been together in every lifetime they've lived?"

His eyes widened, and he fought to keep his expression neutral. Did she feel the same connection he felt to her? Was *that* what she was getting at? "Werewolves use the term fate-bound."

"Because fate binds your hearts. I like that." She smiled and traced her thumbs across the backs of his hands. "This isn't our first life together, James. We're soul-mates." She tightened her grip on his hands as if she were afraid he'd run away.

But he wasn't going anywhere. Hearing her confirm what he'd known—at least in the back of his mind—since he first knocked on her door sent electricity running up his spine. He squeezed her hands in return hoping to imply that at least the man in him agreed. Now to convince his wolf. "How do you know?"

"Would you believe me if I said I just do?"

"I'd like to, but I have a feeling there's more to it than that."

"I've done a few past-life regressions with Natasha, trying to…figure things out. When you came into my life, I had a feeling you were the man from my previous lives. The Mambo confirmed it with a reading, and then Erzulie Freda, the loa of love, spoke to me about you at the cere-mony. You're my soulmate." She shrugged, not looking at all as happy as she should have.

The corners of her mouth twitched, and she swallowed hard, her gaze darting about, looking at anything but him.

"That's good news, right?" He tried to catch her gaze, but she stared at their joined hands.

"Yes and no. I'm kinda glad to have found you." She finally looked into his eyes. "My feelings for you grow stronger every day."

"Kinda?" If they truly were soulmates, there would be no kinda about it. That type of connection was all or nothing. If she wasn't fully on board, and his wolf wasn't fully on board, maybe it was time he stepped off this train before it headed for certain disaster.

He rubbed his forehead and glanced at the door. The best escape would be honesty. Tell her they should slow things down and then stop seeing her after working hours. Now was the time to stand up and walk away, but he couldn't make himself move.

"Please let me finish." She rested her hand on his knee, the light pressure gluing him to the spot. "We seem to be stuck in a cycle, and it always ends in tragedy. That's why I said kinda. Because I know how this is going to end."

He'd been prepared to bolt, but her mention of being stuck in a cycle drew him back in. "You asked about the readings I've had done? They've told me the same thing. That I have to break the cycle. But no one knows what the cycle is."

"I do." Her brow furrowed, pity filling her eyes. "You said you thought those imps were a precursor to something bigger that hasn't fully formed yet?"

"Yeah?" A sinking sensation formed in the pit of his stomach.

"That *bigger thing* is going to kill us both. First me, and then you. It's happened in every past-life I've visited. I'm going to die in your arms, and I don't know how to stop it from happening."

"Wha—" The words stuck in his throat. *Hell no.* His wolf sprang to attention, the deep need to keep her safe rousing it to the surface.

She couldn't die; he wouldn't let it happen. He'd fought plenty of monsters, vanquished nasty demons that would have sent most wolves running with their tails between their legs. "Come here. I'm not going to let you die. Whatever this monster is, I'll protect you from it." He sidled next to her and wrapped her in his arms.

Resting her head on his shoulder, she draped her legs across his lap and snuggled into his side. "It's going to kill you too. That's the cycle."

Nope. Couldn't happen. The cycle ended now. "There's a hole in your theory."

She lifted her head to look at him. "How so?"

"You said we're both going to die because you've seen it in your past-life regressions. But if you always die in my arms, how can you know that I die too?"

"Because I've researched it. I discovered my name in the regression, then I looked up the records. It's always the same, reported as a double murder or murder-suicide. Two mangled bodies are found with their throats slit or their hearts punctured, but the killer is never discovered."

He held her tighter, letting her words sink in. She'd called the murderer a monster. "Do you know who the killer is? Another reincarnated soul who's out to get us?"

"It's not a human. The memories always grow fuzzy when I recount my death. Probably my brain's way of trying to spare me from the horror. But it's horrible anyway. I'm always with you when it happens. The monster is fast and grotesque. From what I've seen, he looks part-human, but his head has melted onto his shoulders in some way." She shivered.

"I feel teeth and claws. Sometimes I think I see a knife, but it could be a long claw. I don't know if it's a reincarnated beast or if it's the same one, living all these years in seclusion."

"Teeth and claws. Could it be a werewolf?" Could someone in his own pack be out to get him? It wouldn't be the first time a lower-level wolf had challenged for rank, nor the first time a mate had been targeted. James wasn't first-family. He didn't have an ounce of alpha blood in his body, but his solid track record and his friendship with the alpha had raised him in the ranks.

Not high enough to be challenged, though.

"It's possible. I don't know, but whatever it is, our coming together has awakened it."

"Do you know what started it? If it's a cycle, it must have a beginning. Maybe that's the puzzle we need to solve. If we can figure out what started it, then we can stop it."

She shook her head. "The farthest back I've gone is 1897, and I don't think that was the beginning." She rubbed at the goose bumps on her arms. "My death came as a surprise that time. Every time that I've experienced. If we did something in the past to trigger it, to make the monster come for us, I haven't regressed to that life."

"You need to do more then. Keep regressing back until you find what started it, and then we'll stop it together."

She dropped her face into her hands. "I can't."

"Why not?"

"For one, the older the life, the fuzzier the memories. Nothing is clear. The main reason, though…I can't experience another death again. It takes a toll on me. My connection to death is strong as it is, so actually experiencing my own death affects me as if I'm really dying. I need days to recover, and I'm not sure we have that much time."

From what he'd learned about imps, once they showed up, their master wasn't far behind. They couldn't spare days for her to recover. "I'll do it then. We'll call Natasha first thing in the morning and set up an appointment. I'll go back as many times as it takes to figure this out."

"No. You won't just be experiencing your own death. You'll have to watch me die too."

His heart sank. He'd endure his own death as many times as he had to in order to keep her safe. But to watch

Odette die again and again? He might not be able to handle that.

He had to, though. "Then I better get it right the first time."

She searched his eyes, the uncertainty in her own transforming into resigned acceptance. "You'd better."

He took her face in his hands, pressing a kiss to her lips. "We'll figure this out together, okay? Solve the puzzle. Stop the cycle. Live to see tomorrow. We've got this."

"We do, don't we?" She smiled and slid her hand halfway up his thigh. "The monster never attacked during the day in the past, so I think it's safe to assume daylight is our friend. And the house is protected, so we're secure inside at night." Her grin turned devilish. "I think it might be best if you stayed here tonight...to be cautious. What do you think?"

His stomach tightened as her fingers inched higher up his leg, his heart pumping a flush of heat through his veins. "I think you might be right. Safety first."

"I'm glad we agree." The words barely escaped her lips before she took his mouth with hers. She kissed him urgently, her right hand squeezing his thigh as she slid her left behind his neck to pull him closer. Her warm vanilla scent tickled his senses, and the feel of her tongue tangling with his was enough to drive him mad.

His jeans grew tight across his groin, and he couldn't hold back the moan that rolled up from his core. He needed this woman. God, he wanted her to be his fatebound, and at the moment, his wolf seemed to agree.

Sliding a hand behind her back, he leaned into her, hoping to lay her on the couch. She resisted, pushing him back instead and climbing into his lap. Straddling him, she roamed her hands across his chest, down lower...

lower, until she reached the waistband of his jeans. Magic shimmied across his stomach as she slipped her fingers beneath his shirt and pressed her palms against his skin.

She broke from his mouth to glide her lips along his jaw, nipping at his earlobe as she tugged his shirt upward. Leaning back, she pulled it over his head and dropped it on the floor. Her pupils dilated, and her tongue slipped out to moisten her lips as her gaze wandered from his eyes down to the bulge in his pants, then back up to his chest. Good lord, the woman was sexy.

"I like your tattoo." She grazed her fingers over his left pec, tracing the pack emblem, a wolf head centered in a fleur-de-lis. "Is it a requirement to be in the pack?"

"No, but it shows our allegiance…"

She dipped her head and licked his nipple, sending a shock of electricity straight to his dick. A groan vibrated in his throat, and she grinned wickedly as she lifted her head and trailed her hands down his stomach.

As she locked eyes with him and popped the button on his jeans, he groaned and reached for her hands. "Are you sure you're ready for this?"

"You're my soulmate; I've always been ready." She tilted her head. "You're the one who's hesitant. Is something wrong?"

"No." His answer came quickly, but his wolf didn't hesitate to show him the image of the dream woman, which he immediately shoved to the back of his mind. "I'm making sure this is really what you want. That was quite a revelation you laid on me."

"Our souls are entwined, and I don't know how much time we have left. Let's not waste a minute of it. I want you, James."

Her sultry words wrapped around him like an electric

blanket, filling him with warmth, caressing his skin, stroking his... Nope, that was her hand rubbing his cock through his jeans.

With a deep inhale, he squared his gaze on hers. "I want you too." That much he could honestly confirm.

Her lips curved into a mischievous grin. "Good." She tugged her shirt over her head and dropped it next to his.

Her black lace bra cupped her full breasts, and he glided his hands up her sides to tease her nipples through the fabric. She made an *mmm* sound and tilted her head back, leaning into his touch.

With her hands on his chest, she slid from his lap, lowering to her knees in front of him. His stomach clenched as she reached for his jeans, tugging them over his hips and down his legs. She pulled down his boxer-briefs next, her brow lifting as she licked her lips.

Oh, to have those perfect red lips around his dick...

Lifting from the floor, she leaned into him, taking his mouth in another kiss. The feel of her body pressed to his was enough to send him over the edge, but there was too much fabric between them. That needed to change.

As he reached for the clasp on her bra, she laughed and slid to the floor again. "You first." She ran a single finger down his dick from tip to base, sending a shudder through his body. As she wrapped her hand around him, his ability to form a coherent thought crumbled like cheap mortar on a poorly-made house.

Her tongue felt like velvet against his shaft, and as she took him into her mouth, the sensation of being engulfed in warm, rich honey had him dropping his head back onto the couch and moaning from somewhere deep in his core.

He needed to stop her. She should be the one to come first, but damn it, he'd lost the ability to form words.

She slid her mouth up his cock, rolling her tongue around the tip before taking him in fully again. He wouldn't last five minutes like this, so he lifted his head, placing a hand on her shoulder. But the electricity jolting through his core forced his eyes shut with the ecstasy.

A pounding on the window behind him drew him from his trance as Odette released her hold. Another bang, this time from the one to his left, sounded like it should have shattered the glass. "What the hell?"

She stood and peered through the pane. "There's something out there."

"No kidding." He rose to his feet, but with his pants around his ankles, he stumbled, catching himself on the arm of the loveseat before he could topple to the floor. "Damn it." He fumbled for his pants, yanking them the rest of the way off, and joining her at the window.

A black mass darted into the side yard, but in human form, James couldn't make out its shape in the darkness.

"You're sure nothing can get in?" He wrapped a protective arm around her.

"Positive. The spell is unbreakable." The confidence in her voice didn't mask the worry in her eyes.

"Stay inside this time, okay? I'll take care of it." He strode out of the room toward the back door.

CHAPTER ELEVEN

THE MOMENT HE SHUT THE DOOR BEHIND HIM, JAMES shifted and bounded down the porch steps toward the fiend. He paused before he rounded the corner, angling his nose upward to catch its scent. The faint smell of swamp —decomposing foliage and mud—greeted his nostrils, but he didn't detect a trace of the rotting garbage odor that normally clung to demons.

The low growl in his throat was barely audible above the banging on the window. Whatever it was, it wanted inside badly.

James crept around the corner, and the entity whirled around to face him. He barely got a glimpse of the some-what-human-shaped figure before it sprang from the ground, leaping over him and darting into the backyard.

What the hell? Hackles raised, James spun, ready to give chase.

But the entity had vanished.

Crouching low, he crept into the backyard, his senses on high alert. A shuffling sound emanated from above, and before he could lift his head, the creature dropped onto him, sinking its teeth into his neck.

Dammit, not again. Searing pain tore through his right side, and James yelped, spinning in a circle, jaws snapping until he finally connected with flesh. A garbled squeal—half-animal, half-human—ripped from the beast's throat before it released its hold and leaped over the fence.

James glanced over his shoulder and glimpsed Odette watching through the window, worry furrowing her brow. He hesitated, torn between the instinct to stay and protect her and the need to catch the creature who'd threatened them.

He trusted her magic, but could he trust her to stay put? He took the slight dip of her chin as confirmation she wouldn't leave the house, and blowing out a hard breath, he took off after the beast.

The monster moved faster than anything he'd encountered before, gaining a three-block lead on James before he'd cleared the fence. Even with his enhanced werewolf vision, James could barely make out the silhouette of a humanoid figure with a massive, oddly-shaped head sprinting up Treme Street toward Louis Armstrong Park.

At two a.m, most of the residents were inside their homes, but James kept to the shadows as best he could, running from tree to tree to keep himself hidden. The houses along the way quickly changed from the mansions of Millionaire's Row to small one and two-story cottages in shades of red, purple, and yellow. He ducked behind a parked car as a dilapidated truck ambled through the intersection, losing precious seconds in his chase.

If he continued to keep to the shadows, the monster would be out of sight within the next minute. *Screw it.* James sprinted down the center of the street. Whatever that *thing* was, it would draw more attention than he would. A werewolf sighting could be written off as an enormous dog.

James slowed as he reached St. Philip, where Treme ended and the park began, but movement behind the wrought-iron fence caught his attention. He increased his speed, hurdling the fence and plowing toward the creature.

Damn, this thing was fast. He searched his mind for another wolf to help him. Though they couldn't exactly hear each other's thoughts, werewolves had an almost tele-pathic connection. He briefly considered calling for Luke, but with Odette involved, this situation was too sticky to contact the alpha yet.

Come on, Cade. Where are you? He focused, feeling his way through the were energy like sifting through the sand to find a shell. When he found his friend, their minds connected, and he relayed the information. He needed help, or the bastard would get away.

With Cade on the move, James followed the creature out of the park and across Basin Street. *Please don't go into the cemetery.*

The beast vaulted over the concrete barrier and entered St. Louis Cemetery Number One. *Shit.*

With a running start, James leaped at the wall, catching it with his front paws and scrambling his back legs up and over. He landed on his side with a *thud*, knocking the breath from his lungs, and pain from his neck wound flashed from his skull to his shoulder.

He lay still for a moment, focusing on the sounds around him: a rat scurrying across the concrete walk, tires turning on the asphalt and the hum of an engine as a car passed, the wind whistling through the rows and rows of above-ground graves that housed the remains of multiple generations of New Orleanians.

Of all the places the beast could have picked to hide… James grunted and rose to his paws. He'd never find the bastard in the city of the dead. The only good thing about this situation was that the cemetery gates locked at dusk, so he didn't have to worry about any humans discovering him.

From massive mausoleums to short, single-family tombs, the graves rose from the ground, creating a labyrinth of twisting paths and dead-ends. Many of the tombs were well-cared for, with new plaster and fresh paint that made them gleam white in the moonlight. Others were crumbling, the plaster decaying to show the brick and mortar beneath.

His chest tightened as the fond memories of his weekends in the cemetery with his dad flooded his mind. Though he'd spent his time in a different cemetery, during the day, something about a graveyard always brought a sense of calmness over him. His dad too. Even through all the turmoil and heartache his mom had caused, James and his father could always find peace in the cemetery.

If he weren't on the trail of a murderous monster, he might have slowed down to enjoy the stillness. Instead, he focused on his senses, searching the darkness for evil.

With no sign of the beast, James wandered amongst the graves, pausing as he reached the end of a row and peering around the corner in hopes of catching the monster off-guard. But with the tombs laid out in no discernable pattern, he soon found himself backtracking, covering the same spaces with no luck.

"James, you still in here?" Noah's hushed voice came

from a few rows over, and James searched his mind for Cade.

Connecting with the other wolf, James relayed his location, and the three of them met in front of the famous Voodoo priestess, Marie Laveau's, tomb. Cade's deep-red fur stood in a ridge along his back, and his ears twitched.

Noah looked from wolf to wolf. "What's the plan?" He paused as if they could answer. Because Noah was second-born and couldn't shift, he lacked the telepathic connection that shifting wolves shared. "Let me guess. We split up and scour the place. Yell if we find it?"

What he lacked in ability, Noah made up for in intelligence. James bobbed his head to indicate his agreement, and the men went in different directions, searching for the monster.

Half an hour later, James returned to Marie Laveau's tomb and sat in front of it. Though it had been repainted several times, the small black Xs still showed through. Rumor had it that if a person drew three Xs on the tomb, spun around three times, and left an offering, the Mambo's Spirit would grant his wish.

He'd always thought it hokum, but after spending time with Odette and learning about Baron Samedi, he couldn't help but wonder if there was any truth to the tale. Cade returned in human form, and Noah joined them shortly after.

"What the hell were you chasing?" Cade scanned the area, still on high alert. "The image was fuzzy in your mind."

James rose to all fours. He'd never gotten a clear look at the creature, but it seemed to match Odette's description. When he didn't answer, Cade furrowed his brow.

"C'mon, man. Shift and let's get out of here. This place gives me the creeps."

James growled low in his throat. They'd have to walk ten blocks to get back to Odette's, and he had a slight problem with doing that in human form.

"Do you know what's wrong with him?" Noah asked Cade.

Cade crossed his arms and shook his head. "Are you hurt? There's blood in your fur."

James let out his breath in a huff. Yes, he was hurt, and if he were a full werewolf, it would have healed by now. His injury wasn't the problem, though if his friends tried to coddle him, it would become one—for them.

The corner of Noah's mouth twitched before turning into a full-blown grin. "Wait a minute. You said he was coming from Odette's place, right?"

Cade shrugged. "Yeah."

Noah chuckled. "You're naked, aren't you? You were banging the Baroness when it happened."

Baring his teeth, James let out a menacing growl. Noah needed to show respect for his girlfriend, and if he could form words, he'd tell him so.

Cade guffawed. "Oh, man. This is classic. Give him your pants, Noah."

"No way. You give him yours."

"I don't think he wants mine. I'm commando underneath."

Noah groaned and crossed his arms. "He's not getting my pants. He made it here in wolf form; he can make it back. We'll meet you at Odette's."

At least one of them was making sense. Backing up a few steps, James sprang onto a tomb and then vaulted over the cemetery wall.

Not the smartest move he could have made.

He overshot his target and landed in the road. A horn blared as a car speeding down St. Louis street slammed on its brakes. James scrambled onto the sidewalk, cursing himself for his lack of caution, and the passenger rolled down the window and stared, wide-eyed, as the vehicle crept past. Damn it, he didn't have time for this. He needed to get back to Odette.

Another car passed, and he raced across the road, determined to get his ass out of view. But he wasn't fast enough.

"Holy shit." A police officer with dark hair and a beer belly rounded the corner and nudged his partner, gesturing toward James as he unclipped his gun from its holster.

The taller man stopped and cocked his head, his right hand resting on his firearm. "Is that a wolf?"

Shit. Shit, shit, shit.

Ten more feet and he'd have made it to the public parking lot where he could have hidden amongst the vehicles. Instead, he stood, fully exposed, beneath a street lamp, two cops cautiously approaching with their guns drawn. If he took off now, they'd shoot. Hit him in the heart or head, and he'd be dead.

Sucking in a deep breath, he forced himself to relax to get the ridge of hair running down his back to lay flat. Best to not look menacing to innocent humans with the power to kill him.

"There you are." Noah took off his belt and jogged toward him. "You can't run off like that, buddy." He sweetened his voice, talking to James like he was a dog.

A goddamn dog.

"I told you that leash was a piece of crap." Cade strode

up and stopped by Noah. "Snapped in half the first time you used it, didn't it?"

"The leash snapped because you yanked it so hard. Pulled the poor guy's collar right off his neck." Noah held the belt toward James.

James huffed and backed up. No way in hell was he pretending to be a domesticated house pet.

"You don't have much of a choice here, man," Noah whispered under his breath.

One of the officers holstered his gun. Beer belly held his tight by his side. "This your dog?"

"Yes, sir." Noah plastered on a smile and slipped the belt around James's neck. "We're on our way home."

"Why's he bleeding?" The tall guy nodded toward James's shoulder.

"Oh, uh…" Noah squinted at his blood-soaked fur. "He tried to squeeze through a broken fence. Sharp edge of wrought-iron got him. We'll take care of it when we get home."

"Biggest damn dog I've ever seen." Chubby adjusted his grip on his gun, and sweat beaded on his upper lip.

Cade moved to James's other side, flanking him. "He's harmless." He scratched him behind the ear, and James gritted his teeth to stop himself from snapping at his friend.

"Holster your weapon, LeClerc." The taller officer stepped closer, while LeClerc did as he was told. "How'd you domesticate him? He's a wolf, right?"

"He's half-wolf. His domesticated side drains the wild right out of him, doesn't it, buddy?" Cade patted his head, and James held in a growl. "He's not nearly as tough as a full-wolf would be."

James jerked his head from Cade's grasp. That

comment better not have been a jab at his lineage. His mom's humanity was common knowledge, but James worked overtime to make up for what he lacked. No one called him a lesser wolf.

"Can I pet him?" The cop reached a hand toward James.

"Uh…" Noah started, but Cade cut him off.

"Sure. He's a sweetheart."

Noah tightened his grip on the belt. He couldn't have held James back if he tried, but the gesture reminded him to play the part in front of the cops. As soon as he was alone with Cade, though…

His friends exchanged a few more words with the officers, and then they headed back toward Odette's. James tugged from Noah's grasp, but his friend clutched the belt again.

"Do you want to draw any more attention? Just a few more blocks."

Cade laughed. "Yeah, buddy. Be a good boy." He rubbed the top of James's head.

He didn't hold back this time. A menacing growl rolled up from his core, and he snapped his jaws, clamping onto Cade's hand, his teeth penetrating to the bone.

"Ow! Damn it, what was that for?" As if he didn't know. Cade tried to pull his hand from James's maw.

Coppery blood oozed into James's mouth, and he tightened his grip, his growl turning into a snarl.

"The half-wolf comment was a low blow," Noah said.

Cade sucked in a breath through his teeth. "I'm sorry, okay? But you knew I was joking."

James released his hand and blew out a hard breath. A sliver of truth laced every so-called joke, and Cade needed to remember his place. James would always out-rank him.

They reached Odette's and searched the perimeter, but they found no sign of the creature. Cade's wound had healed by the time they made it to the front porch, and he lifted his hand to knock as the lock disengaged and Odette opened the door.

She started to speak, but whatever she'd planned to say got stuck in her throat when her eyes met James's. She flicked her gaze to Cade and then Noah before opening the door wider and ushering them all inside.

James narrowed his eyes at his friends, a silent message for them to stay in the foyer, before trotting through the kitchen to Odette's bedroom.

She followed on his heels. "Is everything okay? What happened?"

He shifted to human form and fumbled to right his inside-out jeans. Anger fumed in his chest. Anger at Cade for being an ass. At Noah for the idiotic idea of acting like he was a dog. But most of all at himself for not killing the creature when he had the chance.

"Here. Let me do that." She took his jeans and righted them while he yanked on his underwear. "I take it the demon got away?"

"That was no demon." He shoved his legs into pants, and Odette brushed her fingers across his neck.

"It hurt you."

He touched the wound. Two scratches were all that remained of the gash the creature had torn in his shoulder. He'd healed, but not fast enough to hide it from her or his friends. Then Cade called him harmless because he was only half-wolf… He'd show the jackass harmless.

"I'm fine." He pulled on his shirt and clutched her shoulders. "Did it come back here?"

"I don't think so. It hasn't tried to get in if it did."

Nodding, he took her hand and led her to the foyer. As soon as his gaze met Cade's he dropped her hand and lunged for him, slamming his back against the closed door, his forearm pressing the air from his lungs. "If you *ever* pull a stunt like that again, your ass will be mine. Understood?"

Cade scowled. "What about him?" He gestured with his head toward Noah. "The whole thing was his idea. Aren't you going to bite him too?"

Odette gasped. "You bit him?"

"He was treating me like a dog." He leaned his weight into Cade, showing his dominance.

"We saved your ass and kept the pack's secret safe." Cade's voice strained under the pressure.

"He's right." Noah placed a hand on James's shoulder. "I'm sorry it had to be that way, but the pack does come first."

He glanced at his friend. When did Noah become the voice of reason? "I see your point." He looked into Cade's eyes, holding his gaze, asserting his dominance again. James may have been wrong to challenge his friend, but he wasn't about to lose a fight.

Cade glared at him briefly before lowering his head and dropping his gaze to the floor, ending the confrontation.

Odette clutched his arm, gently tugging until he stepped back, and Cade brushed the front of his shirt as if brushing off the threat.

Wrapping his arms around her, James kissed her fore-head and unclenched his jaw. "I'm sorry I didn't end this today."

She leaned into him, resting her hands on his shoulders. "I didn't expect you to. If it's going to end, we have to do it together."

She was right. In his attempt to prove himself capable of protecting her, he'd blown their chance at defeating the monster. They were stuck in this cycle together, so they'd have to work together to end it. No more leaving her behind while he tried to fight the bad guys.

He turned to Cade and offered his hand. "Sorry, man. Thanks for your help out there."

Cade accepted the handshake. "Me too." He glanced at Odette. "Are you going to call Luke?"

James raked a hand through his hair. As the alpha, Luke needed to know what was going on, but as his boss… "Shit. It's complicated. I…"

"You broke the no sleeping with clients rule." Noah failed at hiding his smile.

Odette laughed and slid an arm around James's waist, resting her other hand on his chest. "It's okay. We haven't slept together…yet." She pinched his side as she said the last word, and he jumped.

Noah chuckled. "He still has to explain to the alpha why he was at your house at two a.m…naked."

She laid her head on his shoulder. "I think he'll make an exception in this case. This isn't our first life together. We're soulmates."

Oh, hell. She went there.

"She's your fate-bound?" Cade cracked a smile and slapped James on the shoulder. "Why didn't you say so? Congrats."

James slipped from Odette's hold and ushered his friends toward the door. "We've got it under control here. Why don't you give Luke a preliminary report and tell him I'll call him tomorrow?" He opened the door and shoved them through, following them onto the porch.

"Congratulations." Noah shook his hand. "It's about time."

"Like I said, it's complicated. Just…don't say anything about this, okay?" He gestured to the door. "Tell him about the monster; I'll fill him in on the rest later."

Cade looked at him incredulously. "What could possibly be complicated about finding your fated mate?"

How about the fact that his half-human wolf insisted he needed two mates? He gripped the doorknob. "Thanks for your help tonight. I'll talk to y'all tomorrow."

He went inside to find Odette waiting for him in the foyer, wringing her hands and biting her lower lip. "That was it, wasn't it? The monster that wants to kill us both? It was too big to be an imp."

"I'm afraid so."

Her brow lifted, and for the first time since he'd met her, true fear glinted in her eyes. "What was it?"

"I don't know. It smelled like swamp, so it wasn't a demon. It was human-shaped. Kinda. Its limbs were longer than a person's, and its head was… It's hard to say because it moved so fucking fast, but its head looked like it had melted onto its shoulders like you described. It stayed in the shadows, so I never got a good look at it, but when it bit me, it felt like a wolf bite."

"It sounds like it's the same beast."

He took her in his arms and hugged her tight. "Sure does. What are we going to do?"

"Are you still up for doing a past-life regression? The monster always kills me first, so maybe you'll see more than I do."

His breath hung on her words. Reliving her death and his own wasn't the slightest bit appealing. Could he even handle the trauma? If it would help them fight the thing in this life… "Now?"

She shook her head. "It's three-thirty in the morning. I'll call Natasha tomorrow to set it up."

"Sounds like a plan." He stood still, holding her, memorizing the way she fit in his arms. Like she was made for him. "What should we do until then?"

She slid her hands into his back pockets and gave his ass a squeeze. "How about we finish what we started?"

That he could handle.

CHAPTER TWELVE

THE OVERCAST SKY BLOCKED THE MOONLIGHT FROM illuminating the bedroom, but the hall light filtering in through the open door cast enough glow for Odette to see the seductive smile on James's lips. He removed his shirt for the second time tonight, and she couldn't fight her own smile as she took in his chiseled features. Perfectly defined abs rolled down his stomach, accented by the V disappearing into his jeans.

Oh, that delicious V…

The monster had found them. Death was knocking on their door, but if her time on this Earth was limited, she wanted to get more than a taste of him before she had to go. Slinking toward him, she ran her fingers down his chest, lightly grazing his soft skin. His stomach tightened as she reached his jeans, the muscles becoming even more defined as he held his breath.

When she popped the button and slid down the zipper, a slow hiss escaped his lips. He caught her hands and brought them to his mouth. "This time, you have to get naked too."

"I suppose that's fair." She hadn't begun to have her way with him, but if he wanted to see her, she could afford him that.

She stepped back, peeling her shirt over her head and unclasping her bra, letting it fall to the floor. "Better?"

An appreciative growl rumbled in his chest. "Getting there." He pulled her into an embrace, taking her mouth in a kiss.

Leaning into him, she allowed herself a moment of vulnerability, getting lost in the feel of his strong arms wrapped around her, the warmth of his bare skin against hers and the magic sizzling between them making her shiver with need.

Before she could get too lost, though, she pulled away. "Take off your pants."

James grinned. "My pleasure." He removed the rest of his clothes and stood before her, holding his hands out to his sides. "Your turn."

She let her gaze travel the length of his magnificent body, lingering on his dick, hard and ready, before she stepped toward him and took him in her hand. She stroked him, pressing her lips to his neck and running her tongue up to his ear lobe.

His eyes fluttered shut as a moan slipped from his throat, and he reached for the button on her pants. Stepping away, she pushed him onto the bed. He chuckled and scooted to the center of the mattress. When she didn't move, he arched a brow. "You are planning to join me, aren't you?"

"I have lots of plans for you, James." She unbuttoned her slacks and slid the zipper down. As she worked them over her hips, he rolled onto his side, his blue eyes smoldering in the dim light.

"You are the most beautiful woman I've ever met." His baritone voice wrapped around her, his words encircling her heart, holding it tight. He opened his mouth as if to say more, but his brow furrowed, a look of confusion tightening his eyes briefly before he composed himself.

"Everything okay?"

He blinked. "It would be a lot better if you climbed into bed with me."

She slinked toward him and crawled onto the mattress. He rose onto an elbow, taking her face in his hand and leaning into her as if to put her on her back. When his lips met hers, she clutched his shoulder, pushing him to the sheets and straddling him.

He laughed. "You like to be in control, don't you?"

"Always." She kissed his neck, nipping at his skin as she worked her way down to his shoulder, the taste of him, his intoxicating, warm scent making her blood hum.

"So do I." Faster than should have been possible, he wrapped an arm around her and flipped her onto her back. Clasping a hand in each of his, he raised them above her head, pinning her to the pillow.

She gasped, her first instinct tempting her to wiggle free, to regain control. But she couldn't deny the thrilling quivers shooting through her core, sparking like fireworks inside her. "You're strong."

"I'm a werewolf, and right now, both man and beast want to ravish you." He glided his hands down her arms, across her chest to cup her breasts. As his thumbs teased her nipples, another explosion of sparks ricocheted through her core.

She could do this. She was in control of every aspect of her life. If she were to let go somewhere, here in the bedroom, with her soulmate, was the best place to do it.

He lowered his mouth to her breast and took her nipple between his teeth. Tugging gently, he released her and moved to the other side. He teased her with his tongue, roaming his hands across her body, the roughness of his palms reminding her what a strong, capable man he was. His deep, woodsy scent. The way he touched her. The appreciative growls rolling up from his chest as he caressed her... He was everything she'd dreamed he would be.

"Are you on birth control?" His lips moved against her skin.

"Of course."

"Then we only have one problem." He pressed a kiss between her breasts and rose onto his elbows to look at her.

"We do?"

"You're still not naked." Sitting up, he grasped her panties and slid them down her legs. "I like black lace, but it's time for these to go." He dropped them on the floor and lifted her leg, running his hand from her ankle up to the center of her inner thigh.

Her pulse sprinted as he settled between her legs. She was completely naked, on her back. Vulnerable.

But that was okay. It was her choice to let him take the lead, so she was still in control. She could do this.

He rubbed his cheek against her thigh, the scruff on his skin tickling her. His breath warmed her center, and a war waged between her body and her mind. She wanted him to touch her—to lick her—like she'd never wanted anything in her life. But to allow him to do that to her. To let him take her to the edge, at his pace and not hers, would mean completely letting go.

She was about to die anyway. For once in her life, she could do it. Just this once. With James.

He slipped out his tongue and tasted her, the sensation of warm velvet enveloping her as a moan vibrated across his lips. He licked her again, and a shudder ran through her entire body.

"I can feel your magic getting stronger." His lips moved against her. "It's incredible."

Incredible didn't begin to describe the way he was making her feel, but…

Her heart pounded, icy panic flushing through her veins. She couldn't do this. Couldn't lose control. She'd made a promise to herself. "Please stop."

He froze, his mouth hovering above her center.

"I can't do this." She sat up, scooting back to lean against the headboard.

Confusion contorted his features as he rose onto his knees. "Did I hurt you?"

"No." She shook her head. "I just can't."

Pressing his lips together, he blew out a hard breath. "Should I leave?"

"No. Stay please." She pulled up the sheet, covering herself.

He rubbed his forehead. "If I did something wrong…"

"You didn't do anything wrong. Everything you've done has been amazing. It's…" How could she explain this?

"Wait…are you a virgin?"

She laughed at the dumbfounded expression on his face. "Of course not. Lie down with me. Come here." She pulled back the sheet and patted the space next to her as she lay on her side.

He settled near her, face to face, but not touching. She needed his touch. If she didn't explain her little freak-out quickly, she would ruin the night. Taking his hand, she reached a leg to his, planning to drape it across him. As soon as she touched him, he moved, entwining her leg between his. Holding her.

"What's going on?" Concern filled his eyes, making her heart ache.

She felt like such an idiot. She'd never put herself in this position before. The few men she had slept with had been much more passive than James, allowing her to take the lead. They also didn't have as much interest in her pleasure, none of them protesting when she'd made sure all the focus went to their orgasms and not her own. "I've never let anyone do that to me before."

"Why not?"

She bit her bottom lip and searched his eyes. His puzzled expression morphed into one of compassion, and her reservations dissolved. She could trust this man. It was time to tell him the truth about her past. Some of it anyway. "I'm a bit of a control freak."

He chuckled. "Really? I couldn't tell."

"I have a good reason."

He pressed a kiss to the back of her hand and scooted closer to her. "What does that have to do with what we were just doing?"

"I felt…vulnerable. Exposed. Letting you do that to me…you were in control of my body. That's scary."

Gliding his fingers down her side, he rested a hand on her hip. "I wasn't trying to hurt you. If I did, I'm very sorry."

"You didn't hurt me." She was doing a terrible job of explaining this. *Tell the man. He's not going anywhere.* "Losing control is something I haven't allowed myself to do since I was a kid. Since I moved away."

"What happened when you were a kid?"

She bit her lip, hesitating. "It's a long story."

"I want to know."

Sweet Spirits, she was going to tell him. Lifting her head, she propped it up with her hand. "My dad is Catholic. Completely mundane."

He moved to mirror her posture. "I never would have guessed you didn't have magic from both sides."

"When my mom died, my dad wanted me to continue with Voodoo, but he didn't have a clue how to teach me. So, he sent me to stay with my uncle on the weekends. He had a place out in the swamp." She inhaled deeply to calm her sprinting heart.

"This is your mom's brother?"

She nodded.

"Why did he live in the swamp?" He looked at her intently, his eyes gleaming in the dim light.

"He was a *traiteur*. An extremely powerful faith healer." She stared at their hands entwined on the sheet as the memories came flooding back, and she swallowed the thickness from her throat. "He claimed to be a *traiteur* anyway. Turns out he was much more than a healer, though I didn't know it at the time. My mom had died. I was weak, and he preyed on my weakness, using my powers in ways Baron Samedi never intended them to be used."

"You can do more than communicate with the dead." He continued to hold her gaze, his silence willing her to elaborate.

A normal person, even a werewolf, would turn tail and run if he knew the extent of Odette's power. Her aura alone intimidated most, leaving her with few friends and a distillery full of employees who walked on eggshells.

James was different. He was the first person who wasn't

afraid to stand up to her. Even when she'd allowed her power to build, and he'd felt it, he didn't run. She hadn't scared him off yet, and if she planned to spend the rest of her life with him, no matter how short that life may be, he deserved to know her.

"I can control the dead." The words rushed out like a river breaking down a dam, and as the last one left her lips, the constant pressure building inside her for years flooded out with it.

He blinked. "Control?"

"Bend them to my will. Make them do whatever I want them to. My connection to the spirit world is constant. I'm like a conduit. I can channel the energy from that realm and feed it to spirits that are trapped here, giving them abilities dead people shouldn't have. I…"

She inhaled deeply, trying to quell the nausea churning in her stomach. He hadn't recoiled yet. Not that he could have with the vise-grip she had on his hand. She relaxed her fingers and continued, "My uncle was a *bokor*."

"He practiced black magic?"

"Yes, but I didn't know it at the time. I was doing what I was told. I didn't…"

"Hey." He traced his fingertips down her cheek, lifting her chin so she looked at him. "You don't have to defend yourself to me. We've all done things we aren't proud of. You were a kid."

"It's very rare to be crowned by Baron Samedi. If I hadn't died the day I was born, I…" She shook her head. Now wasn't the time for what-ifs. "My uncle recognized my power. He used me to…" She brushed the hair from her forehead, giving James ample time to mull over her words. To get the hell out if he wanted to.

When he didn't move, she continued. "He used black

magic to take a piece of a person's soul. But once the soul fragment was severed, he couldn't do anything with it. It would pass on to the spirit realm, and the sick person, who had come to him for help, would die. But I could control the spirit energy. He forced me to put the soul pieces in *ouangas*, jars created to hold spirits. He told me it was for safekeeping. That the people were sick and storing part of their soul would keep them alive."

She lowered her head to the pillow. "I thought it was wrong, but I did it anyway. I mean, they were dying if I didn't store their souls, so why not? And using my power feels so good. It's like a…spiritual orgasm. Stress, worry, all my earthly emotions dissolve, and I feel nothing but bliss."

"I've felt that coming off of you. Why is that?"

"Baron Samedi, and all the loa of the Ghede family, understand that death is the one guarantee in life. All the things we stress about really don't matter, because we're all going to die one day. So we should live life to the fullest. Enjoy every minute of the time we have here because that time is borrowed. When I use my magic, their philosophy fills me, and it's the most amazing thing I've ever felt."

"But you seem to live in opposition to that philosophy."

"Because my uncle wasn't helping the people by storing their souls. He kept them so that when they died, he could control their spirits. He wanted my power, but since Baron Samedi wouldn't grant it to him, he found a loophole. Own a piece of the soul, control the spirit. He was an evil man, and I helped him."

She rolled onto her back and squeezed her eyes shut, the shame of what she'd done raising heat in her cheeks. "But I stopped. Baron Samedi was angry with me, and I stopped. I got away. I…" A shudder ran through her body, and she clamped her mouth shut. He didn't need to know all the gory details.

"How old were you?"

She stared at the ceiling fan whirring above, her gaze latching onto a single blade and following it on its dizzying, circular path. "Twelve."

"That must have been scary." He rested a hand on her shoulder, the warmth of his skin pulling her from the memory and into the present.

"You have no idea. Anyway, I begged my dad to take me away from New Orleans. I wanted nothing to do with Voodoo, my powers, or Baron Samedi ever again."

He scooted closer, pulling her body to his. "So you ran away from everything?"

She'd been on the verge of tears, ready to make a beeline for the bathroom so he wouldn't see her cry, but the warmth and firmness of his embrace grounded her, giving her strength. She didn't need to hide from this man. "I turned my back on my religion and my home, but I couldn't run from myself. My magic follows me wherever I go. Spirits will always be drawn to me."

He kissed her forehead, her cheek, her lips. "I'm glad you came back."

"I had to. The Baron came to me in my dreams. The distillery was about to go under. I owe my life to my *met tet*, and I'd abandoned him. I thought coming back and making his distillery successful again would put me back in his good graces, but I was wrong. He's been appeased, but he's still not happy with me."

"Because you're so uptight?" One corner of his lip tugged into a tentative grin.

She opened her mouth to argue, but what could she say? She was the most uptight person she knew. It was a miracle this rough-around-the-edges werewolf found her attractive at all. "I've been in total control of every aspect of my life for as long as I can remember, and it's worked for me. Then you came along and started chipping away at my façade, restoring the real me that I've kept suppressed all these years. It's terrifying, but I also kinda like it."

And it was time she went with it. She trusted James down to her bones. Relinquishing a little bit of control with him would be good for her; she could control her magic with him. She traced her finger down his nose to his lips, tugging the bottom one down before pressing her mouth to his.

Sliding his hand to her hip, he opened for her, tangling his tongue with hers. He leaned into her, the evidence of his desire pressing against her thigh, sending a flood of warmth through her core. As he broke the kiss, she couldn't stop the moan of protest from escaping her throat.

He twirled a curl around his finger and glided the back of his hand down her cheek. "I would never try to control you or to make you do anything you didn't want to do."

"I know." She kissed him again, trailing her lips across his jaw and down his neck, inhaling his intoxicatingly masculine scent. His pheromones were tuned specifically to her senses, and each inhale brought on a fresh wave of desire. "James?"

"Hmm?" He slid his fingers into her hair and tilted his head, giving her better access to his neck.

That small gesture made her breath catch and pressure build in the back of her eyes. For a werewolf to willingly expose his neck, to make himself even slightly vulnerable, showed a level of trust she would never deserve.

When she didn't move, he pulled back to look into her

eyes. "You were going to say something?" Did he even realize what he'd communicated with his body language?

It was time she did the same for him. "Do you think we could try that again? I promise not to freak out this time."

A crooked, kissable grin lit on his lips. "I would like nothing more than to make you come, my dear." He rolled her onto her back, his gaze locking with hers as he ran his hand down her body. If he was looking for signs of fear or panic, he wouldn't find them. She was ready this time.

His eyes smoldered as he settled his shoulders between her legs. "Where were we?" His breath tickled across her center, tightening her core.

She was *so* ready.

As he flicked out his tongue to lick her, she gasped at the electrical sensation pulsing through her core. He paused, giving her plenty of time to change her mind, but there was no turning back now. She was in this, and they were going all the way.

An *mmm* vibrated across his lips as his tension eased, and he licked her again, gently sucking her into his mouth and working her in circles with his tongue. Goose bumps pricked at her skin, every nerve in her body firing on overdrive as she allowed the enthralling sensations to overcome her.

She let go, giving in to the passion as her soulmate took her to the edge. He slipped a finger inside her, and she moaned. When a second finger slid in, she screamed his name. Her orgasm exploded inside her, unraveling her senses, tearing down her walls, making it impossible for her to hide. Her body was his to command, and he was a master. *Sweet Spirits*, was he good.

He slowed his pace, gently bringing her down from the wave of sheer ecstasy. Her breathing under control, she opened her eyes to find him watching her, a hunger in his eyes so palpable she could taste his need.

He growled as he mounted her, and with one swift thrust of his hips, he filled her, sending another explosion of fiery energy flowing through her veins. Nuzzling into her neck, he began moving, slowly at first, the delicious friction sending a shock of electricity through her core.

His pace quickened, and she clutched his shoulders, wrapping her legs around his waist and giving herself to him. His magic caressed her skin, seeping into her core to mingle with her own. For the first time in her life, she didn't hold back. She let her power build, the peaceful emptiness of the spirit world channeling through her, vibrating in her aura.

James moaned and pressed his lips to her ear. "God, this feels so good, Odette."

The thick, raspy tone of his voice sent her over the edge again. As her climax ripped through her, James moved faster, harder, until he found his own release and collapsed on top of her, panting.

They lay there, holding each other, a tangle of pounding hearts and liquid limbs, until their breathing slowed and he rose onto his elbows. "You are one amazing woman, Odette Allemand." He rolled to his side, tugging her body to his. "That was…wow."

"*Wow* is the perfect word to describe it." A bubbly, giddy sensation rose from her stomach to her chest, and she smiled as he moved to his back and held her even closer. She had let go, surrendered control and let James take her to a place she thought she'd never experience in her life. She'd put her trust and faith in him, and he did not disappoint.

Of course he didn't. He belonged with her.

Snuggling into his side, she let his warmth and his woodsy scent envelop her, calming her. They were perfect together, and if they got along this well in the bedroom, surely, they could work together to defeat the monster. She'd been resigned to her tragic fate before, but for the first time, the hope that she could change it lighted in her heart.

CHAPTER THIRTEEN

JAMES LAY ON HIS BACK, NESTLED IN THE CENTER OF Odette's bed, listening to the melodic rhythm of the rain falling against the window panes. With her leg draped across his, her head resting on his shoulder, he could've lain there all day, basking in the afterglow. It was Saturday morning, so he just might. He kissed the top of her head.

Making love to her had been more intense than he'd ever imagined. No doubt they had a soul-deep connection. Once they'd begun, his wolf hadn't interrupted him with visions of the dream woman...until the very end as Odette fell asleep in his arms. He'd pushed the image aside, and he would continue to do so until his wolf relented and would be satisfied with one mate. With Odette.

With a sleepy sigh, she snuggled in closer and pressed a kiss to his chest. Lightly grazing his skin with her fingertips, she tilted her head toward his. "If this is what it's like being mated to a werewolf, I think I'm going to like it."

His heart missed a beat before slamming against his chest. He wasn't ready to *officially* become mates. Not when his wolf's heart was still divided. Scrambling through their conversations, he searched for anything he might have said that would give her an idea like that. She'd called them soulmates, but he'd been careful not to confirm it. *Shit.* He needed more time.

She propped her head on her hand and smiled. "Normally it would be way too soon for this, but considering the circumstances, I'm going to say it. I love you, James."

He opened his mouth, but he couldn't make a sound pass over the baseball-sized lump in his throat.

Her brow furrowed as her smile twitched and then faded. "You don't have to say it back. I know it's rushed. I just wanted you to know, in case anything happens before…" She shrugged and swallowed hard.

"Um…" He let out a nervous chuckle. "We might not live to see tomorrow. No sense in rushing into anything." Pushing to a sitting position, he leaned his back against the headboard. "Taking a mate is a big step. It's not something to do because you're scared."

"I'm not saying it because I'm scared." Hurt flashed in her eyes before she sat up and pulled the sheet to her chest. "I'm saying it because I mean it, and I wanted you to know."

He chewed his bottom lip and stared at his hands clutched in his lap. He wanted, more than anything, to take her in his arms and tell her he loved her too. That they'd spend the rest of their lives together.

But he couldn't make a promise like that unless he knew he'd be able to keep it.

When he didn't say anything, she slid out of bed and put on a dark-purple satin robe, cinching it at her waist. "I'm not wrong. We are soulmates, and you may not love me yet, but if we have time, you will. It's fate. And what we did last night…that meant something to me. It meant everything."

He groaned and rolled out of bed to pull on his underwear. "I know. It was special to me too, and it's not that I don't love you."

She crossed her arms. "Do you love me?"

"I…" His phone rang from the heap of clothes on the floor, and he cut his gaze toward it.

Odette narrowed her eyes, daring him to answer it. "What is it then? Is there someone else?"

The phone quieted, taking his one hope for a time-out from this conversation with it, and he hesitated. He wanted to tell her no, that she was the only one for him, but she took his immediate silence as confirmation.

Her mouth dropped open, her eyes widening in disbelief. "You're seeing someone else?"

"No." This time the answer came instantly. "I'm not seeing anyone else. My wolf…"

"Your wolf is seeing someone else? What? You've got a girl wolf out in the swamp that you screw when you go hunting?"

"No. That's not it." Frustration grated his nerves. He'd never been good at vocalizing his emotions, and his lack of eloquence wasn't helping this conversation. "There's something—"

His phone rang again, and he rose from the bed. "I need to answer that. It could be the alpha."

"By all means." She gestured toward the sound, her irritation obvious in her jerky movements. Could this situation get any worse?

He pressed the phone to his ear. "Hey, Luke. I was going to call you—"

"We've got a problem. Six people dead. Looks supernatural. Get your ass to the bar. Now." The alpha ended the call. Yep, things got worse.

He raked a hand through his hair and turned to Odette. She stood rigid, her arms crossed over her chest, the power building in her aura causing his neck hairs to stand on end. The pull of death around her hollowed out the space, and for a brief moment, his self-preservation instinct persuaded him to run. But she couldn't scare him into submission.

"That trick doesn't work on me."

She dropped her arms to her sides, her posture relaxing slightly. "I didn't realize I was doing anything."

"That was Luke. I have to go, but this conversation is not over." He had to come clean about his problem, but telling the woman who loved him—who was convinced they were bound by fate—that there could be another would crush her. Hurting Odette was the last thing he wanted to do, but he owed her the truth.

He shoved his legs into his jeans and pulled on his shirt before taking her shoulders in his hands and kissing her cheek. "I will be back as soon as I can, but know this… I am not seeing anyone else. What we did last night was special, and I don't regret a thing. But I do have a problem, and I will tell you all about it when I get back, okay?"

She chewed her bottom lip and nodded.

"Will you be here?"

"I'm not going anywhere."

Sliding his fingers into her hair, he kissed her forehead. "Good. Hopefully this won't take long."

James parked two blocks from O'Malley's and shoved his hands in his pockets as he trekked up the sidewalk to the werewolves' HQ. The rain had stopped, and the morning sun hadn't risen above the buildings, sparing him from its sweltering intensity, but enough humidity hung in the air to make his skin feel like he was walking through a sauna.

A thin layer of water and soap coated the street from its daily early-morning washing from city services, and a mass of dirt-tinged bubbles collected around a storm drain. Situated on St. Philip, O'Malley's sat far enough away from the party end of Bourbon Street to avoid most of the mess and sour smells the tourists deposited overnight, but James welcomed the fresh scent of soap each day, reminding him every morning was a fresh start.

And he'd royally screwed his start to this morning.

A blast of cold air from above mussed his hair as he stepped through the pub door, but he didn't bother smoothing it into place. He hadn't even glanced in a mirror before he left Odette's.

Amber gave him a solemn nod of her head as he stomped past the bar and pushed open the swinging door that led to the back rooms.

Six people dead? If the monster that showed up at Odette's house last night was responsible and he'd missed his chance at stopping it… Damn him and his inadequacies.

Two exposed light bulbs lit the narrow, brick-lined corridor, and his shoes thudded on the concrete floor. He found Luke's office door ajar, the lights inside turned off, and his stomach soured. The people invited to this meeting wouldn't fit inside his office, so he must have summoned the entire demon-hunting team. *Shit*.

He used his shoulder to shove the heavy door to the

meeting room open and strode inside. Yep, every werewolf on the team, plus a few extras, filled the folding chairs that sat in a semicircle around a podium. Cade acknowledged him with an eyebrow raise, and Luke nodded as James took a seat next to Macey, the alpha's mate.

"Now that everyone's here, we'll get started." Luke swept his gaze across the pack. "Like you were told on the phone, we've got six bodies with lacerations to the throats and chests that look like teeth and claw marks."

Chase, the pack's second-in-command and James's old hunting buddy, stood next to the alpha. Colorful tattoos sleeved both his arms, and his eyebrow piercing glinted in the overhead light as he stroked his dark-brown beard. "They were all couples, three men and three women. Two couples were found last night and one the night before."

James sank lower in his chair. Had the monster come looking for him and Odette the night before, and the unlucky couple had been its consolation prize when it couldn't find them? No, it was possible the events were unrelated. He hadn't seen hide nor tail of the monster the previous night. Then again, he hadn't spent the night with Odette.

Luke looked at his mate. "Macey, what's happening with the police?"

She stood and strode to the podium. The detective wore her long, blonde hair slicked back into a bun at the nape of her neck, and her bright-green eyes held a fierce determination. Though she was second-born and stood nearly a foot shorter than the alpha, she was a hell of a fighter and as tough as any shifter James knew. "At the moment, we have one witness, though her credibility is in question. The roommate of the second pair of victims claimed to see a deformed man climb in through the living room window and walk right past her to the couple in the back bedroom. She described him as tall and lanky, with longer-than-normal arms and a head that looked like it had melted onto his shoulders."

Oh, hell. James pinched the bridge of his nose and squeezed his eyes shut. This was his fault. Every goddamn bit of it.

"But the markings, if they were teeth marks," Luke said, "didn't come from a human mouth. If the witness really saw what she claims, the demon must have shape-shifting abilities. The teeth marks looked canine."

"The witness had been drinking," Macey added, "so I'm leading the investigation team toward dismissing her claims."

"But it sounds demonic." Chase crossed his arms and looked at Luke for confirmation.

"Agreed. After Cade's report last night, I want to hear the rest of the story." Luke's gaze landed on James, and the hair on the back of his neck pricked. This wasn't the first time he'd been in the hot seat with the alpha, but if he didn't get his act together, it would be the last.

James held Luke's gaze for a brief moment before glancing at Cade. "It's not demonic."

"So you saw it?" Luke crossed his arms. "Cade reported that you were giving chase to a demon, but you lost it in the cemetery. Then Macey told me about the murders, and I put two and two together. Tell me what you saw."

Shit. Shit. Shit. "I saw exactly what the witness described, but it didn't smell like rotting garbage; it smelled like swamp." He described the pursuit through the park and into the cemetery, blaming his inadequacy on the monster's incredible speed and not on the injury that slowed him down. "I should have taken it out last night, but I was sloppy. I'm sorry."

"Do you have any idea where it came from?" Macey returned to the chair next to him. "What it's after?"

He rubbed his sweaty palms on his jeans. "It's after me."

"You?" Luke moved his hands to his hips.

"Me and Odette. It's hard to explain, but we're stuck in this cycle. In every lifetime, when we meet, this monster rises and kills us both. I don't know how or why it happens, just that it does and it's going to keep happening until we're both dead or we kill it first."

Luke held up a hand to quiet the murmur of the pack. "Then I suggest you kill it first."

"I'm working on it. I need to get back to Odette. She's taking me to her Mambo to do a past-life regression to figure out how the cycle started so we can end it." If she'd even speak to him after the mess he made and left behind this morning.

The alpha nodded. "I trust you to do what needs to be done. Bryce and Chase are on first patrol tonight. I'll take Cade on second. You keep me posted."

Luke dismissed the meeting, but as the werewolves filed out the door, he held James back. "Is that scar on your neck from your altercation last night?"

Shit. He couldn't let the alpha know how bad the monster had gotten him, so he instinctively covered it with his hand. "Nah, this is nothing."

"If you need backup with this thing…"

"C'mon, man. You know me. I didn't earn my status in the pack by needing backup." He worked his ass off to prove himself worthy of his position.

"You're right about that." He nodded. "Go find out

what you can. We'll discuss the *other* thing that happened last night later."

Did he mean the fact that he was sleeping with a client or that he'd nearly exposed the werewolves and had to act like a domesticated house pet to get out of the predicament? It didn't matter; his ass would be grass for either one.

James ground his teeth and knocked on Odette's door. She didn't say a word when she opened it; she didn't even look at him as she stepped aside for him to enter. Her posture ramrod straight, she closed the door and crossed her arms, the tendons in her neck protruding as she clenched her jaw.

He rubbed the back of his neck and looked into her eyes.

Her posture relaxed, and her eyes softened, her brow furrowing as she dropped her arms to her sides. "What happened?"

He lifted his hands palms up. "Either three other couples are stuck in the same cycle, or they got caught in the crossfire when the monster couldn't get to us."

She covered her mouth. "Six people died?"

"Two couples last night, one the night before. We have to stop this thing."

She nodded and strode past him. "My phone is on the nightstand. I'll call Natasha, and we'll go do that past-life regression."

He followed her into the bedroom. "Hold on. That can wait a few minutes; we need to finish our conversation from before." *If* he could make himself spit it out and tell her the truth. His palms slickened with sweat, and he fisted them at his sides.

She snatched her phone from the nightstand and turned to him. "If people are dying because of us, we need to—"

"We need to talk about us. You said the loa told you we have to fix this together, so let's fix *us* first, okay? Let me explain why I couldn't tell you I love you this morning."

She swallowed hard and gave her head a tiny nod.

Shit. If he wanted to admit his inadequacies to anyone, Odette was the one he could tell. Of course, he'd rather not admit anything, but he didn't have a choice at this point. She deserved to know. He raked a hand through his hair. *Might as well cut to the chase.*

"My wolf is broken. I'm not a full werewolf, so *I'm* broken, and I don't know how to fix it." He dropped onto the sofa, leaning his head back and covering his eyes with his forearm, embarrassment making him wish he could disappear. "I'm sorry."

The cushion next to him compressed as she sat down and rested a hand on his leg. "Don't apologize. You didn't do anything wrong, and you're not broken."

He pressed his arm harder against his eyes. She deserved so much more than he could give her. She deserved someone whole.

"James." She pried his arm from his face and held his hand. "I've seen you shift. You look like a full werewolf to me. Please talk to me."

Lacing his fingers through hers, he chewed the inside of his cheek to keep his mouth closed. A battle raged in his mind, his thoughts volleying between laying it all out, baring his soul…or zipping his lips and keeping his problems to himself where they belonged. The concern in her eyes urged him to spill the truth, but... Where could he even begin?

She cut her gaze to the side. "Not now, Nicolas. Will you give us some privacy?"

"I forgot he was here. Was he around last night?" It hadn't felt like they'd had an audience, but he hadn't been paying attention to much else.

"If he was, he kept himself hidden. He's usually respectful of my privacy, now that we've set up some ground rules." She caught James's gaze. "Please tell me why you think you're broken." She ran her finger over the spot where his pinkie should have been, and the scar tissue tingled.

He stared at their entwined hands. Odette had never asked him what happened to his finger. She'd simply accepted him, flaws and all. She loved him, and...damn it, he had to tell her. "My mom is human."

"So is my dad. Him being mundane doesn't make me any less of a vodouisant."

He blew out a hard breath through his nose. "When only one parent is a were, there's a fifty-fifty chance their firstborn will be a shifter. The chance is even less when one of the parents is human."

"So, you're rare. That doesn't make you broken." She offered a small smile, but he couldn't hold her gaze.

"I don't..." He closed his eyes for a long blink. He trusted Odette to his core, but it didn't make the admission any easier. Opening his eyes, he squared his gaze on her. "I can't heal as fast as the others. You saw the marks where the monster bit me when I came home last night. If I were a full werewolf, they'd have been healed before I reached the cemetery."

Her lips quirked into a smile, and she pressed her fingers to her mouth.

"What?" How could she possibly find this amusing?

She shook her head. "You said when you came *home* last night. You came here."

He'd admitted the one weakness he tried desperately to hide from everyone, and his confession didn't faze her. Her acceptance warmed his heart, tightening his chest, and he chuckled. "I did say that, didn't I? I guess it's starting to feel like home to me."

Her smile widened, and his heart pounded harder. As he looked into her eyes, something unspoken passed between them. She wanted this to be his home as much as he wanted it to be.

Her lips parted on a quick inhale, and she straightened, composing herself. "Do all werewolves heal at the same rate?"

"No, but I might as well be second-born with the way I heal. This." He tightened his grip on her hand and lifted it so she could see his missing finger. "When I lost it on a construction site, I should have been able to reattach it. My body should have stitched it right back on when I touched it to my hand, but it didn't."

He lowered their hands to his lap. "Luke was there, his eyes all full of concern, asking me why it wasn't healing. I couldn't let the would-be alpha see my weakness, so I dropped it in the cement mixer."

She blinked. "You threw away your finger so Luke wouldn't think you weak?"

His ears burned. "I know it's stupid, but yeah, I did. I can't say for sure if it would have healed anyway, so…" He shrugged. "My dad always told me to hide it, not to let anyone know I'm the weakest wolf in the pack. He kept me sheltered when I was a kid so no one ever saw me get injured. When I became an adult, I was tired of hiding, so I did everything I could to prove my strength. I joined the demon hunting team, volunteered for the toughest assignments. I've worked my ass off to prove I'm worthy of my rank, but nothing I do changes who I am. Are you sure you want to be soulmates with a broken werewolf?"

"It wasn't stupid, and you're not broken or weak. I understand not wanting to show weakness. I've spent my entire adult life hiding mine."

"That's not the only way I'm broken." Now for the hard part. The reason he couldn't commit to her, even though every fiber of his human being knew she was the one. "My mom, being human, didn't take the mating bond seriously. Didn't know what she was getting herself into. They weren't fate-bounds, but my dad loved her. He still loves her, and I think somewhere in her twisted heart she loves him too. They're still mates, but she disappears for months, sometimes years, at a time. She wanders. She cheats on him."

"Why doesn't he leave?"

He let out a dry chuckle. "He couldn't if he wanted to. Werewolves mate for life. So I made a promise to myself when I was old enough to understand what was going on that I would never let that happen to me. I would never take a mate unless my wolf was one hundred percent on board. Unless I was certain she was my fate-bound."

"I see." Her jaw tightened, and she inclined her chin. "Because you think you've inherited your mom's wandering eye?"

"I don't want to be that way. I'm not, but…it's the only explanation for…" He lowered his gaze. God, he didn't want to hurt her, but he didn't have a choice.

She pulled from his grasp and folded her hands in her lap. "What's her name?"

"I don't know. I've never met her." He pleaded with his eyes, willing her to understand.

She laughed, unbelieving. "What?"

"About three months ago, I started having dreams about this woman. In my dreams, my wolf has claimed her. My wolf was convinced she was my fate-bound, that I would find her one day…until I knocked on your door. Now he wants you both, and that's not possible. You can't have two fate-bounds, but the stupid beast won't let go of the dream lady."

Silence stretched between them as she processed his confession, her mouth screwing up on the side like she was chewing the inside of her cheek. He scrambled for something else to say, but she finally responded, "Where does that leave us then?"

He took her hands. "Odette, if I were just a man, I'd get down on one knee right now. I do love you. My wolf loves you, but I don't want to hurt you. I can't take you as my mate while my wolf insists there's another. What if I meet her? What if…?" He couldn't finish the sentence. He'd be an idiot to leave Odette. She was meant to be his.

"You can't help him, Nicolas." She shook her head. "Our ghost friend wants to talk to you, but…" She lowered her voice to a whisper. "He thinks I'm his lover… the one who murdered him, though he doesn't know she did it."

He looked toward the empty space where she'd been speaking. "If he thinks he can help, I'd like to hear what he has to say." He'd take anything he could get at the moment. Hell, it couldn't hurt.

"He can't say much. He's strong, but he's so confused."

She narrowed her eyes. "I haven't seen him act this way since the first time you came into the house. He's so frantic."

"What's he saying?"

She shook her head. "'He knows me.'" She looked at James. "He keeps repeating it. He thinks you know him."

"Damn it, I wish I could hear him. If he really can help…" If the ghost had even a sliver of information—a single piece of this massive jigsaw puzzle—James would do anything to learn it. He straightened and glanced from Odette to the place where she stared. "Can't you help him? Give him some of that power you told me about? Be the conduit so he can show himself to me?"

She stood and paced toward the bed. "No. I told you I don't use my powers like that. No one should have that kind of control over the dead."

"You don't have to control him. Just give him a little boost. Open up like when you were trying to scare me the other day." As he rose and moved toward her, an icy emptiness enveloped him. A feeling of familiarity clawed through his chest, making his heart race. A tiny piece of an image flashed through his mind, the scene so recognizable it felt like it had happened yesterday. A woman…the dream woman…stepping out of a horse-drawn carriage.

He jerked to the side, and the cold dissipated, taking the image with it. Warmth slowly returned to his skin, and he rubbed at the goose bumps on his arms.

That image felt nothing like the ones he'd seen before. The recognition made it seem as though it hadn't come from his own mind, but rather it had been waiting for him inside the pocket of cold as if the ghost had generated it. His wolf stirred, hovering near the surface, as anxious for answers as James was himself.

"Did he try to jump me again?"

Odette sank onto the edge of the bed. "No. You walked through him. He won't jump you."

"He won't or he can't because you told him not to? He hasn't bothered me again because you're already controlling him, aren't you?" And if she was controlling him, surely, she could find out what he knew.

She lifted her hands in a show of innocence. "I had no choice. He knocked you out and was trying to get inside you. What was I supposed to do?"

Sitting on the bed beside her, he took her hand and inhaled a slow, deep breath. "Thank you for that." He had to stay calm despite the adrenaline coursing through his veins. The ghost could be the answer to his problems. If Nicolas knew something...*anything* about the dream woman or how he could get his wolf to forget about her, James needed to hear it.

And Odette could make that happen.

"Do you trust me?" He held her gaze, searching for signs of doubt.

"Of course I do."

"Release him. Let him jump me. You don't have to give him any more power, but you have to let him go. I need to know what he has to say."

"No." Fear flashed in her dark-brown eyes. "It's not safe. Ghosts that can get inside people like that...they can make you crazy."

James balanced on the edge of crazy on a daily basis. He'd take his chances. "He won't hurt me."

Her mouth hung open in disbelief before she snapped it shut. "He's already knocked you out. There's no telling what else he might have done to you if I hadn't ordered him to leave you alone."

James dropped to his knees on the floor and faced her. "Because I wasn't ready. This time, I'll be prepared for impact, and I know you won't let him hurt me." Resting his hands on her thighs, he gently squeezed them. "I trust you to keep me safe."

Pressing her lips together, she let out a slow breath through her nose. "You're insane. You know that?"

He rose to his feet. "I've never claimed otherwise."

Standing, she gestured to the bed. "Lie down. You'll probably lose control of your muscles while he's in you."

He crawled onto the bed and lay on his back, fisting his hands at his sides to stop them from trembling. She was right, he was nuts for trying this, especially after what happened the first time. But something deep inside him said he had to.

She rested her fingertips on his shoulder. "The second you show any signs of distress, I'm pulling him out. Whether you've gotten the information you're looking for or not."

He nodded in reply, afraid a tremble in his voice would betray his apprehension.

Turning to face the empty room, Odette pushed her shoulders back. "You be gentle with him. Go ahead and tell him what you need to say."

In less than a second, the temperature around him plummeted. James gasped as the sensation of 220 volts surged through his veins, and his body stiffened like a corpse in rigor mortis before his limbs fell limp at his sides. He tried to move. To fist his hand or open his eyes, but his body was no longer his.

The shock subsided to a mild tingle, and the spirit's energy gathered in his mind, swirling and undulating like a storm on the sea. Emotions not his own rolled through his body—confusion, betrayal, despair—until an image took form behind his eyes.

"Serafine." His mouth formed the word before the thought registered, and her image grounded him, clearing his thoughts and allowing his mind and Nicolas's to join. For that brief moment, for the first time in his life, he felt a sensation he'd never experienced before.

He felt whole.

CHAPTER FOURTEEN

"James?" Odette rested a hand on his chest and patted his cheek. He didn't move. "Wake up. Come back to me."

She shook his shoulder, and his head lolled to the side, his eyes darting back and forth beneath his lids. "Please wake up." Her throat tightened, and she raked in a ragged breath as tears formed in her eyes.

What had she done? Allowing Nicolas to jump James, even for a minute, was an idiotic move. She'd let the ghost linger too long. She should have pulled him out at the first twitch of James's arm, but the way he'd said, "Serafine," had frozen her.

The name had rolled off his tongue like he'd said it a thousand times, and so much adoration had filled those three syllables, her breath had stilled in her chest. He'd sounded like a man in love.

Now she was paying the price for her hesitation. No, James was paying the price.

"James?" She shook him again, harder this time, but

he still didn't respond. The pressure of a hand on her shoulder startled her, and she snapped around to find Nicolas hovering next to the bed. "What did you do to him?" More venom laced her voice than she'd intended, but if James didn't recover, she'd unleash her wrath on the spirit. How dare he harm her soulmate?

"Well?" She shot to her feet, fisting her hands at her sides. "What did you show him? Why won't he wake up?" Her voice hitched on the last word, and she covered her mouth as Nicolas faded away.

"Oh, that's perfect. Run away when things get heated." She would fix this. Her powers had caused enough harm to last twenty lifetimes, and she never should have used them with James. She knew better. *Please, Baron, I can't do this alone.*

Hooking her arms through James's, she tugged him off the bed and dragged him through the house. He was 190 pounds of pure muscle, but she had enough adrenaline coursing through her veins to give her the strength to get him out the door.

Getting him down the back steps proved the problem. His weight shifted as she descended, and her foot missed the second step. She fell backward, taking him down with her, and he landed on her chest, her right arm barely keeping his head from smacking the concrete. Sharp pain shot through her spine, the impact of the slab on her back and the pressure of his weight on top of her making her rib cage feel like it would snap.

She lay still, staring at the sky as the fluffy, white clouds drifted into the shape of a wolf head. Another puff of cumulus started to take the form of a person's body beneath, and she squeezed her eyes shut. She had no time for delirium. As she opened her lids, the shapes her mind had formed vanished, leaving nothing but tufts of cotton candy in the sky.

James moaned, sending her heart into a sprint. Sitting up, she wiggled from beneath him and held his head in her lap. She ran her fingers through his hair, brushing it from his forehead, and he shook his head, his brow furrowing as if he were in pain.

"Come on, love, open your eyes for me." Her insides quivered, her mouth going dry as her fear tipped to panic. He should've been okay by now.

He continued shaking his head, his lids fluttering as if they might open, but he didn't wake up.

Scrambling to her feet, she dragged him to her car and opened the back door. Sliding herself in first, she pulled him onto the back seat and exited the other side. With both doors shut, she climbed into the driver's seat and sped toward the French Quarter.

She called Natasha on the way, and when she arrived at the temple, two vodouisants met her outside and carried James into the back room, laying him on the couch.

The men left, and Odette knelt at James's side, holding his hand and resting her other on his forehead, cursing herself for letting this happen. "Stay with me, James." Her voice cracked.

"What happened?" Natasha gathered an armful of herb jars from a cabinet and set them on the table by her mortar and pestle.

Odette stared at his handsome face. "The ghost. Nicolas wanted to communicate with James, and James…" She sucked in a shaky breath. "He insisted, so I let the ghost jump him." She looked at the Mambo.

"James trusted me to keep him safe, and look at him. Look what I did." The tears collecting on her lower lids spilled down her cheeks, her lip trembling as she watched Natasha work.

Natasha ground a mix of herbs in the bowl, and the sharp scent of rosemary filled the air. "You said you let him? You were stopping him from doing it before?"

Biting her bottom lip, Odette nodded. The Mambo didn't say a word, but the expression on her face conveyed her thoughts: *So, you are using your powers.*

"Can you help him?" Her voice sounded tiny, like the helpless little girl sitting in the road by her momma's body.

"Of course." Natasha mixed the herbs with a light blue liquid and poured the concoction into a shot glass. "This will help get him out of his head and into the present."

Tugging on his chin, Odette trickled the potion into James's mouth. As she emptied the container, he swallowed, and a deep moan rumbled from his chest.

Natasha beat a rhythm on a small drum—two slow taps followed by a quick percussion—and chanted a prayer in Haitian Creole. Her magic filled the room, the buzzing electricity prickling across Odette's skin, swirling around her and seeping into James.

Odette pressed her lips to her soulmate's cheek, and his eyes opened.

James gasped as his lids flew open, the cool air raking down his throat like forty-grit sandpaper. "Serafine," he croaked, his heart pounding relentlessly as his mind scrambled to comprehend what he'd seen. The sound of his own name swirled delicately in his ears, and familiar energy vibrated on his skin as soft hands cupped his face.

He squinted through his blurred vision until a figure came into focus. "Odette?" He blinked and then stared into her dark eyes, her presence grounding him, bringing the world into focus.

He glanced about the room, but nothing looked familiar. An old wood and glass cupboard lined one of the walls, and an array of hand-made burlap dolls sat upon one of the shelves. Colored glass jars filled the rest of the space, and as he swept his gaze over his surroundings, he took in an old tribal-looking drum set and an altar of some sort against the other wall. "Where are we?" He focused on Odette, and a look of relief smoothed the tight lines in her forehead.

"We're at the temple. Are you okay?"

He stared at her for a moment, and the confusion clouding his thoughts dissipated like a fog burned away by the sun. "I'm fine." He sat up, swinging his legs over the side of the couch and resting his feet on the floor. The room tilted on its axis, and he closed his eyes until the dizzying sensation subsided.

Odette sat next to him, taking his hands in a firm grip. "Do you remember anything?"

He smiled, and his heart filled with joy, making his chest feel like it would explode. He remembered everything. "It all makes sense now."

"What makes sense?" Natasha put a bowl in a cabinet and closed the door. He hadn't noticed her presence before.

"Everything." He looked at the Mambo. "The puzzle. The pieces fit. The woman from my dreams." Turning to

Odette, he cupped her cheek in his hand. "She's you. That's why Nicolas called you Serafine. You *are* Serafine."

She shook her head. "That's not possible. You would have to be…" Her eyes widened.

"I was Nicolas, and you were Serafine. It makes perfect sense. I'm connected to the ghost, and when you bought that house, that's when I started seeing Serafine in my dreams. Because Nicolas saw *you*."

Her mouth hung open, but she didn't speak.

"When he got inside me, for the first time in my life, I didn't feel like a piece of me was missing. My wolf recognized it too. Nicolas is part of me. The logic doesn't make sense, I know. But I feel it in my bones. How can a ghost of my former self be haunting your house when I'm here in the flesh?"

The muscles of her throat worked as she swallowed and glanced at Natasha. "Did you see how you died?"

"I didn't really *see* anything, aside from her face. I felt his emotions: love, betrayal, desperation. As our minds connected, I *knew* things. Like how I know you're Serafine."

"She killed him. That's why he felt betrayal. If a person's death is tragic enough, his soul can fracture." She shook her head. "It's so rare. I've heard of it happening, but I've never met a ghost who had a soul shard before. If you really are Nicolas, then a piece of him stayed behind when he died, and when you reincarnated… James, you've always felt incomplete because the ghost has a piece of your soul."

He stopped breathing mid-inhale as her words settled over him. He'd always felt like a piece of himself was missing, because it was. And that missing piece was the answer to it all. He didn't heal as fast as a normal werewolf, not because his mother was human, but because he himself wasn't complete. And his wolf didn't want two mates. The beast had claimed Serafine because of Nicolas's memories…and Odette *was* Serafine.

Holy hell. He'd finally found his fate-bound.

"James?"

His name on Odette's lips pulled him from his thoughts, and he finished a deep inhale. "This is fantastic." He laughed and pulled her into a hug.

"No, it's not." Her voice was muffled against his chest.

"But it is." Gripping her shoulders, he pushed her far enough away to look at her. "My wolf doesn't want another woman. It's always been you. *You* are my fate-bound."

"That's what I've been trying to tell you." She trailed her fingers down the sides of his face and pressed her lips to his.

Warm and soft, the gentle caress raised goose bumps on his skin and his heart thrummed in his chest. He wrapped his arms around her and coaxed her mouth open with his tongue. Her lips parted for him, and he drank her in, reveling in the overwhelming sensations of love. She was his now, and he would do everything in his power to protect her.

She broke from the kiss, clearing her throat and straightening her shirt as she cast a glance to Natasha, who fought a smile.

"Sorry about that," he said to the Mambo. "Got a little carried away."

"No need to apologize." Natasha's smile faded as she glanced at Odette and gestured with her head to James.

The pained expression on Odette's face popped the

bubble of elation in his chest. "What aren't you telling me?"

Odette took a deep breath and blew it out hard. "I am thrilled that you and your wolf got the soulmate issue worked out, but we've got a bigger problem. With a piece of you stuck in limbo like this, the cycle is going to keep repeating forever. And..." She cast her gaze to her lap.

"And?"

"If Serafine killed Nicolas, then she didn't die in his arms. But in every life I've regressed to, I did die in your arms. What if Nicolas is summoning the monster to kill me every time I reincarnate to get even with me?"

"No." The word left his lips before the thought formed in his mind. "Nicolas loves Serafine. He would never do anything like that."

"I don't know James. It would explain—"

"No, he wouldn't. He was inside me. I felt what he felt...nothing less than utter adoration. He's not doing this." And he refused to let Odette even consider it. Her research was wrong.

Natasha pulled a chair next to the couch and sat down. "I think it's time we found out what really happened to Nicolas and Serafine."

Odette squeezed his hand. "Are you still up for that past-life regression? It will be painful."

"Ain't nothing a werewolf can't handle, right?" Natasha winked.

James straightened his spine. He'd relive a thousand deaths before he'd allow anyone to harm his fated mate. "Bring it on."

Natasha instructed James to lie on the sofa, and she scurried to the cupboard and gathered jars of herbs.

Odette sat on the edge of the cushion next to him, resting both her hands on his chest.

He placed his hands over hers and squeezed them. "Thank you for making that happen." Tugging a hand to his lips, he kissed her palm. "I'm sorry for not realizing you and the dream woman were the same person. Even though she doesn't look like you, it seems so obvious now."

"There was no way for you to know. Nicolas doesn't look like you either. Souls don't change, but appearances do." Her brow pinched, concern filling her gaze. "Are you sure you want to do this? You'll feel your death…and mine…like it's really happening."

"Death doesn't scare me."

"It doesn't scare me either, but dying sure as hell does. Nicolas was stabbed in the chest and beheaded, and I… Serafine did it."

He chewed the inside of his cheek and studied her, trying to imagine a situation where Odette would be inclined to murder him. She wouldn't. "I don't think she did it."

"But the police report said—"

"We'll soon find out." Natasha handed him a mug of liquid. Rising onto his elbow, he sniffed the contents. "This smells like rum."

"Just a splash to help you relax. The herbs will open your mind. Drink up." The Mambo waved her hand, indicating he should lift the cup to his mouth.

He cringed as he swallowed the bitter liquid. It burned on its way down to his stomach like it was taking a layer of his esophagus with it. "Remind me never to order that in a bar."

Natasha dragged another chair to the end of the couch

near his head and ordered Odette to sit. He reached for his fate-bound's hand as she sank into the seat, but she pulled from his grasp.

"My energy could affect your visions. I'll be here, but we can't touch while you're regressing."

"Okay." He smiled, but it probably didn't mask the worry churning in his gut. He was about to watch his fate-bound die.

"I'm not going to leave you, and you'll be in control the whole time." Odette half-smiled, the uncertainty in her eyes disheartening.

He let out a half-hearted chuckle. "I'm not scared."

"You don't have to wear that mask for me. I'd be terrified."

Really reassuring words from the woman he was supposed to spend the rest of his life with. He nodded and swallowed the thickness from his throat.

"If it gets unbearable, you can open your eyes and bring yourself to the present whenever you want. But the longer you can stay under, the more information you'll gather." She kissed his forehead and leaned back in her chair, out of his reach.

Natasha closed her eyes and mumbled something in a language he didn't understand. He tilted his head to look at Odette, and his vision swam. "What's she saying?"

"It's a Haitian Creole prayer to Papa Legba, the guardian of the crossroads. When she's done, she'll guide you through a meditation and into your past life. Close your eyes and relax."

He settled into the cushion and let his lids drift shut. Whatever was in that drink made his limbs feel heavy, and the tension drained from his muscles. As he lay there, listening to the Mambo's rhythmic prayer, he sank deeper and deeper into the couch, until he couldn't tell where his body ended and the fabric began.

The air around him grew heavy, pressing into him as the scents of patchouli and something sharp that he didn't recognize filled the room. Natasha's chanting quieted, and her voice drifted toward him, lightening the pressure on his body. "Clear your mind of everything but the color blue—so dark it's almost black. Let your mind drift into your subconscious and take a deep, cleansing breath with me."

The Mambo inhaled, and James followed her lead, focusing on the color, until liquid warmth flowed through his veins, melting him into an altered state.

"Imagine a pin-prick of light in the corner of the blue." Natasha's voice seemed to come from somewhere inside his mind...all around him, but from nowhere at the same time. "As the light brightens, I want you to focus on Odette's house. Not as it is now, but as it was when you were there long ago."

The scene in his mind brightened into crisp focus. He stood in the foyer of the house on Esplanade. Dark-green paper with intricate gold designs covered the walls, and a crystal chandelier—not unlike the one he'd recently installed—glittered in the rays of the setting sun entering through the open door.

"What do you see, James?" Natasha's voice whispered in his mind.

He worked his jaw, prying his lips apart through the sluggishness in his muscles. "I'm in the house."

"What time period is it? Present day?"

Casting his gaze into the living room, he focused on the brick fireplace. A small clock sat on the mantle, but Odette's altar wasn't there. A pair of intricately-carved, dark-wood chairs with deep-red upholstery faced the hearth, and a chaise lounge sat beneath the window. "No. It's in the past."

"Focus on Serafine, the woman from your dreams. Try to bring her into the picture."

Shuffling sounded at the top of the stairs, and then she appeared, a vision of beauty in a maroon ball gown. She'd swept her hair up into a twist, and shiny, dark curls spiraled from her temples to brush her dark-brown shoulders. A timid smile played on her lips as she descended the steps, and James's chest tightened, so much love filling him he felt like he'd burst from the pressure.

Serafine may have started as his servant, but Nicolas would have moved heaven and Earth for this woman.

"Do you see her?" Natasha asked.

"Yes." His voice cracked.

"Let the scene play out. See what information you can gather."

He took a deep breath and let his thoughts slip away, focusing on the woman in his mind and the emotions intensifying in his heart.

As Serafine reached the bottom floor, he kissed her hand and laced it into the crook of his arm. "We do not want to be late for the party, mon cher."

She hesitated. "I'm still not sure this is the best idea. It will not be good for your reputation."

"I don't give a damn about my reputation." He toyed with the ring on her finger. "You are to be my mate. My wife."

"People will talk."

"Then let them talk, mon cher." He twirled a curl around his finger and brushed her cheek with the back of his hand. "They know better than to cross me."

With Natasha's guidance, James followed the scene as Nicolas and Serafine climbed into a carriage that took them to a mansion down the road. Painted bright blue, with white gingerbread trim, the two-story house boasted a wrap-around porch and a grand gallery on the second floor.

With Serafine on his arm, Nicolas stepped through the doorway, and a hush fell across the crowd. A few dozen people in suits and gowns paused to stare as he led his fated mate deeper into the house.

Serafine tightened her grip on his arm. "They are staring at me."

"Of course they are. You are the most beautiful woman in the room." He picked up two glasses of champagne and offered her one.

"A word, brother." A stocky man with blond hair and deep-blue eyes glared at him and jerked his head to indicate he should follow.

Antoine.

"One moment, mon cher. Let me see what he wants." He kissed her hand, and her eyes widened as she swallowed hard. With a tiny nod, she stepped away from him, and he followed his brother into the next room.

"How dare you bring her here?" Antoine spoke through clenched teeth, the muscles in his neck tight like cords. "Are you trying to ruin everything we have worked for?"

He lifted his chin, narrowing his eyes. "Serafine is my fate-bound. You and everyone else will have to get used to it sooner or later."

Antoine glanced through the doorway and leaned toward him, lowering his voice. "She is your servant."

"She is my fiancée."

His brother narrowed his eyes, and one of them twitched

with his agitation. "We are to be the first family in New Orleans. You are to be alpha. You cannot take her as your mate."

Nicolas downed his champagne in one gulp and set the glass on a table. "Her father was a were. I will not taint the bloodline."

Antoine stepped closer, taking him by the arm. "Her mother was a slave."

He jerked from his brother's grip, a low growl rumbling in his chest. "I am aware of her lineage." He turned to leave the room.

"You will ruin us, bringing attention to yourself like this. The alpha cannot afford to be in the human spotlight."

Nicolas stopped and looked over his shoulder. "I don't care the cost. The full moon is tomorrow, and we will become mates. You cannot stop this."

James gasped. "Nicolas was alpha." His lids fluttered, his head shaking as he tried to open his eyes.

"Stay under." Odette's voice calmed him, caressing his temples, and sending a wave of relaxation through his body. "Try to go to the night of their deaths. We need to know what happened."

With a long exhale, James let his mind drift back in time.

A bedroom. Serafine in a long, white nightgown. He lay next to her, his mind spinning with thoughts. His brother was right, but Nicolas didn't care the consequence. Serafine was his fate-bound; they would make this work.

Nicolas slipped into a dream, rolling onto his back as the sound of boot heels thudding on the floor echoed somewhere in his mind. Serafine gasped, and as the bed jerked, Nicolas awoke.

His fate-bound's scream ripped through the night, dragging him into full consciousness, and he sat up, shock not allowing him to comprehend what was happening. Antoine stood over Serafine, his bloody dagger raising and lowering into her heart.

Bright-red blood pooled from her chest, staining her gown as life drained from the wound. Searing pain tore through Nicolas's heart, shredding him.

Agony. Betrayal.

He scooped her into his arms as Antoine backed against the wall, his chest heaving. "My sweet Serafine." A sob lodged in his throat, and he swept the matted hair from her face. Blood trickled from the corner of her mouth, taking her life force with it. Her head fell back, her eyes wide, the light in them gone. His entire world shattered into nothingness, and hot tears trailed down his cheeks as he lifted his gaze to his treacherous brother.

Numb with grief, he pushed the question through the thickness in his throat. "Why?"

"I will not have you ruining our lives over a woman." Fear flashed in Antoine's eyes, and he gripped the dagger tighter. "You will thank me for this when the pack is formed."

"Thank you?" Laying his fate-bound onto the mattress, he focused on the single spark of anger burning in his soul. The only sensation palpable through the emptiness of his despair. He stoked the flame until his rage consumed him, vengeance his sole focus.

He rose from the bed, a growl rolling up from his chest as he called on his beast. His brother would pay for what he had done. But in his grief, he'd grown numb. As he leaped toward Antoine, he failed to shift. His brother plunged the dagger into his chest, piercing his heart.

Falling backward onto the bed, he gasped for breath, but the fatal puncture refused to give him air. Searing pain spread *through his body, and he choked on his own blood as Antoine jerked the knife from his chest and brought it down on his throat.*

"Serafine!" James shot up, raking in a ragged breath and grasping for his fate-bound. His vision swam, and nausea lurched in his stomach, making him double over.

"James." Odette sat next to him and wrapped her arms around his shoulders, running her hand across his back. "Breathe, honey. Just breathe."

Squeezing his eyes shut, he sucked in a breath, then another, until his head stopped spinning and he straightened. Blinking his gaze into focus, he found Natasha across the room, grinding herbs into another drink.

He looked at Odette, and cool relief flooded his veins, spiraling up his chest and coming out as something between a sob and a laugh.

Holding his face in her hands, she wiped the dampness from his cheeks and kissed his forehead. "Are you okay?"

He rubbed his chest where the knife had been, and a faint burning sensation spread across his skin. "I'm...fine. Are you...? That was intense."

Natasha handed him a cup. "This will help with the nausea and the fog in your brain."

He sipped the warm licorice-flavored liquid and leaned into Odette's side. Her presence grounded him, bringing him fully back to the present as the drink eased the physical strain the regression had put on his body. He drained the cup, and Natasha returned it to the counter.

Odette rested her hand on his thigh. "Did you see the monster?"

"It wasn't a monster. It was his brother. Antoine killed both of them." He explained what he'd seen in his vision.

"You were right then." She shook her head. "Serafine was innocent, yet she was blamed for it all. Typical."

"There's got to be more to the story, though." James rubbed his throat, trying to relieve the burning sensation left over from his regression. "The Dubois didn't become the first family. The Masons did."

She frowned. "If Nicolas was the shifter, Antoine couldn't have become alpha, could he? A second-born alpha? Is that possible?"

James raked a hand through his hair. "If a first-born dies prematurely, the shifter magic in the second-born is triggered. Antoine should have inherited the ability when Nicolas died, and he should have become alpha. They were the first werewolves to inhabit New Orleans."

Odette's eyes widened. "But Nicolas's soul fractured. Part of him has been stuck in the house since his murder."

"And that could have kept Antoine from inheriting the ability to shift." It made sense, but it didn't explain the murders recurring in every life. "What happened to Antoine afterward? Did you find anything in your research?"

"There was nothing about Antoine after that. He seemed to have disappeared."

"Werewolves aren't immortal, so we know he's not still alive. Could his ghost be doing this?"

She shook her head. "In my regressions, the killer was always solid. A ghost can't strangle someone unless it's getting help from the living."

"So someone living is involved?"

"You know who could answer these questions." Natasha crossed her arms and lifted a brow at Odette. "I'll set up another ceremony for tonight, but you're gonna have to get right with your *met tet* if you want him to show."

Odette groaned and leaned into James's side.

"Unless you're both ready to join the Baron on the other side, you've got work to do."

James cut his gaze between the women. "How do you get right with Baron Samedi?"

Odette took in a deep breath and blew it out hard. "I'm going to need your help."

CHAPTER FIFTEEN

"HEY." JAMES REACHED ACROSS THE CONSOLE AND pried Odette's hand from its death-grip on the steering wheel. His skin was warm, a stark contrast to her ice-cold fingers. "You're going to be okay. I don't think Baron Samedi would give you powers he didn't think you could control."

"I know." Her voice was a whisper over the lump in her throat. How many times had the Mambo said those same words? She chewed her bottom lip and stared out the windshield at the cemetery across the street. Growing up, her mom brought her here every Saturday to show their respects for the Baron and leave him offerings at the gate. As an adult, she'd paid tribute here once, the day she moved back to the city, and she hadn't returned since.

She'd been gone for far too long. Scared for too long too. Not just scared of her powers and what she was capable of doing with them, but afraid of life. She was living on borrowed time, and she'd spent so much of it trying to control everything that she'd forgotten what a gift life was. Especially her life.

It was time she made amends with the giver.

She looked at her fingers entwined with James's and focused on the magic seeping from his skin. Magic that blended so well with her own it felt as if her soul connected to his. With this man, she was whole, and she would do whatever it took to make him whole too.

Her stomach soured at the thought of what she would probably have to do. Only with the Baron could she mend the fracture in James's soul, and to do that, he'd...

"Are you ready?" James squeezed her hand and rested his fingers on the door latch. He caught her gaze, and the deep blue of his eyes grounded her. She could do this.

They could do it together.

"As I'll ever be." She slid out of the car.

Slinging her bag over her shoulder, she took his hand, and they darted across the street. James strolled toward the weathered concrete walls and nearly crossed the threshold, but she held him back.

"We can't go in yet. The Baron is a gatekeeper, so we start at the entrance to honor him." Setting her bag near the wall, she took a deep breath to calm her sprinting heart.

"Right. I saw you do this when we were kids. Sorry." James shoved his hands into his pockets and gave her a sheepish grin.

"Don't apologize." She knelt on the sidewalk and dug through her bag to find a thick piece of purple chalk. Settling in the entryway, she pressed the chalk into the concrete and dragged down and to the right. It made a scraping sound as the fine powder marked the ground, and Odette let down her carefully constructed walls, allowing her powers to manifest.

Her arm hairs stood on end, goose bumps pricking at

her skin as the cross and coffins of Baron Samedi's *vévé* took shape. Her *met tet's* presence surrounded her, the emptiness of death overpowering the natural humming energy of life.

"Is it just me, or is it getting colder?" James knelt beside her and rubbed his arms. "I've never felt this happen around you before."

She exchanged the chalk for a bottle of spiced rum from her bag and twisted the cap. "The Baron hasn't come this close in a long time." A shiver ran up her spine. "He's listening." She held the bottle in both hands and ran her thumb across the label. "I was stupid to think the distillery was a fair trade for my life. It's a small tribute for the gift you've given me, Baron, and I'm here to make amends."

Pressing the bottle to her lips, she took in a mouthful of rum. The warm undercurrents of cinnamon and nutmeg danced on her tongue, and James's eyes widened as she leaned forward and spit the alcohol across the *vévé*.

"I never saw you do *that* when we were kids."

She handed him the bottle. "My mother did it on special occasions. Your turn."

He gave her a wary look. "Spit it?"

"As an offering for the Baron. We aren't going to make it without his help." Facing the monster wasn't optional. They would either kill it, or it would kill them, but they couldn't let another couple die in their place.

Gazing at the bottle, he chuckled. "Normally, I'd say that's a waste of good rum, but in this case, I suppose it's the best use of it." He took a swig and spit it on the ground before offering the bottle to her.

She shook her head. "Now take a drink for us."

Locking his gaze with hers, he drank deeply and put the bottle in her hands. His eyes held her still, calming the sprint of her heart as she raised the container to her lips. She took a gulp, and the rum burned its way down to her stomach. It had been years since she'd swallowed a sip of alcohol. Too many to count.

Capping the bottle, she picked up her bag and rose, leading James across the threshold into the cemetery. Then, she set the bottle by the wall along with an expensive cigar and a top hat she'd bought at a party store. "We offer you rum and tobacco for listening to our prayers."

James stood next to her and rested his hand on the small of her back. "What now?"

She stared out into the cemetery, at row after row of above-ground tombs. Dingy white plaster covered many of the graves, while others had worn away until the brick beneath was all that remained. Stone urns filled with colorful flowers adorned many of the tombs, a symbol that though the dead may be gone, they were not forgotten by the living.

A weeping angel sat atop a 150-year-old tomb, watching over the remains of its inhabitants. Did the loa ever weep for her?

She looked at James. "Now I beg for forgiveness."

Running her fingers along the sectioned graves in the wall, she traced the names engraved on the plaques, stopping at a recent burial. While the standing graves within the cemetery housed the remains of generations of family members, the law stated a new body could only be entombed at least a year and a day after the previous one. If a family member passed away within the year, his body was housed in a temporary grave in the wall until enough time had passed to move him to the family plot.

No one in Odette's family had died since her mom. Not on her father's side anyway. Their family tomb was ready to receive, and hopefully she wouldn't be its next inhabitant.

"I've made it a point to never say 'I'm sorry' unless an apology is actually warranted." She stood in front of her offerings and gazed at the shiny, black top hat. "In this case, I can't say 'I'm sorry' enough to make up for what I've done. You gave me life and some powerful gifts, and I've squandered them. After…everything that happened… I thought if I denied my powers and lived in contrast to the Ghede way I could control not just my life, but everyone's around me."

Pressure built in the back of her eyes. "But there are some things that are beyond my control, and I've got to learn to accept them. I *will* learn. This man…" She took James's hand. "He's teaching me. I know you know him. He spent a lot of time here as a kid, he and his dad honoring you without even realizing it. His life is in danger because of me, and if I…"

A sob lodged in her throat, and she swallowed it down. "If I don't change my ways, we're both going to die, and for that, I am deeply sorry." She looked into James's eyes. "I'm so sorry I dragged you into this. I was supposed to die as a baby. If my mom hadn't made a deal with death, we never would have met and we wouldn't have awoken whatever it is that's after us. I'm so sorry, James."

The first tear trailed down her cheek, and he wiped it away with his thumb. "I'd take a single day in love with you over a lifetime of having never met. We're soulmates."

Something between a laugh and a sob rolled up from her chest. "Yes, we are." She sniffled and wiped another tear from her cheek. "I'm sorry, Baron. I'm sorry for abandoning my faith, and I'm sorry for not living in your image. Today, I'm offering my apology, this rum and tobacco…and I'm offering my life. If you will help us, come to the ceremony tonight and speak to us, guide us, tell us how to fix this, I swear on my mother's grave that I will start living. I will embrace my magic, and damn it, I'll learn how to have fun."

"I'll make sure she follows through on the fun part." James slid an arm around her waist. "Oh, shit. Is it okay if I address him too? Or did I ruin your prayer?"

She laughed. "It's fine. I have a feeling he's been watching over you too."

She looked at James, and the pressure of all the emotion, all the built-up magic and energy that she'd been suppressing for years exploded in her chest like a water balloon bursting on the pavement. The floodgates opened, and tears streamed down her cheeks as she buried her face in his shirt.

He held her as she sobbed, and a weight seemed to lift from her chest as she let go. She didn't have to hold it in anymore. Didn't have to always be in control. For the first time in as long as she could remember, she was relinquishing the wheel, letting the loa and fate steer her life.

She pulled back to look at James. "First thing I want to do when this is all over is go dancing."

He grinned. "You got it."

A frigid wind kicked up, swirling around them before settling into stillness. The Baron's way of letting her know her prayer had been heard. Tonight, she'd learn if she'd been forgiven.

"Thank you for not being afraid of my powers."

"Fate knows better than to bind you to a scaredy-cat. Lucky for you, there isn't much that scares me." He pressed his lips to hers.

She expected a quick kiss, but he lingered, his sweet

breath warming her skin. Snaking her arms behind his neck, she pulled him closer, pressing her body to his and deepening the kiss. With James by her side, she could do anything.

He pulled away and chuckled. "We probably shouldn't be making out in a cemetery."

"Want to head home? The ceremony doesn't start for another two hours."

A tour guide's voice drifted on the air, "That's a *vévé* for the god of death. It's a symbol a Voodoo practitioner draws on the ground to summon the god. We better be careful in here and stick together…" The guide flashed a mischievous grin. "Unless you want to end up hexed."

"Oh, please." Odette rolled her eyes and strode toward the exit. "I hate it when they get things wrong on these tours. I wish they'd do a little more research. Maybe *ask* someone before they start spreading rumors."

James chuckled. "I'm not sure they could handle the truth."

"You're probably right." As she slung her bag over her shoulder a chill formed in the air behind her. Contrary to popular belief, ghosts didn't tend to congregate in cemeteries; they generally followed people or objects. With this group of twenty shadowing the tour guide, the spirit probably belonged to one of them.

She turned and took in the spectral form—an eighty-something-year-old man with hunched shoulders and dark-brown eyes. From the looks of him, he had to be recently deceased. Long-dead ghosts usually showed themselves as they appeared in the primes of their lives.

James looked at her quizzically, and she sighed. As much as she wanted to spend what little time she had left with her soulmate, this ghost appearing now could be a test from the Baron. "Give me a minute?" she said to James. "I think I need to help someone."

He looked toward the spirit, though he probably saw an empty space. "Ghost?"

She nodded. "Do you need help, sir?"

The ghost gazed out over the crowd of tourists.

"Is someone you know out there? A loved one?"

The spirit nodded and drifted toward the crowd. Odette followed, with James on her heels, and joined the group as the guide explained the history of the cemetery.

"Has anyone here ever had any experiences with ghosts?" the guide asked.

A few hands went up, and people described various experiences of things moving, as well as hearing voices.

"I wish my grandpa would pay me a visit," a woman in an LSU T-shirt muttered. "Or at least tell me where he hid his stash."

The ghost's eyes brightened, and he looked at Odette. She hung back as the crowd moved on, and she whispered, "Is that who you're here for?"

He opened his mouth to speak, but no sound formed.

Odette closed her eyes and rubbed her forehead. This had to be a test. Make a promise to the Baron, and be ready to pay up. She let out her breath in a long exhale.

James rested his hand on her back, grounding her again, and she had to wonder if he realized how calming his touch was for her. He must have, because he always did it at just the right moment. "He needs more energy?"

"How'd you know?"

"Call it a hunch." Stepping behind her, he rested both hands on her shoulders. "You've got this. I'm right here if you need me."

Nodding, she closed her eyes and opened up the channel. Weightless, empty energy from the underworld flowed through her, chilling her veins and making her shiver. James wrapped his arms around her, pressing his front to her back, grounding her even more.

She pushed the energy outward toward the spirit, and it grew solid. She could have given the ghost enough energy for all the tourists to see—wouldn't that have made their day—but she reined it in, only giving as much as was needed for him to speak. "I can pass on a message if you have one."

The ghost told her about his death, and a little too much about his life. He'd never trusted the banks, so his entire life savings, cash and gold coins, lay hidden inside his home.

The ghost followed Odette as she approached the woman, his granddaughter, his energy fading as she closed the channel along the way.

"Excuse me, Elizabeth." She touched the woman's arm.

Elizabeth's eyes widened. "Do I know you?"

"Your grandfather says his savings is in a safe in the Northwest corner of the attic, behind the framed map of the Gulf."

Her mouth dropped open. "Who are you?"

Odette smiled. "No one important. Have a nice day."

Taking James's hand, she strolled toward the exit, and the woman pressed her phone to her ear.

"Yes!" The excited voice echoed off the cemetery walls, and Odette smiled. She'd passed the test.

"I'm curious." James followed Odette up the front steps and into the foyer. "If Baron Samedi shows up at the ceremony, will he be in ghost form? Will everyone be able to see him or only you?"

With the ghost approaching her in the cemetery as a test, the loa's appearance at the ceremony seemed likely, and his mind had been churning with questions ever since.

She took his hand and led him toward the bedroom. "No one will be able to *see* him. He'll communicate through ritual possession."

"Possession?" He stopped in the hallway. Plenty of rumors about what went on at Voodoo rituals circulated through New Orleans, and that was one he'd hoped wasn't true. "You mean he'll do like Nicolas did to me? Get inside your head and show you things?"

Stepping toward him, she smiled softly and cupped his face in her hand. "He, and any other Spirit that makes an appearance, will get inside someone and take over their body, moving and speaking through the host." She laughed softly. "We call the host a horse, and the loa is the rider."

His eyes widened. No way in hell was a Spirit getting inside him. He opened his mouth to suggest he wait outside while the vodouisants did their thing, but she caught his lips in a kiss instead.

Her magic shimmied across his skin, and warmth bloomed in his chest, chasing away his fear. As she moved closer, pressing her soft curves into his body and slipping her arms around his waist, all logical thought dissolved from his brain.

"Don't worry." She kissed his jaw, trailing her lips up to his ear. "The loa won't ride you unless you're open to it, and you haven't been initiated. You'll be a spectator." Sliding her hands beneath his shirt, she nipped at his lobe.

His knees nearly buckled with the sensation. "Good, because the only person I want riding me is *you*."

"I can make that happen." Running her hands up his chest, she pulled his shirt over his head and stepped back, admiring him. Her eyes filled with hunger, and she licked her lips as her gaze traveled up and down his form.

His stomach tightened, blood rushing to his groin. "Saddle up, sweetheart."

"Hmm…" She unbuttoned his jeans, letting them fall around his ankles before pushing him against the wall and reaching into his boxer-briefs to grip his dick. "I prefer bareback if you don't mind."

He held her gaze for a moment, trying for a witty comeback, but the feel of her soft fingers wrapped around his cock scattered his thoughts like sawdust in a summer wind. She stroked him, and electricity shot through his core. He leaned his head back against the wall and closed his eyes as she explored his body with her mouth.

Gliding her lips along his neck, she moved down to kiss his chest, her warm breath raising goose bumps on his skin. As she flicked out her tongue to lick his nipple, a shudder ran through his entire body, a possessive growl rumbling in his chest.

This was his woman. His fate-bound. And his wolf finally agreed she was the *only* one for him. Forever. He belonged to her, body, mind, and soul, and it was time he gave himself to her fully. No more holding back on his emotions. On anything.

He was hers to do with as she pleased, and as she straightened and stepped back, the mischievous look in her eyes said there was plenty of pleasure to come.

"Bedroom. Now." Not waiting for a response, she

strutted through the doorway, dropping her clothes to the floor on her way to the bed.

"Yes, ma'am." He toed off his shoes and stumbled out of his jeans before going to her and running his hands along her curves. "You are so beautiful." He kissed her, sucking her bottom lip into his mouth as he unclasped her bra.

A soft moan escaped her throat, and she leaned into him, her body molding to his. This woman was made for him, and he intended to spend the rest of his life showing her how perfect she was.

She grinned and pulled down his underwear before removing her own. Then, she tugged him toward the loveseat and gently pushed him down onto a cushion. She straddled him, sandwiching his dick between his stomach and her center, and kissing him like this was their last moment together.

Running his hands up her back, he drank her in, the thrilling sensation of her growing magic enveloping him, heightening his senses. She rocked her hips, and her soft folds rubbed against his cock, sending a shock of passion rocketing through his core.

He broke the kiss to press his lips into her ear. "I want you, Odette." He needed her like he needed air to breathe.

"Tell me what you want, James." She moved her hips again, teasing him, igniting a desire so deep within him he could think of nothing else.

"You." His voice rumbled in his throat. "I want you." He trembled as she took his length in her hand and rose onto her knees.

"Is this what you want?" She lowered onto him until his tip slipped between her folds.

"Yes. God, yes." Gripping her hips, he pulled her

down, lifting his own until their bodies met and he filled her completely, her wet warmth squeezing him, fire shooting through his veins.

He drew out slightly, and she gasped. Folding forward, she gripped his shoulders and leaned into him, following him down as he settled onto the cushion. Then he leaned back and let her take control.

And man, was she good at being in control.

She lifted her hips, sliding up his shaft until only his tip remained inside her luscious folds. Then she took him back in, her heat wrapping around him, enveloping him in rapture. He couldn't help but match her thrusts with his own.

With his hands on her hips, he slid his thumb between her legs to find her clit. She moaned as he circled the sensitive flesh, and her rhythm shifted, her movements growing shorter and harder until his climax coiled inside him like a tightly-wound spring.

"Oh, James." She threw her head back as she tightened around him, her orgasm making her entire body shudder.

The breathy sound of his name on her lips pushed him over the edge. His release ricocheted through his core, shattering his senses until he and Odette were the only people left in the world.

Wrapping his arms around her, he held her tight to his chest, showering her in kisses until she laughed and sat up. Her dark curls spiraled down to her shoulders, and he coiled one around his finger and watched it unravel as he caressed her soft cheek.

"I love you." The words tumbled from his lips without a second thought. Pure truth. Every bit of it.

"Took you long enough to figure it out." She smiled and gave him a quick kiss. "I love you too."

"Cut me a little slack." He gazed out into the empty room. "There's a piece of my soul floating around in here somewhere."

She moved to sit sideways in his lap and snuggled into him. "And I am going to figure out how to put you back together. If the Baron makes an appearance at the ceremony, I'll ask him for help. Whatever the price."

"What should I expect tonight? Will he be possessing you?"

She drew in a quick breath and slid from his lap. "No. I won't be possessed." Rising from the couch, she shuffled about the room, gathering her discarded clothes.

He seemed to have hit a nerve. She disappeared into the hallway and returned with his jeans and T-shirt, laying them on the bed. Without making eye contact, she dressed, and he rose and picked up his pants.

"Have you ever been possessed?"

Her hard swallow was audible as she clutched her shirt to her chest. As she lifted her gaze to his, her eyes tightened with concern. "That's a long story."

He shoved his legs into his jeans. "Will you tell me on the way?"

Pressing her lips together, she studied him, but what was she looking for? Wondering if he could handle the truth? How bad could it be?

He took her hand. "Whatever it is, I want to know. I can take it."

She glanced at their hands and then into his eyes. "You're right. You deserve to know."

CHAPTER SIXTEEN

"I'D LIKE TO KNOW WHAT HAPPENED TO YOU BEFORE we go in there." James shifted into park and looked at Odette. His deep blue eyes held concern and compassion, and she couldn't blame him for the hint of apprehension emanating from his aura.

Fear of the unknown could be the worst kind of fear.

She glanced at her watch; they had twenty minutes to spare. A fluttering formed in her stomach but not the usual butterflies that took flight when James was near. This felt more like a swarm of angry wasps. "No time like the present." Clearing her throat, she took a deep breath and blew it out hard. "Remember when I told you about my uncle and the pieces of souls he was keeping in *ouangas*?"

He shifted in his seat to face her. "I remember." His eyes widened. "Wait. You put them in the containers. If you can force a soul into a jar, you can force one into a person, can't you? My body is a container for my soul."

The hopefulness in his voice tore at her heart. "I can't. That part of you is attached to the house. It's trapped there, and only Baron Samedi can mend a broken soul."

"Oh." His posture deflated. "Well, a guy can hope. Anyway, what happened with the *ouangas*?"

She took his hand. "When Baron Samedi found out about my uncle's soul collection, he was furious. He insisted the souls be set free so they could rejoin with their rightful owners, but like I said, I don't have that power. I can help spirit energy cross over, but I can't mend an actual soul. Since these souls were residing in *ouangas,* Baron Samedi had to cross over into our world, and in order to do that, he had to act through a conduit. Through me." Her voice trailed off, her will to tell this story crumbling. What would James think of her if he knew the entire truth?

He placed his free hand on top of hers. "He possessed you when you were twelve years old?"

She nodded. "It was the only way. I had to give up control of my body, let Baron Samedi take over. Things got out of hand. Jars were shattering. The spirits I'd trapped were angry with me. My uncle was livid." Her lip trembled, and she blinked back the tears collecting on her lower lids.

"That must have been scary for you."

"Most of the time, during a ritual possession, the horse doesn't remember the ride. When a loa takes over, the host loses consciousness along with their control." She held his gaze. "I remember everything, and it was terrifying. I was there, but my body wasn't my own. I couldn't move. Couldn't speak. But I was acting. Moving. Destroying the *ouangas.* Releasing the souls."

Her heart sprinted in her chest, and she took a few slow breaths to calm herself. That was all he needed to know. Only two other living beings knew the rest of the story. Her father would never utter a word, and she would never see her cousin again. No need to add a third to the mix. "When it was over I swore I would never let it happen again." She laughed. "Now you see why I have control issues."

He shook his head. "I can imagine, but…" His eyes narrowed, and she could practically see the questions forming in his mind. He could tell she was holding back.

Time to change the subject. "What about when you're in wolf form? Does the animal ever take over? Do you lose control?" She pressed her lips into a tight smile and prayed the deflection would work.

"Never. My wolf and I are the same being. Whether we're in his form or mine, we work together. That's why I couldn't commit to you at first, before I knew the other woman he'd claimed was also you. When fate binds a werewolf's heart, there is no fighting it, so I was confused as hell as to how I could be bound to two women."

She grinned. "Bound to two mates. Sounds like a sexy romance novel."

He chuckled. "Well, this is real life, sweetheart, and you are the only woman for me."

"That's good to know." She cupped his face in her hand and ran her thumb across the dark stubble that was turning into a beard. "I like this look. Very rugged, handsome."

Holding her hand to his face, he turned his head, rubbing the softening hairs against her palm before kissing it. "Maybe I'll stop shaving then."

She held his gaze, and the corners of his eyes crinkled with his smile. His sky-blue irises held little flecks of gold, like treasure in an infinite sea she wanted to swim through for the rest of her life. Her stomach tightened, a feeling of elation expanding in her core, slowly making its way into her chest. How could she get so much satisfaction from staring into someone's eyes?

She could have sat in the car all afternoon simply looking at this man, but if she wanted more afternoons with him to come, they had work to do. "Are you ready to go in now?"

"I was born ready."

"Such a tough guy." She mussed his hair and climbed out of the truck.

The smell of burning incense greeted her nose as they entered the Voodoo temple. Taking James's hand, she led him through the front of the shop into the altar room, where she stopped in front of Papa Legba's dais.

"Please allow Baron Samedi to cross over today, Papa. I need to speak with him." Tugging an old house key from her pocket, she kissed it and dropped it in a bowl next to a walking stick.

"Do I need to do anything? Say a special prayer or…" He rested his hand on her back tentatively. Nervousness rolled from his aura, and she slid an arm around his waist.

"Get right in your head. Outsiders like to write these rituals off as hokum, but I assure you everything you're about to see is real. No one is faking."

"You realize you're asking a man who turns into a wolf to believe in magic, right?"

She smiled. "You'd be surprised how easy it is for your brain to convince you something isn't real."

"I'm a believer." He pressed a kiss to her temple.

She tightened her arm around him. "Understand that these are Ancestral Spirits, and we must hold them in reverence. Show them respect at all times. Follow my lead. I'll let you know if you need to do something specific."

"I'll follow you anywhere, sweetheart."

The conviction in his voice would have melted her doubts, but she didn't have them anymore. He would follow her into certain death. Now it was up to her not to lead him there.

As they entered the ritual room, Natasha knelt on the ground, drawing a *vévé* to Papa Legba. Never lifting her gaze from her creation, she said, "Welcome back, you two," and continued with her masterpiece.

"How'd she know it was us without looking?" James's voice was a whisper, his eyes tight with worry as he glanced about the room at the other vodouisants.

"She knows things." Odette rubbed his back, trying to ease his fear the way his presence always soothed her own.

The same drummers and dancers from the previous ceremony were preparing to begin, and three more female members of the house had joined them this time. A sour sensation churned in her stomach. She'd rather the entire Voodoo community *not* know about her situation, but there was strength in numbers, and the Baron did enjoy the women when they danced. If this didn't entice the loa to pay her a visit she…

No. Don't even think like that. This would work. They were out of options.

"Are we waiting on anyone else?" Natasha scanned the crowd, and the vodouisants shook their heads. "Alrighty then. Let's get this party started." The Mambo began her chant, and the drummers, Jackson and Tyrell, joined in, matching her rhythm.

"She's going to ask Papa Legba to allow the loa to cross over, and then we're going to pray that Baron Samedi will come." She caught James's gaze. "Keep him in your thoughts, and stay beside me, no matter what happens."

His lips quirked into a hesitant smile. "I won't leave your side."

He had no idea how much strength that simple sentence gave to her. She hadn't spoken to the Baron in person since the incident, and a brick settled in her stomach at the thought of all the things he might have to say. Things she deserved to hear.

As the beat continued, the dancers congregated in the center of the floor and moved along with the rhythm. The melodic cadence called to Odette, her body swaying before she realized what was happening. Instinct stiffened her, the usual fear of losing control taking over and bringing her mind into sharp focus. She had to keep it together. Panicking would do no good for anyone.

Natasha knelt again, grabbing a handful of cornmeal and drawing Baron Samedi's *vévé* on the floor in front of Odette.

A flitting sensation bubbled in her stomach, reaching up to her throat, but she swallowed it down. She'd made a promise to her *met tet*, and she had to keep it. Slipping her hand into James's, she relaxed her mind, allowing the music to penetrate her soul. As she swayed, her thoughts cleared, and she drifted into a semi-meditative state.

The energy around her shifted, an emptiness in the vibrational field increasing in strength. Was it her own magic intensifying with the ritual, or was her *met tet* joining the party? The darkness contracted, deepening and gathering into a cantaloupe-sized sphere.

The Baron was here.

Pressure built in Odette's chest as her heart sprinted and her palms slickened with sweat. An electrical current pulsed up and down her spine. Though she'd only experienced it once, she would never forget the feeling of being ridden by a loa.

Panic tightened her throat, and her stomach turned. This couldn't happen. Not now. She wasn't ready. The last thing she wanted to do was renege on her promise to the Baron, but agreeing to live her life in his image and allowing the Spirit complete control over her body were nowhere near the same thing.

Tightening her grip on James's hand, she turned her head toward him. He looked into her eyes, and she focused on the deep-blue color, the tiny flecks of gold glittering in the light. His aura, his presence, sharpened her mind and gave her the strength to let the loa know, in no uncertain terms, that she was not a horse to be ridden.

"I need to talk to you, Baron," she whispered. "I can't be your host."

James raised his eyebrows, silently asking if she was okay.

She nodded, letting out a breath of relief as the loa's presence dissipated, but a pang of regret flashed through her chest the moment his energy left. She may have ruined her one chance to receive Baron Samedi's help.

Tyrell stopped drumming, his face falling slack and his shoulders slumping. The Mambo dashed toward him as his body stiffened, and she caught him before he collapsed on the floor.

"Is he okay?" James squeezed her hand tighter.

"He's being possessed." *Please let it be the Baron.* She'd never forgive herself if her irrational fear had screwed up their one shot.

Odette held her breath as Tyrell regained his footing. Slipping the strap over his head, he set the drum on the floor and rolled his shoulders, stretching his neck from side to side. He ran his hands down his stomach to lift his shirt and peer at his abs.

"Not bad." He gave his wash-board stomach an appreciative nod and straightened, sweeping his gaze across the room. He paused on James for a split second, a look of recognition flashing in his dark-brown eyes, before focusing on Odette.

She gasped, and his lips curled into an un-Tyrell-like grin. Her pulse sprinted, and her lunch threatened to make a reappearance. Her prayer had been answered, but it didn't make facing her *met tet* any easier.

He looked at Natasha and spread his arms, speaking in a thick Haitian accent. "What have you got for your Baron, Mambo?"

Natasha bowed her head and presented him with a bowl of white powder. He dipped his fingers in the substance and smeared it on his skin, making circles around his eyes and mouth until his face took on a skull-like appearance. Strutting toward a table, he picked up a pair of round sunglasses, popped out one of the lenses, and settled them on his nose. Then, he placed a silk top hat on his head and ran his fingers across the brim.

"He looks like the guy on the rum bottle," James whispered, but no one responded.

Every vodouisant in the room had stopped to stare as Tyrell transformed into Baron Samedi, and the loa lifted his hands, palms up. "Why did the music stop? You know I love a party."

Natasha picked up Tyrell's drum, and she and Jackson played an upbeat rhythm.

Baron Samedi smiled, gyrating his hips and grinding on each of the dancers in turn as he made his way toward Odette. Stopping in front of her, the Baron pointed and then crooked his finger, indicating she should join him. Heat crept up her neck, and a low growl rumbled from James's chest. Her werewolf didn't want her to dance any more than she did, but she didn't have a choice.

She leaned into James's side. "Remember, he's not Tyrell right now. I'm dancing with an Ancestral Spirit."

He released his grip on her hand, but his gaze bore into her back as she stepped toward Baron Samedi and swayed her shoulders from side to side. Dancing with him was no different than an offering of rum or tobacco. She did it to honor her *met tet*. She needed to remember that.

"You call that dancing?" The Baron gripped her butt and pulled her body to his, circling his hips until she had no choice but to move along with him.

"I'm trying." She rested her hands on his shoulders and forced a smile. "I promise I am."

He laughed and released her, and James put his hand on the small of her back, reminding her he was with her no matter what.

"Your promise ain't gonna be an easy one to keep, is it?" Baron Samedi arched a brow, and the white powder creased in the lines on his forehead.

She straightened. "Nothing worthwhile is easy. I brought you an offering." She handed him a bottle of her newest white rum. "I hope you'll accept it, along with my sincerest apology."

The Baron uncapped the bottle and pressed it to his lips. Tipping his head back, he gulped down half the contents before handing it back to her. "Not bad."

James's mouth dropped open as he eyed the half-empty bottle. "Tyrell's not gonna know what hit him."

Baron Samedi grinned, snatched the bottle, and drank three more gulps. "I like this guy." He gestured to James.

"He's good for you. Let's talk." Draping his arms over their shoulders, he led Odette and James to some chairs in the back of the room. He gestured for them to sit, so she sank into a seat between her *met tet* and her soulmate.

The ceremony continued across the room, and Baron Samedi moved his shoulders, dancing along to the drumbeat. "You need my help."

She clutched her hands in her lap. "Yes. Something is trying to kill us, and it happens in every life cycle."

The loa nodded. "I know. I've seen it every time. Happens when you two meet." He looked at James. "I almost hated seeing you reborn, knowing what would happen to you."

"But…" She let out an exasperated sigh. "If you knew this would happen, why didn't you take me the first time I died? Why let me live, only to curse him too?"

"Because, child, you were a baby. Even the loa of death doesn't like to take the souls of children. And your mother made such a tempting offer." He took another swig of rum. "An entire distillery dedicated to me? I had to save you. Besides…" He patted her shoulder. "Your other half had already been born. This was willed by fate."

"So, our fate is to die?" Irritation edged James's voice, but he cleared his throat, lowering his gaze and keeping it under control.

The Baron grinned. "Not necessarily. You have the power to stop him this time. You've been second-born in every life between then and now, and it takes a shifting werewolf to defeat the Rougarou."

"You can't be serious," Odette said.

"He can't shift?"

"Yes, he can, but…" Everyone knew the Rougarou was nothing but a legend. Some centuries-old folklore from the bayou passed down through the ages. She gaped at the loa, expecting him to laugh at the preposterous idea. When he kept a straight face, she looked at James.

He rubbed at the scruff on his chin. "Maybe it's something different in Voodoo, but for werewolves, the Rougarou is the equivalent to the boogeyman. It's a story parents tell their kids to keep them in line."

Baron Samedi shrugged. "Eh, call him what you want, mon. The Rougarou is real, and he's fully awake."

Skepticism snaked into her mind, but she knew better than to doubt the word of a loa. At least out loud. But this cycle started with a power-hungry man. "Why is it after us? It must have something to do with Antoine, the one who killed Nicolas and Serafine. Did he make a deal with the monster?"

"Antoine *is* the Rougarou." He looked at them both, holding eye contact with her and then with James as his words sank in. "He's cursed."

She sucked in a breath. Why didn't she think of this before? "Serafine was a vodouisant."

"Now you're catching on." He straightened his shoulders as if her statement made him proud. It was just like a loa to make a vodouisant find her own answers to her questions.

Odette wasn't about to complain, though. She was lucky he'd shown up at all. Glancing at James, she chewed her bottom lip as the pieces of the puzzle clicked into place. "She didn't curse him, though; she wouldn't have had time. A family member did it."

The loa looked at his hand and rubbed his fingers together as if rolling something between them. More answers would require more offerings.

She patted James's leg. "Will you get the cigar out of my bag?"

"I'm on it." He strode to her bag and returned with the cigar and a lighter. Handing the smoke to the Baron, he held out the lighter and lit the end as the loa puffed away.

Returning to his chair, James leaned forward, resting his elbows on his knees. "How did it happen? And more importantly, what can we do to stop him?"

Baron Samedi examined the cigar and nodded, seemingly satisfied with the quality. "You were supposed to be the first alpha, yeah?"

James rubbed the back of his neck, his unease at the statement apparent in his pinched expression. "According to the past-life regression, I was, yes."

"With Nicolas out of the picture, Antoine should have inherited the ability to shift, but he didn't." Odette cut her gaze between the Baron and James.

James scratched his head. "That's how it usually works."

Odette's eyes widened. The puzzle was nearly complete. "Antoine didn't realize he'd fractured Nicolas's soul. When he didn't inherit the ability, he went to a *bokor*, didn't he?"

Baron Samedi nodded, tapping a finger to his nose.

"You mean like your uncle?" James asked.

Her breath caught, and she lowered her gaze to her lap. She glanced at the Baron, and his smile faded. "Yes." She forced out the answer, her heart pounding against her breast. "But the *bokor* was related to Serafine, wasn't he? Her uncle?" She nearly choked on the last word.

"He may have served the loa with both hands," Baron Samedi puffed on the cigar. "But he did love his niece."

Her chest ached at the memory of what happened with her own uncle, and she couldn't help but wonder if the Baron's statement was meant for both. "I'm sorry." Her whisper was barely audible, but James heard it. He rubbed his hand across her back, comforting her, but she could never change what had happened that day. If it were possible to go back in time and undo all the damage she'd done, she'd go in a heartbeat. Instead, her sins would weigh heavy on her shoulders for the rest of her life.

"Doesn't mean he didn't get what he deserved in the end." Baron Samedi winked, implying the double-edge of that statement as well. "Antoine went to the *bokor* to have the wolf gene activated, and he did get what he asked for. But the curse that came as the price was far higher than poor old Antoine ever imagined."

"He became the Rougarou." She reached for James's hand.

"That he did." The Baron extinguished the cigar and dropped it into the nearly-empty rum bottle. "Stuck somewhere mid-shift, he can't take on a complete human form, but he can't become a full wolf either. His body is in limbo, along with his soul."

"Damn." James shook his head. "I'll never tell that story to scare the pack kids again."

Baron Samedi rose to his feet. "Now the Rougarou sleeps somewhere in the swamp until the two of you meet. Then, he wakes up with nothing but revenge on his mind. As his power builds, demons feed on it and rise up from the underworld to come after you, weaken you."

"Shit." James leaned back in his chair. "But I can kill him? In wolf form, I can take him out for good?"

"There's a Spirit guardian in the swamp that watches over the Rougarou, does his best to keep him sedated after his revenge is exacted. But the Spirit ain't strong enough to make him sleep forever. The Rougarou's hatred for the ones he feels are responsible for his condition is powerful. When you're together, he knows, and he will kill you. Unless…"

James stood eye to eye with the loa. "Unless what?"

Baron Samedi's eyes fluttered and began rolling up—a sure sign the loa was done with the conversation and taking his leave. Odette stood and motioned for Natasha to help catch Tyrell when he fell.

"Work together, and you can kill the Rougarou. You'll need *L'Acallemon*. The *traiteur* in the swamp can lead you to him." Tyrell collapsed, and James caught him by the shoulders.

Natasha helped them settle him in a chair and wiped the white chalk from his face with a damp rag.

Odette's stomach soured, and she ground her teeth until sharp pain shot through her temple. *Please don't let it be the traiteur I think it is.*

"Who's *L'Acallemon?*" James asked.

Odette scrunched her brow. "The Gator Man. Another myth."

"He's no myth." Natasha held Tyrell's face as his eyes fluttered open.

"Who?" Tyrell tugged the glasses from his nose and took off the top hat. A grin tugged at the corners of his mouth as he examined the articles. "Baron Samedi?"

Odette nodded.

Tyrell chuckled. "That's a first."

"How you feeling?" James gestured to the nearly-empty rum bottle.

Tyrell held it up, his eyes wide. "The Baron drank all that?"

"With your body. Can you stand?" James tugged him to his feet and held his arm until he stood steady.

"Huh." Tyrell looked at the bottle again. "He must've taken it all with him. I feel fine."

James gave her a quizzical look, and Odette shrugged. "It happens," she said.

"I hope you got what you were looking for." Tyrell hugged Odette and returned to his drum.

She turned to Natasha. "What do you mean the Gator Man is no myth? He's a story told to tourists along with the Rougarou."

"If Baron Samedi says they're real, then they are." Natasha leaned in, her voice hushed. "Don't doubt your *met tet.*"

"Then which *traiteur* in the swamp is he talking about? There must be dozens." There had to be. This situation was a mess as it was. If they had to seek help from the *traiteur* her gut told her the Baron meant, they were screwed.

"Twenty years ago, maybe, but times have changed. There's one *traiteur* left near New Orleans, and it's Emile."

The name pulled the breath from Odette's lungs. She struggled to inhale, but a vise-grip held her chest, squeezing until her lungs felt like they would collapse. Not Emile.

Anyone but Emile.

A gasp from across the room drew her attention, and one of the dancers collapsed as a loa possessed her.

"Good luck." Natasha squeezed Odette's shoulder and scurried back to the ritual.

"Who's Emile?" James furrowed his brow, concern dancing in his gaze.

"He's…" Her cousin. The one other living being who

knew the truth about the day she turned her back on Voodoo. She hadn't dared speak to him since it happened.

Her head spun, and she blinked rapidly as thoughts tumbled through her mind. She might as well seek out the Rougarou and offer herself to him now. Her cousin wouldn't help her. Hell, he probably wanted to kill her. Raised by a *bokor*...no telling what the man was capable of.

Was this Baron Samedi's way of punishing her? Sending her back to the place where she ruined everything?

"Talk to me, sweetheart." James cupped her cheek in his hand, lifting her gaze to his. "We're in this together, remember?"

She swallowed the bitter bile creeping up her throat and nodded. "Let's go somewhere quiet. It's not an easy story to tell."

CHAPTER SEVENTEEN

JAMES SHIELDED HIS EYES FROM THE SUMMER SUN AS he followed Odette out the door and onto Dumaine Street. Humid heat enveloped him, coaxing sweat from his pores the moment he stepped out of the shade. A bicycle bell rang, and he jumped back to avoid being run over by a grubby-looking guy with a scraggly beard, riding an old Schwinn. The scents of body odor and weed trailed behind him like the tail of a kite, and James wrinkled his nose as he jogged to catch up with Odette.

She stared straight ahead, her determined strides propelling her to her destination at a fast clip. Her fluid dancer's posture tightened, her shoulders drawing toward her ears as she clenched and unclenched her fists.

Catching up to her, he matched her pace. "Why don't we find somewhere to sit, so we can talk." He rested his hand on the small of her back, and she slowed, blinking at him as if she'd forgotten he was there.

"Let's walk and talk. I need to keep moving or I'll..." She shook her head. "This is bad, James. Emile is... I don't even know where to begin."

"Take your time." He slipped his hand into hers and strolled beside her. His presence seemed to calm her like it usually did, bringing her down from the steep cliff she teetered on, but he'd never seen her this worried.

Her palm slickened, and she chewed her bottom lip, glancing at him occasionally as she composed her thoughts. Whoever this Emile guy was, Odette was afraid of him...and her fear commanded his wolf's attention. If Emile had done something to hurt her...

"He's my cousin." Her voice was thin, but as she relaxed her shoulders, it grew stronger. "The *bokor's* son. He was there when Baron Samedi set the souls free, and when I killed his father."

"You—?" James stopped, tightening his grip on her hand and tugging her to face him. "You killed him?"

She held his gaze for a moment, and a five-piece street band started up a brassy rendition of "When the Saints Go Marching In."

"Come on." She pulled him around the corner onto Royal Street.

"When you were twelve?" His childhood memory of her battled with this new information. Odette wasn't a murderer. There was no way. She may have lived with one foot in the spirit realm, but she'd never send someone there intentionally. She didn't have it in her. Not now and especially not as a kid.

She drew in a deep breath and blew it out hard. "I've told you my uncle was livid when Baron Samedi released his souls."

"Yeah?"

"Once the souls were free to return to the bodies of the living, the Baron took his leave. I collapsed from the possession...like Tyrell did at the ceremony." She rubbed at her throat. "I was weak and vulnerable, and when I came to, my uncle was on top of me, choking me. A few of the souls belonged to people who had already died, so their spirit energy lingered. They were as mad at me for trapping them as my uncle was for setting them free."

She shivered. "Emile helped me. He dragged my uncle off of me, and then the asshole turned on him. He was in a fit of rage, going after his own son. I don't think Emile even knew the souls had been trapped."

James pulled her to his side. "What happened then?"

She hesitated, pressing her lips together, the muscles in her mouth working like she was chewing the inside of her cheek. "I used my magic. I was terrified, and I didn't know what else to do. He was going to kill both of us, so I commanded the spirits. I gave them the energy to act and ordered them to attack him." She stared straight ahead, her gaze growing distant. "The ghosts grew so strong they turned solid. They bombarded him, and one of them broke his neck. He was lying there dead, and the ghosts floated above him, waiting for their next command."

She stopped and faced him. "They were like mindless soldiers. I could have made them do anything I wanted. It was the most terrifying thing I've ever done. I was trembling and crying, and Emile lay there, his eyes as wide as dinner plates, staring at me. I was scared, James, but it felt so good. All that power running through me."

Shaking her head, she took both his hands in hers. "I crossed them over. No matter how good the power felt, I knew it was wrong, and I sent them to the Baron. To the other side. Emile didn't say a word. We carried his dad's body to the swamp and sank it with some cinder blocks. I tried to talk to him, but he wouldn't even look at me. I left, told my dad what happened, and we packed up and moved away."

And she'd been harboring that secret for nearly twenty years. No wonder her powers terrified her. He couldn't imagine the pain she'd endured. The guilt. The suffering. He brought her fingers to his lips and kissed them. "Sounds like you did what you had to do. You saved Emile's life."

"By killing his father. I haven't spoken to him since the day it happened. How can I go to him for help after all these years? Why would he want to help *me*?"

"It looks like we don't have a choice. If we don't stop the Rougarou tonight, someone else will die. He won't be just helping you; he'll be helping everyone in New Orleans."

She huffed. "If he's anything like his dad, he doesn't care about anyone but himself." She laughed, but there was no humor in it. "Natasha convinced me to do these past-life regressions to help me figure out why I was afraid of my powers. Of course, *I* knew what the problem was, but I couldn't let the Mambo know I'd killed a man. I went through a few regressions to humor her, but when the pattern of death started emerging, I quit."

He kissed her cheek. "It's a good thing you did them. Otherwise, we'd both be dead by now and neither of us would have seen it coming." He couldn't fault her for not telling him before. He'd thought his wolf's issues were too tragic to share, but this… He couldn't imagine going through that at twelve years old.

Wrapping his arms around her, he inhaled the warm, sweet scent of her hair. A scent he wanted to experience every day for the rest of his life. "This is all going to work out. I've got your back with Emile…and after we kill this thing, we'll go home, and I'll have your front too."

Her laugh vibrated in his chest, and she pulled away to look at him. The tension around her eyes eased, the worry lines on her forehead smoothing. "If we make it through this, you can have any side of me that you want."

He cocked an eyebrow. "Whenever I want?"

"Forever." She gestured to a wooden sign hanging from the gallery above. "Have you been inside the Voodoo museum?"

He peered at the *vévé* carved into the plaque. A series of stars and swirls embellished two straight lines intersecting at a ninety-degree angle, much like the one Natasha had drawn in cornmeal to start the ceremony. "Can't say that I have."

"Come with me. I want to show you something." Taking his hand, she led him through the door and handed a ten-dollar bill to the attendant for the entrance fee.

They paused at the entry as a line of tourists exited the narrow hallway, and then they continued into the museum. On the right, a row of portraits hung, each one representing a famous Mambo from the past. A twenty by thirty-inch frame contained a painting of Marie Laveau herself, with a white scarf wrapped around her head, a snake draped over her shoulders.

He shuddered. The only animals not afraid of werewolves, snakes didn't hesitate to bite his legs when he got too close in the swamp. Their venom didn't slow him down, but it burned like hell until his body expunged it. "What is it with Voodoo and snakes?"

She slipped an arm around his bicep. "The snake represents Damballa, the creator of all life."

The beady, red eyes of the snake in the portrait stared back at him, and its forked tongue protruded between its fangs. "Ah, so kinda important then."

"There's a live one in the back. A python. Would you like to see it?" Her lips quirked into an adorable, kissable grin.

"No thanks. I see enough snakes when I'm hunting."

She wandered down the hall, and he followed her into a small room filled with life-size portrayals of various loa. A science class skeleton wearing a top hat, black jacket, and sunglasses with a lens missing stood in the corner. They'd spoken to the guy in person; why did they need to look at a replica? "Why does Baron Samedi have cotton in his nose?"

"It's a Haitian funeral tradition, but he's not who we're here to see. Look." She pointed to two figures standing side by side.

He moved closer to the statues. "Wolf head, human body, red eyes. That's the Rougarou my dad used to tell me about when I wouldn't go to bed." The same boogeyman he'd warned little Emma about when she'd thrown a fit in the bar a week ago.

The fake wolf's lips drew back in a snarl, and its hunched posture and pained expression in its eyes almost made James feel sorry for the guy. Almost. "Hard to believe I'm related to that thing."

He studied the other figure. An alligator head with a red mohawk sat atop a moss-stuffed mannequin wearing white coveralls. A small placard read, *"The Gator Man (L'Acallemon) protects people from the Rougarou (werewolves)."*

James huffed. "The Rougarou is *not* a werewolf. Nobody needs protection from us."

Odette chuckled. "Relax. No one believes any of this is real, werewolves included. When you live in secrecy, outsiders make up their own stories."

"But these." He gestured to the statues. "These aren't stories."

"Apparently not." She glanced at her watch. "We've got three hours of daylight left. We'd better pay Emile a visit."

Nausea churned in Odette's stomach on the twenty-minute drive out of the city. Curiosity had led her to research Emile when she'd returned to New Orleans a few years ago. That and her desire to avoid running into him by chance.

His website proclaimed him a *traiteur*, which was odd in itself. Faith healers usually didn't advertise their services. Then again, word of mouth traveled mostly online these days. Maybe it wasn't so odd after all.

His list of services didn't include anything that alluded to black magic, but that didn't mean anything. His father had kept his dark side hidden unless the price was right.

"Make a right here." She pointed to a narrow dirt road, and James turned, his truck bumping along the uneven path.

Cypress and pine trees rose on either side of them, creating a canopy over the road, their needles filtering the soft sunlight, making it appear darker than it should have at six-thirty in the evening in July.

James rolled down the windows and inhaled deeply. "I love the smell of the bayou in the summertime. Don't you?"

The earthy aromas of moss, mud, and arbor took her back to her childhood. To the tragedy she was about to return to. "My nose isn't as sensitive as yours."

"You're missing out." He reached across the seat and took her hand, trying to lighten the mood, to calm her, and his presence did help.

But nothing could tame the hurricane-strength anxiety blowing through her mind that returning to the scene of her crime had induced.

"There it is." She pointed ahead as the house came into view.

The wooden cottage looked exactly like she remembered it. Thick coats of white paint, applied over the peeling layers beneath, gave the panels a bumpy, mottled appearance. The corrugated-tin roof had rusted, and a blue tarp covered one corner to stop it from leaking.

An herb garden took up twenty square feet of the front yard, the rich, green plants overflowing the railroad tie barriers to take in another two feet. Emile had inherited his father's green thumb.

James parked the truck on the side of the road and looked at her with raised eyebrows, his silent question giving her pause.

Was she ready for this? Not really. Not at all.

She climbed out of the truck and walked hand-in-hand with James up the front steps. He reached for the screen door, but she tugged him along the porch to the side of the house.

"Always enter a *traiteur's* house through the back door. It's considered rude to go in through the front."

"Interesting." James rubbed at the scruff on his chin. "I'd have thought the opposite."

"I think it's safe to let go of everything we *thought* from here on out."

A wooden "open" sign hung on the door, so she twisted the knob and gave it a push. A set of chimes hanging from the ceiling jingled, announcing their presence.

She peered up at the wood and metal instrument. "Chicken bones."

"What?" James slid past her into the room and followed her gaze to the ceiling.

"When my uncle lived here, those were chicken bones. They rattled when the door opened." Her uncle had said the rattle of bones was significant because the people who came to him for help were on their deathbeds.

She knew better now.

"Have a sit. I'll be out in a minute." The man's voice was deeper than she remembered Emile's, but he was seventeen the last time she saw him.

Odette's heart slammed against her breast before crawling into her throat. James gestured to the worn sofa beneath the window, and she sank onto the edge, her back straight, muscles tense and ready to flee. What was she doing here? No good could come from this.

James rested a hand on her knee. "We've got this."

"I know." She scanned the room, searching for signs of black magic. A shelf filled with books on herbalism and healing lined one wall, and a lush array of herbs, too delicate for the Louisiana heat, filled an assortment of clay pots on the windowsill. No animal bones. No signs of blood sacrifice. Even the energy in the room felt lighter than she remembered.

Had Emile moved, taking her only chance of survival with him?

A woman in a pale-yellow dress entered the waiting area from a side door. Her shiny black hair flowed to her shoulders, and a white daisy pinned near her temple matched her necklace and bracelet. She smiled warmly. "Can I help you?"

Odette stood, the quick movement more aggressive than she'd intended. "We're here to see Emile. Does he still live here?"

The woman took a step back, her smile faltering before she composed herself. "Yes, he does. I'm his wife, Brooke. Do you have an appointment?"

"No, we don't." She tried to relax her posture, to tone down the off-putting aura of death that usually scared people away.

Unfazed, Brooke took a tablet from a shelf. "Would you like to make one?"

"This is an emergency." James stood next to Odette, so close his shoulder brushed hers.

Brooke's smile widened as she glanced at James and then looked at Odette. "Let me guess, you need a fertility spell?"

Odette glowered at the woman.

"I'm James, and this is Odette." He held out his hand, and Brooke shook it. "She's human," he said, as if assuring her the woman was harmless.

Brooke raised her eyebrows. "I take it you aren't?"

"Just a few more sessions, and it should be cleared up." Emile's voice drifted through the door first. Then his patient stepped through, a woman in her eighties with silver hair and bright blue eyes.

"I still think you should charge a fee for your services," the woman said. "Donations aren't a stable income. You can't count on people's generosity."

Emile smiled. "It's worked so far. See you next week."

As the woman shuffled out the door, Emile's gaze landed on Odette. His smile slipped into a frown, and he cut his gaze to James and then to his wife before looking back at Odette. "What are you doing here?"

The fear and guilt she'd kept bottled inside all these years erupted in her gut like someone dropped a Mentos into a bottle of Diet Coke. The little girl in her screamed to run, to leave New Orleans, her past, and everything behind. Running away had worked before; it could work again.

But the Rougarou would keep killing until it found her.

She straightened her spine and drew upon her magic, letting it build, gathering a static charge in the air, reminding her cousin of her power. "I need your help."

Emile crossed his arms. "Death isn't welcome in my clinic, and I've got bigger things to worry about. You need to leave."

"I'm not here to bring death. I want to stop it."

He scoffed. "Like you stopped my father?"

Brooke gasped and covered her mouth. "She's the one?"

"She is, and she's leaving. I've worked too hard to rid myself of my father's *bokor* legacy for you to come in and ruin everything. And to bring a werewolf with you?" He shook his head and ushered them toward the door. "Out you go. Scoot. And don't come back."

James crossed his arms, refusing to budge. "Tell us where to find the Gator Man, and we'll be happy to leave."

Emile narrowed his eyes. "What do you know about *L'Acallemon?*"

"We know he's the only one who can stop the Rougarou," James said.

"And that he can't do it on his own." She reached toward her cousin and touched his elbow. His magic vibrated up her arm before he jerked away. "Please, Emile. Will you help us?"

Her cousin's fingers curled into his palms as he ground his teeth. "My father took you in when the House didn't want you. He taught you how to use your magic, how to control it so you didn't bring death everywhere you went. He may have served the loa with both hands, but he…"

He clamped his mouth shut and took in a deep breath. "Yes, my father practiced black magic, and while he may not have been the most honorable man, he loved you… more than he loved me."

Odette blinked, scrambling for something to say. Emile had no clue what she'd suffered at the hands of his father. Crossing her arms, she inclined her chin. "If that's what you believe, then why didn't you turn me in?"

"No one missed the crazy old man from the swamp. Anyway, the magical community takes care of their own problems." He cut his gaze to James. "I bet your *boyfriend* can tell you some stories. I've heard about werewolf justice."

James stiffened, taking a step toward Emile, but Odette caught his hand.

"You could have turned me in to the House since you say they didn't want me anyway. Why'd you let me get away with it?"

"Your dad paid me for my silence." He crossed his arms to mirror her posture. "But, since there's no statute of limitations on murder, maybe I should call the police."

A growl rumbled in James's chest. "She was defending herself."

"He was attacking *me* when she killed him." Emile jabbed a finger at his own chest.

"Okay, let's all take a deep breath." Brooke put up her hands to stop the argument, but a sharp look from Emile had her backing up.

"He loved my magic, not me," Odette said. "I had enough bruises to prove it, but I hid them. So, go ahead and call the police. Are you going to tell them a twelve-year-old broke your dad's neck or that a bunch of ghosts did it? Which do you think they'll believe?"

Emile's mouth opened and closed a few times, his eyes losing focus as he processed her words. "Bruises?"

Her chin trembled, so she snapped her teeth together. "He beat me into submission whenever you weren't around because he wanted my power. He thought if he could control a child of Baron Samedi that he could control the dead." Her own uncle. Her *family.* Pressure built in the back of her eyes as the knife of betrayal twisted in her chest. A knife she'd thought she'd gotten rid of but had apparently just been ignoring.

This argument was pointless. No matter how justified she'd been, she did kill Emile's father. She didn't deserve his forgiveness, nor did she need it. Asking for his help had been a mistake. She tightened her grip on James's hand and stepped toward the door. "You know what, Emile? Never mind. If I could survive two years under your father's thumb, I can survive anything. Come on, James. We'll figure something else out."

She tugged James out the back door and rounded the corner, stopping on the side of the house. Her head spun, and what little she'd eaten today threatened to make a reappearance as she leaned against the porch railing. That confrontation had gone about as well as she'd expected it to.

"Are you okay?" James faced her, resting his hands on her hips.

She sucked in a trembling breath, shaking her head. "I knew he wouldn't help us. He'll never forgive me for what I did."

"He might if you ask him to. Have you ever apologized?"

"I…" she dropped her gaze to the ground. "I guess I haven't. I've been too busy defending myself, making sure nothing like that could ever happen again."

He tucked a spiral curl behind her ear. "Maybe you should. According to Baron Samedi, *L'Acallemon* is our last hope for defeating this thing. Without him, we're screwed."

She chewed her bottom lip as she held his gaze. Funny how James had turned into the sensible one. "I'll try. But I don't think it will help."

"Odette." Emile trotted around the corner, stopping when his gaze locked with hers. "Good. You're still here."

She pushed from the railing and faced him. "You've got access to *L'Acallemon*, and we're offering to help him defeat the Rougarou. If you really want to end your family's black magic legacy, this is your chance." It wasn't exactly an apology, but it was the best she could do at the moment.

James cleared his throat. "I think what she's trying to say is…"

"I know what she's saying. I heard every word, and you're right."

Of course she was right. He may have cleansed himself

of his father's black magic, but she was offering him the means to stop a two-hundred-year-old curse.

"Give us the Gator Man, and we'll put an end to the reign of the Rougarou."

Emile let out a dry laugh as Brooke stepped onto the porch. "You don't know what you're offering. You'll die trying to defeat him."

James put his hand on her shoulder. "We'll die if we don't. We're the reason he's awake."

Emile's eyes widened as Brooke squeezed his arm. "I'll get some tea. You all better come inside." She scurried to the kitchen, and Emile led them to his living room. As they settled onto the sofa, Brooke returned with four tall glasses of sweet tea.

Emile sat in a teal accent chair, and Brooke perched on the arm beside him. "So you're his target this time." He chuckled and rubbed his mouth as if to rub the humor away. "No wonder it's taking so long. He's up against a shifter and child of Baron Samedi. How did you figure it out?"

She told him about her past-life regressions, James's dreams, the imps, and the ghost. "And Natasha said you're the keeper of *L'Acallemon*. That your family has been since the beginning."

"We have been because we're the ones who made him." He pressed his lips together, eyeing her as if he wasn't sure he should divulge the information. "We made the Rougarou too."

Emile paused, but if he was waiting for her to act shocked, he'd be sorely disappointed. She was in this mess up to her eyeballs, so it made sense that her cousin's side of the family would be too.

"Curses are made with black magic, which is unstable

in itself," Emile continued. "From what I've read, the *bokor* who cursed the man into the Rougarou had a grudge, and adding negative emotions into the mix makes it even less predictable."

Odette nodded. "He killed the *bokor's* niece."

Surprise flashed in his eyes before he shook his head. "The Rougarou wasn't supposed to live forever. The curse was meant to make him hideous so he would have to spend the rest of his days in hiding, not quite a wolf but not a man either, and never able to claim New Orleans to start a pack. Unfortunately, with black magic, side effects occur and his strength multiplied, the curse binding his soul to the earth, making him impossible for an earthly-realm being to kill."

James put his hand on Odette's knee. "Has he ever gone up against a werewolf? We slay demons like piñatas. Maybe we don't even need the Gator Man's help."

"Many have tried." Emile's eyes darkened. "The Rougarou went on a killing spree when the curse was complete. Rogue werewolves from the bayou tried to stop him, but he tore them to pieces like *they* were the piñatas."

Emile arched a brow as James leaned back into the seat. Odette took her soulmate's hand and squeezed it. Now was not the time for a battle of egos. "So your family created *L'Acallemon* to fight him?"

"Our ancestors created *L'Acallemon* to defeat him, but their dealings with the black arts made the loa reluctant to help. Their magic wasn't strong enough to create an entity that could kill the Rougarou—only subdue him. Without a body, *L'Acallemon* is no match for the rage inside the monster. The rage that awakens him when the target couple meets."

Emile took a long drink of his tea. "I'm surprised you've lasted this long, even with your power."

Did he not remember what she was capable of? She took a slow, deep breath. Now was not the time for rivalry either. "I have a charm on the house, and we haven't been out after dark since the killings started. He's found us though. James has already fought him once and injured him. With *L'Acallemon's* help, we can—"

He set his glass on the coffee table with a *thunk.* "*L'Acallemon* can't do anything without a host. He has to ride someone."

Her heart dropped into her stomach to swim around with the churning, nauseating mess of emotions she'd been trying to keep down since they walked through the door. Before she could utter a word, James cut in.

"I'll do it. He can ride me."

"No, James. You're not even initiated. You can't…"

"I can initiate him." Emile looked at his wife as she lovingly rubbed her hand across his back. "I'm a *houngan*, so that's not the issue."

"It's settled then." James leaned back on the sofa. "With my fighting abilities and whatever magic the Gator Man brings to the table, the Rougarou won't stand a chance."

"Maybe not." Sadness filled Emile's eyes. "But *L'Acallemon* isn't really a loa. He can't move in and out of beings without harming them, because he was created for a single purpose. If you allow him to ride you, he'll probably sever your soul; it's what he was made to do. The priestess who created him died in the process."

Her stomach, heart, and every other organ in her body plummeted to the floor. *L'Acallemon* required the ultimate offering in exchange for his help—a life. With her hand on James's leg, she squeezed until her knuckles turned white.

"What are you trying to say?" He patted her hand, but she couldn't release her grip.

The one and only way to defeat the plague that had been following them through countless lives would kill the man she loved. She ground her teeth, cursing fate for its sick sense of humor.

Closing her eyes, she blew out a slow breath and swallowed the dryness from her mouth. "He's saying you'll die."

CHAPTER EIGHTEEN

"So, if I let *L'Acallemon* possess me, you're sure I can beat the Rougarou?" James pried Odette's fingers from his leg and held her hand in both of his. Her fingers had turned to ice, so he sandwiched them between his palms.

"According to the notes left behind, yes." Emile looked at his wife. "Get the book, will you?"

Brooke disappeared through a door and returned with a worn, leather-bound volume filled with yellowing paper. It creaked as she opened it and laid it in his lap, and the deteriorating pages looked so brittle they might fall out of the binding.

Emile turned to a bookmarked page and pointed to an entry. "They used a lock of Antoine's hair in the ritual when they created *L'Acallemon*. The Spirit is tied to the beast, they share energy, so he should be able to defeat it."

The warmth returned to Odette's fingers, so he laced his own through hers and swallowed the thickness from his throat. "And why haven't I tried this before in any of my past lives?" Besides the fact that he'd be facing certain death, because death was coming for him either way.

Flipping a few pages, Emile scanned the documents. "I don't think you knew what was happening before. Normally, when the Rougarou wakes up, he finds his target the same night and returns to the swamp where *L'Acallemon* puts him back to sleep."

It made sense. Baron Samedi said James had been second-born in every life since the cycle started. He wouldn't have been involved with hunting the demons that preceded the attack. He'd never had a clue…until now.

Odette's fingers tightened on his hand as she slowly shook her head. "You can't do this, James; I can't lose you. There has to be another way." Her eyes were wide with fear.

"I'm open to ideas."

"We can move away. Go to London or Australia. Somewhere the Rougarou could never get to us." Her brow pinched, the reality that the idea would never work draining the hope from her voice.

"He'll never stop killing."

"Until we're dead." Her expression blanked, a mask of resolve covering her fear as she looked into his eyes. "We have to stop him. People are dying because of our love."

"Not our love, sweetheart." He trailed his fingers down her cheek. "Because of the ridiculous standards of an outdated society and one man's hunger for power. Hate and greed created this monster. Love will take it down."

Emile handed Brooke the volume, and she took it to the other room, returning with a small yellow suitcase. "I'll be back in the morning, love." She blew a kiss to Emile, and he rose and hugged her. "Be careful."

"Always."

"It was nice meeting you two." She waved and shuffled out the door.

Emile took the tea glasses to the sink. "She's been spending the night with her sister two hours away since it started. The beast is looking for couples, and I've been casting locator spells and begging the loa for help. If I'd known who he was after…" He shook his head.

"We'll stop him." James rose and cracked his knuckles. No one else would die because of his twisted fate. "Tell me what to do."

Emile nodded. "Come with me. We'll need to perform a *lavé tet*."

"It's a head-washing ceremony." Odette took James's hand and guided him into another room. "A spiritual cleansing to make you ready to receive a loa in possession."

He sat in the chair Odette gestured to. A row of cabinets with shelves full of herbs lined one wall, and a table holding equipment similar to what he'd seen in Natasha's temple sat next to it. "But the Gator Man isn't a loa."

"Which is why the short version of this ceremony should be enough to make the possession tolerable for you." Emile filled a bucket with water and sprinkled in herbs from the jars. Pressing his palms together, he said a prayer over the mixture, blessing it.

Odette sat next to James, her death grip on his hand letting him know how much she disliked what he was doing. Hell, he didn't like it any more than she did, but what choice did he have?

Emile set the bucket on the floor and pulled up a chair. "Take off your shirt and tilt your head back."

James tugged his shirt over his head, and Odette put her hand on his chest.

Her fingers felt like icicles again. "Wait. What if I carry *L'Acallemon*? You can subdue the creature, and the Gator Man can use me to kill him. Then at least you'll have a chance to survive."

Her lips paled as she spoke, her fear of relinquishing all control causing her shoulders to draw up toward her ears. No way would he let her go through something so traumatic to spare his life.

Holding her hand to his chest, he kissed her temple. "I don't want to survive if it means living without you."

Tears collected on her lower lids. "That sentiment works both ways, you know."

He draped his shirt across his knee and took her face in his hands. "I'm not afraid of being possessed. I'm not afraid of death or of dying. I was made for this."

"The only thing that scares me is losing you." A tear dripped down her cheek, and he wiped it away with his thumb.

"I've got this."

"But I can—"

"No, Odette. You can't." Emile dipped a wooden spoon into the bucket and stirred the contents.

"Yes, I can." She shot to her feet. "Voodoo created the curse, so a vodouisant should be sacrificed to end it. I won't let James die over something *my* ancestor caused."

While James admired her determination, there was no way in hell he would let her die. "Odette." He reached for her hand, but she jerked away.

"Put your shirt back on. I'm hosting *L'Acallemon*."

Emile carried the bucket to James's chair. "You've put up a block; I can feel it in your aura. Baron Samedi himself couldn't ride you in this condition, much less a home-grown Spirit like *L'Acallemon*."

"I can handle it, Emile. I'll do whatever needs to be done."

James reached for her hand again, and this time she let him take it. He pried her fingers from her palm and gave her hand a squeeze. She relaxed a little with his touch, but she was riled up and ready to fight. God, he loved this woman.

"Regardless of what you can or can't handle, it has to be James. You said yourself that Baron Samedi told you only a shifting wolf can kill the Rougarou, and I understand why." Emile dropped the spoon into the bucket and glanced at James, hesitating to continue. "*L'Acallemon* was conjured using werewolf blood."

"Son of a bitch." No wonder this situation was so royally fucked. Blood magic, especially the kind involving werewolf blood, was extremely volatile and always came with a price.

Emile raised his hands. "I didn't write the spell. I read about it in the family journals." He laughed dryly and looked at Odette. "I've been studying this for the past sixteen years, trying to figure out the secret, and then you come along, chat with your *met tet*, and suddenly you've got all the answers. Loa don't lie. If the Baron said it has to be a werewolf, then it *has* to be a werewolf."

"You have no idea what it took to get Baron Samedi to help me. It sure as hell wasn't a simple chat."

Her cousin raised his hands. "Whatever it took, you got the answers. Unless your dad is secretly a werewolf, you know as well as I do that you can't be the host for *L'Acallemon*."

Her breath released in a hiss as she lowered into the chair, the expression on her face one of pure determination. She wasn't going to let *L'Acallemon* take him without a fight.

James leaned back in the chair, and Emile dumped cup after cup of seasoned water over his head, saying both Catholic prayers and Haitian Creole chants. He wiped at the room-temperature liquid to stop it from getting in his eyes, but it ran in rivulets down the back of his neck, soaking his shoulders and half his torso.

The magic in the room intensified, the vibration of the air increasing, raising the hairs on his arms. When Emile used up the last of the water, he wrapped James's head in a white towel and took the bucket to the sink.

Odette clutched her hands in her lap and smiled weakly. "Normally we'd dress you in all white and have you lie down for the rest of the day." She glanced at her watch. "But we've got to get going if we're going to make it home before dark."

"We're not doing this at your house. You've got neighbors." He took the towel Emile offered, and he patted himself dry. Bits of crushed rosemary and sage clung to his skin, making him smell like a Thanksgiving turkey waiting to go in the oven.

"The neighbors won't see a thing. I'll lift the charm; the Rougarou will come inside to find us." She took the white towel from his head and gave it to Emile.

"We'll tear the place apart." He pulled his shirt over his head, slipping his arms through the sleeves and running a hand through his wet hair.

She straightened her spine. "It's a sacrifice I'm willing to make. If you're going to…" Her voice hitched, and she swallowed. "If you're going to die, it needs to happen in the house. I think I can…" She dropped her gaze to the floor, and a sob caused her shoulders to bounce.

James pulled her into a hug and kissed the top of her head, his heart breaking at the sadness in her voice.

"If you die, I think I can make Nicolas cross over with you. If he sees his brother pay for his crimes, he'll be able to move on too. You'll be whole again."

Emile handed him a preserved alligator head, its snout nearly the length of his entire arm. "*L'Acallemon* is tied to this. It's the gator that was sacrificed to create the Spirit, preserved with magic and formaldehyde. For the Spirit to possess you, you'll have to put it on your head. *L'Acallemon* will travel down through your crown and into your body."

James lifted the mummified head toward his own.

"Not yet." Emile put his hand on the gator. "The possession will happen quickly. Wait until the Rougarou is in sight."

"Thank you." James shook his hand.

"Yes, thank you, Emile." Odette clasped her hands together. "I wanted to tell you that I'm sorry about everything that happened. I didn't use any black magic that day. It was the power Baron Samedi gifted me, but I abused it. I am so, so sorry."

Emile pressed his lips together and nodded. "You saved my life, and you kept my father's secret. I should have thanked you a long time ago." He held out his hand, and Odette accepted it. "Good luck. I hope you can end this cycle."

"We will." James shook his hand once more and led Odette out the back door.

Odette sat quietly in the passenger seat as James maneuvered along the bumpy dirt road and back out onto the highway. A tornado of emotions swirled through her body, and she focused on them one at a time, so they didn't overwhelm her.

The easiest emotion to pluck from the storm was her relief that Emile didn't hold a grudge. She'd hoped for forgiveness, but to receive his thanks after all these years of turmoil was like opening a pressure valve on her soul.

She'd made right by her *met tet* and made amends with her last living relative on her mother's side. If not for the impending death of the man sitting next to her, she'd have said things were looking up.

The despair of losing her soulmate tore open her chest, fracturing her heart, and causing a sob to bubble up from her throat. James glanced at her, and she coughed to cover it up. *He* was the one about to die, and no tears streamed from his eyes. If he could be strong, so could she.

She stared out the window as the blur of trees made way for buildings as they approached the city. Who was she kidding? Her strength was a façade. It always had been. Ritual possession was nothing for a seasoned vodouisant like herself to be afraid of. She'd seen it happen to her friends countless times, and none of them were harmed in the process.

Now the one Spirit that would harm its host was about to possess her boyfriend, and there wasn't a damn thing she could do about it. Or maybe there was…

She remained silent as he spoke with his alpha on the phone. Her attempt at protesting his desire to ask the pack for help fell flat when he reminded her that wolves were pack animals. If he was going to die in this fight, she'd let it happen on his terms.

If she let it happen at all.

He tossed his phone into a cupholder and reached across the console to rub the back of her neck. "Luke's gathering a few weres to meet us at the house. If I fight the Rougarou with the pack's help, it will be over faster. Less damage to your home."

She nodded and fought the tremble in her voice. "You didn't tell him you wouldn't be surviving the fight."

The corner of his mouth twitched. "If he knew that, he'd never agree to the plan. You and I both know this is the only way to end the cycle. Sacrificing my life will stop anyone else from dying at the hands of the Rougarou."

"Sometimes I wish you weren't so damn noble."

James chuckled. "You wouldn't have me any other way."

He stopped in the driveway, and they both watched in silence as the sun sank behind the house. The orange and pink of the sky morphed into a deep purply-blue, and an early cricket chirped, its ominous song a harbinger of tragedy.

A ten-ton weight pressed into Odette's chest, squeezing the air from her lungs. She held her eyes wide, but try as she might, she couldn't stop the tears from falling. Turning her head, she slid out of the truck and paced toward the front door.

James caught up to her on the porch, and balancing the gator head on the railing, he pulled her into his arms, wiping the tears from her cheeks. "Hey." He hooked a finger under her chin, lifting her gaze to his. "This isn't goodbye, you know. I'll find you in our next life, and then we'll have our happily ever after, okay? I promise."

She nuzzled her face into his chest, breathing in his woodsy, masculine scent. A scent she'd come to associate with comfort. With home. James had done more than restore this old house; he'd restored *her*. He had chipped away the plaster of her carefully constructed façade and found the woman beneath, bringing her to the surface and reminding her how to live.

James was right; this wasn't goodbye. Emile had said the Gator Man would drain James's life force and *probably* sever his soul. That qualifier was her ray of hope, and she planned to hold onto it until the end.

Pulling herself together, she faced the front door and whispered a banishing spell, asking Papa Legba for help opening the gateway to her home, breaking the protection charm. Magic vibrated in the air, gathering in front of the door, condensing and expanding until the pressure popped like a bubble and dissipated into the air. "It's done. The Rougarou, and anything else for that matter, can get inside." The fact sat heavy in her stomach like a block of dried-up mashed potatoes.

"Then we'd better get ourselves in and get ready."

As if she could prepare for the impending death of her soulmate. Living the rest of this life without James would be unbearable, and she refused to continue living alone.

A sense of resolve washed over her as she stepped through the threshold. If defeating the Rougarou, breaking the cycle, meant ending James's life, she knew what she'd have to do. James wasn't afraid of death. Neither was she.

James paused on the porch as Luke, Cade, Noah, and a woman with a blonde pixie cut and bright-green eyes strode up the walk.

Luke shook James's hand. "Chase and Bryce are leading a patrol in case your beast tries to make any pitstops on the way."

James nodded and gestured for them to enter. Odette chewed the inside of her cheek as James set the gator head on a table, and they gathered in the foyer. The woman hesitated to close the door. She looked outside and glanced at Luke before lowering her gaze.

"We need you here."

At the alpha's words, she closed the door and nodded.

James rested a hand on Odette's back and whispered, "Her mate is on patrol. They haven't been together long."

Odette recognized the worried expression. Her own face probably looked the same.

"This is Alexis," Luke said. "She's our healer."

"Healer?" Her eyebrows raised as the tiny ray of hope she clung to grew a little brighter, but James rolled his neck, his back stiffening.

"She'll help us fight, but if anyone gets hurt in the crossfire, she can use her enhanced healing ability on others." Luke flashed a small smile, focusing on Odette. "We'll keep you safe."

James's tension eased, but she hadn't been the slightest bit worried about herself. She'd been caught up in the soul-severing fear and hadn't stopped to think about how the confrontation had gone down in her previous lives. The Rougarou would come after her first.

Luke held a hand above the gator head, but he didn't touch it. "There's a Voodoo Spirit attached to this thing?"

"*L'Acallemon.*" James picked it up and looked into its glassy eyes. Cocking his head, he squinted, studying the object as if he were looking for the Spirit, but even Odette couldn't see the Gator Man.

Was it even attached to it? What if Emile hadn't forgiven her and this was a cruel attempt at getting even? She had killed his father, a man that he loved. Maybe her cousin had infused them with the false hope that they could defeat the Rougarou, when his true intention had been ensuring their timely deaths. Bile crept up the back of her throat, but she swallowed it down. Her cousin's intent didn't matter at this point. The beast would be there soon, and the house was unprotected.

Cade shoved his hands first in his front pockets and then his back before crossing his arms. "You're sure you want to let it possess you?"

"It's the only way to end this." James looked at Odette, and pressure built in the back of her eyes again, so she lowered her gaze. She would not cry in front of his pack.

"Are you sure it's safe?" Alexis peered at the head and curled her lip.

"He can handle it." Noah clapped James on his shoulder. "This'll be over before midnight, and I'll buy the first round of beers when we're through."

She dared another glance at James, and when his eyes met hers, time seemed to freeze. Her lungs betrayed her, not allowing her breath to pass in nor out, and the force of gravity multiplied, threatening to crumbled her. She would not live a single day without this man, and she had all the ingredients she needed to make sure she wouldn't have to in her cupboard. Now, she had to convince Baron Samedi to cooperate.

Shaking herself to break the trance James's gaze had put upon her, she cleared her throat. "We should prepare."

"She's right." James carried the gator head beneath his arm and stood by her side. "Luke, I think it's best if y'all hide. Odette and I will wait in the bedroom since that's where it likes to find its victims. Stay in the laundry room across the hall. There are no windows, so it can't see you, and when you hear the fight starting, then come in. Not before. I don't want the Rougarou to take off before the Gator Man has a chance to take hold."

The alpha squared his gaze on Odette. "Are you sure this is safe for him?"

"It's the only way." James slipped his hand into hers. "I trust her with my life, and I trust that if anything happens to me, the pack won't seek retaliation. I'm doing this voluntarily, and I'm aware of all the risks."

Luke cut his gaze between them and nodded. "Agreed."

"I'll prepare the *vévés*." She shuffled into the kitchen, with James on her heels, as the alpha called his pack into a huddle. "I'll be right back." She kissed James on the cheek and glanced out the window at the final rays of light disappearing behind the horizon.

He clutched her hand. "We're out of time."

Out of time before the Rougarou arrived, before their lives ended, their love lost. "I'll be fast."

Taking a sack of cornmeal from a cabinet, she hurried to the bedroom and drew Papa Legba's *vévé* in the entrance.

"Please, Papa, allow *L'Acallemon* to enter our world and take James as his host." She glanced over her shoulder to be sure she was alone. "And please allow Baron Samedi to cross over, should he so desire."

Nicolas appeared before her, a confused expression pinching his ghostly brow.

"Stay with me. You'll be free from this place soon." She returned to the hallway as the werewolves headed to the laundry room to hide, and James gave her a questioning look. "One more minute. I need a word with the Baron."

James nodded, and she rushed to her altar room. Pausing to take a deep breath and center herself, she dropped to her knees and drew her *met tet's vévé* in corn-meal on the floor in front of his altar. "Please Baron Samedi, name your terms. I'll pay any price if you'll allow me to be with James, if not in this world, then in yours."

His pack mates squeezed into the laundry room, and James tapped Noah on the arm. "A word?"

"What's up?" Noah followed him into the hallway, his excitement at being included in the fight evident in his casual smile. Hopefully the pack would continue to include him after James was gone.

He guided his friend out of the alpha's earshot and lowered his voice to a whisper. "There's a ninety-nine percent chance I'm not going to make it out of this alive."

Noah's expression fell. "Wha—"

"Shut up, man. This is between you and me." Odette returned from her prayer to Baron Samedi, and he pulled her to his side. "This Spirit is probably going to kill me, and I'm well aware of it. I need you…"

Noah shifted from side to side, opening and closing his mouth like he wanted to protest.

James held up a hand to keep him quiet. "I need you to keep your mouth shut, first of all. Second, when this is over, I need you to make sure she's taken care of. If anyone holds my death against her, you set them straight. Under-stood?" He stared his friend hard in the eyes, willing him to understand. James didn't want to die any more than the next person, but if it meant Odette would be safe and no one else would fall victim to the Rougarou again, he'd gladly make the sacrifice.

He squeezed Noah's shoulder. "I'm telling you this because I trust you. Will you do this for me? Consider it my dying wish."

Noah blinked a few times, his mouth hanging open like his mind couldn't comprehend. "Yeah. Of course, but…damn, James. Are you sure?"

"If one more person asks me if I'm sure, I'm going to punch him." He jerked his head toward Odette. "Whatever she needs, you get it for her. No matter how weird her request."

"Got it. I…" His eyes softened, his brow pinching.

"Don't you dare say you're gonna miss me or any bullshit like that." He was having a hard enough time keeping it together for Odette. If his friend started blubbering, he might lose it right there in front of her. "Get in there and be quiet."

Noah nodded and shuffled to the laundry room to join the pack, and James followed Odette into the bedroom, setting the alligator head on the dresser.

She paused by the bed and ran her hand across the cream-colored duvet. "Now that I've had you in this bed, I won't be able to sleep in it without you."

"Come here." He hugged her tight and caught her mouth in a tender kiss. He started slow, gently brushing her lips with his, but as the reality that this would be their last kiss settled in, he tangled his hands in her hair and drank her in.

Her fingers dug into his back as she held him, and she leaned into him, returning his passion with an unbridled heat like nothing he'd ever felt before. He'd barely scraped the surface of her cool and refined shell. If he'd had more time with her, he could imagine the ecstasy they could have shared.

Her sweet scent. The warmth of her body. The softness of her curves. She was built to be in his arms, and this was the most wonderful, painful moment he'd felt in his entire life. "I love you, Odette."

"I love you too." Her lips moved against his, her sweet breath sending shivers down his spine.

What he would have given to make this moment last forever.

But a bang sounded against the window, the pane rattling with the impact. James spun around, shoving Odette behind his back and widening his stance. The silhouette of a hand with elongated fingers slammed against the glass, and the piercing screech of claws dragging down the pane resonated in his ears. He reached for the gator head, ready to let *L'Acallemon* kill the bastard, but Odette stopped him with a hand on his arm.

"Let him come inside first. If he senses the Gator Man, he might run."

His heart pounding in his throat, James clutched her hand and lowered his arm to his side. His wolf howled inside him, begging to be released, but James held on to his humanity a little longer. His human side had to be fully in control in order to accept the Voodoo Spirit into his body.

The creature outside grunted and shattered the glass with a fist. Uncurling its claws, it gripped the windowsill and hauled itself into the opening. Squatting on the ledge, its legs resembled canine haunches, the knees bending backward with an extra joint below the hip jutting forward. Its fingers extended into sharp, black claws, and its face… Good God, its face.

The skin appeared half-melted, while the bone structure looked stuck mid-shift between human and wolf. Its
nose and mouth jutted forward in a short, malformed
muzzle, and its pointed human ears sat too high on its
head—above the temple, but not quite where a wolf's
would be.

Odette gasped, and the beast jerked its head toward
them, a menacing sneer curving what was left of its lips
over canine teeth. It lowered itself into the bedroom and
straightened to its full six-and-a-half-foot height.

"The bitch dies first." Its gravelly voice sounded more
like a growl.

James released Odette's hand and stepped forward.
"Not a chance." He reached for the alligator head and
shouted, "Now, Odette."

She began the ritual, asking the Spirit for help, and
the beast snarled as its head morphed into a wolf with
glowing red eyes and razor-sharp teeth. The Rougarou
lunged, swiping the gator head from James's hands, and
it slid across the room, slamming into the wall with a
thud.

"Damn it. Noah! Luke!" He was no match for this
beast in his human form, but he needed that head before
he shifted. With his arms stretched wide, he backed
Odette into the hall.

But the beast moved like lightning, gripping James's
shoulders and tossing him aside as if he were weightless.
His head slammed into the hardwood floor, and his vision
spun as he scrambled to his feet. He righted himself, and
the room tilted on its side. *Not now.* He couldn't afford to
black out.

Odette screamed, and his heart stopped for a beat or
two before pounding against his ribs. He would not let

that thing hurt his fate-bound. Grabbing the gator head, he placed it on his own and raced into the hallway.

Luke howled, and the other wolves joined in, charging the Rougarou as it advanced on Odette. Luke swiped a paw across its back, and it reeled, spinning and running into the foyer. Odette locked eyes with him and quickly called on the Spirit, her magic intensifying, filling the room with a static charge.

Noah glanced between them, rubbing the goose bumps from his arms. "I'm going to miss you, buddy, but I know you've got this."

James closed his eyes and invited *L'Acallemon* inside him, relinquishing control and giving himself over to the Spirit. The top of his head heated, and vibrating magic bore into his skull, filling first his head, and then his entire body with Spirit energy.

He looked at Odette and opened his mouth to tell her goodbye, but the Spirit took over, using James's magic to transform him into his wolf, absorbing the gator head into his form.

———

As his paws hit the ground, James darted down the hall toward the fray. Odette started to follow the sounds of snarling beasts, but Noah stopped her with a hand on her arm.

He jerked it away and rubbed his palm on his jeans. "Is he possessed now? Like, that's not James anymore?"

"The Gator Man is inside him. I don't know how much control he has. If *L'Acallemon* were a loa, James would have no control." And a little dizziness would be the only symptom he'd experience when it was done.

She paced toward the fight, keeping Nicolas in her peripheral vision. The ghost needed to see what was about to happen if he was ever to be free from this realm.

"And it's going to kill him?" Noah followed on her heels.

"*Probably* going to kill him. It might not." *I hope it won't.*

She rounded the corner as a sandy-colored wolf and a light-brown one sprang toward the Rougarou, each one clamping onto a shoulder. The beast cried out, hurling its lanky arms in circles, throwing the wolves to the ground. Damn, that thing was strong.

The Rougarou lunged for James, biting into his back as it clung to his gray fur. James spun, snapping his jaws at the beast, but he couldn't reach. Dark-red blood soaked his coat around the puncture, and he stumbled.

Odette gripped the doorjamb to stop herself from running into the fight. Would he heal instantly if his soul were whole? They hadn't mentioned his problem to Emile. How much would his weakness hinder his ability to stop the monster?

The beast snarled, wrapping its arms around James's chest, and he let out a pained yelp. Odette's heart raced at a .hummingbird's pace. The Gator Man Spirit was supposed to make James stronger. He was supposed to kill the Rougarou. She had to do something.

Fisting her hands, she inhaled a deep breath and called upon her power. Her energy built, emptying the room of its buzzing life energy, filling it with the static emptiness of the spirit world.

The Rougarou hesitated, glancing at her, and the reddish wolf rammed into the beast and knocked it to the ground before sinking its teeth into the creature's malformed leg. It cried out in pain, and the two other wolves gripped its upper arms, spreading it out on the floor as James loomed over it, one paw pressing down on its chest.

James growled, peeling his lips back over his teeth, and positioned his head to strike the killing blow.

"Wait." Odette poured her magic into Nicolas, filling the ghost with energy until he became as solid as a living being.

"Holy shit." Noah stood next to her, his eyes wide as he stared at the specter. "Is that a ghost? Has he been here the whole time?"

She ignored him, focusing her attention on Nicolas. The spirit's brow lifted, his expression becoming even more confused. "Serafine?"

"This is who killed Serafine. Look at him, Nicolas. He's your brother. He killed you too."

The ghost floated toward the creature and peered down at it. "Antoine?"

The Rougarou shifted, a sickening sloshing sound filling the room as its face transformed into the half-human abomination it was when it broke in. James growled again, shifting his weight forward, onto the beast.

Turning its head toward Nicolas, the Rougarou winced in pain before its eyes widened. "Brother, have mercy," it croaked.

Nicolas shook, a rage filling his ghostly form as he gathered more of Odette's energy. "You don't deserve mercy." Gripping the table in the foyer, Nicolas flung it across the room. It hit the wall with a crash, the wood splitting and falling to pieces on the floor.

"That's enough, Nicolas." Odette reined in her power,

the high of opening herself to the other realm dissipating as the spirit grew transparent.

Nicolas grasped at a broken table leg, but his hand passed through the wood. He grunted and whirled to face Odette. "He must pay for his crimes."

"He will, but his curse has bound his soul to the earth. *L'Acallemon* can break the bond and end his life."

The Rougarou struggled, yanking its leg from the red wolf's grasp. James snarled and delivered the killing blow, clamping his maw on the creature's throat. He held on, his wolf form convulsing as *L'Acallemon* ripped the curse from the creature's body, scattering the dark magic into the universe.

The Rougarou gasped, a gurgling sound emanating from its throat as its face finally made the full transformation back to human, and the life in its eyes dimmed. Antoine's soul lifted from his body, and Odette called on her power again to force him to cross over.

The spirit disappeared, whisked away to the underworld, where he could never harm a living being. They had broken the cycle. She'd never have to die in her lover's arms again.

She allowed herself a single breath of relief, but no more. Killing the Rougarou had been the easy part.

The wolves released the body and backed away, their gazes locked on Antoine's lifeless form. Seemingly satisfied that the creature was dead, Luke shifted, a mist gathering around his fur, elongating his body until he stood erect, and then disappearing into his human form.

The other wolves followed their alpha's lead, shifting to human form, their faces bright with satisfaction that they'd rid the world of such a terror.

But Odette's nightmare had just begun.

James shifted, rising to his feet as *L'Acallemon* ripped from his body. The mummified alligator head tumbled to the floor, shattering into dust on impact. The Gator Man had been created for a single purpose: to fight the Rougarou. With the threat extinguished, the magic holding the Spirit together dissipated into the atmosphere, leaving James drained and dying.

He collapsed into her arms, and she lowered him to the floor, her heart beating a frantic rhythm in her throat as she held him tight to her chest. "Please, Baron, don't take him yet." If her *met tet* took James, he'd have to take her too.

"What's wrong with him?" Luke dropped to his knees beside them. "Alexis, heal him."

Alexis knelt and put her hand on the bite mark on his back. "Unless that thing was venomous, this wound shouldn't be fatal." She closed her eyes for a long blink and opened them with a confused expression. "The wound is healed. I don't sense any poison, but he's slipping. His heart…it's not beating."

Odette loosened her grip, letting James slide from her lap, and gently laid him on the floor. Sitting back on her heels, she focused on his lifeless body, waiting for his soul to ascend, and a sob lodged in her throat. Or was that her heart wrenching from her chest?

This was not the end. She would be with him forever —one way or another. "Please, Baron Samedi, I need your help. I'll keep my promise; name the price."

She dropped her walls, opening herself to every ounce of magic the loa had blessed her with. No more restraint. No more self-imposed blocks on her power. Rising to her feet, she let it all go and focused on her connection to the spirit realm. She wasn't merely a conduit; she became a portal, an open doorway to the other side, the energy flowing through her like the river Styx through Hades.

"Jesus Christ, it's getting cold in here." Cade rubbed at his arms.

"Well?" Luke gave Alexis a pointed look, but their conversation barely registered. Odette stood with one foot in the spirit world.

"I can't heal him. Nothing is broken." Alexis's tone raised an octave with her panic.

"Start CPR." Luke began chest compressions, and Odette wandered into her altar room.

James and Nicolas stood side-by-side, two parts of a single soul, and Odette's chest ached at the sight of the spirits. Her magic had solidified them, but the werewolves were too concerned with his body to notice his soul. The commotion in the other room dulled to a hum as James drifted toward her.

A sad smile curved his lips, and the love in his eyes made her breath catch. "I told you I wouldn't let you die in my arms."

"Yeah, but you weren't supposed to die in mine." Something between a laugh and another sob bubbled up from her chest. Where was Baron Samedi?

James ran his fingers down her face leaving a trail of warmth on her skin and giving her hope. The heat meant his soul remained, not just his spirit energy. "Why can I touch you? Is your magic doing this?"

She nodded. "I'm giving you everything I've got."

"That's all I ever wanted."

Like it or not, he was about to get more. Holding her arms to her sides in the most open posture she could manage, she lifted her chin and made one final plea to her *met tet*. "Baron Samedi, grant me the power to mend this fractured soul. My body is yours. I open myself to your magic." She absorbed the deep blue of her soulmate's eyes. "I refuse to live without him."

Baron Samedi's presence pressed on her shoulders, building in intensity as the temperature in the room plummeted. She exhaled a breath of fog, and her body hummed with new power: Magic so pure and white that her fear crumbled, her core filling with warm light. The magic to heal a soul.

Holding her arms in front of her, she motioned for the spirits to come toward her. As they approached, she took James's face in her left hand and Nicolas's in her right. Both men were warm and soft to the touch, almost as if they were alive.

"Breathe, dammit," Luke shouted behind her, as the werewolves continued CPR, trying in vain to bring James back to life.

Odette stroked her thumb across her soulmate's cheek and gently pushed the spirits together. "What hate and greed fractured, let love mend."

The spirits glowed, bright golden light surrounding them both as they joined into one. As the light subsided, only James remained, a complete soul, ready to be reborn whole.

"Thank you, sweetheart. I promise I'll find you in the next life."

Odette shook her head. "I'm not living another minute without you by my side."

"What?" He reached for her, but she withdrew her magic, and his arm passed through her. "Odette."

"I'm ready, Baron Samedi. Take me."

"You can't... He won't let you die." Panic creased

James's forehead. "Noah! Cade, stop her!" His friends couldn't hear his screams.

Odette swayed, letting an imaginary rhythm guide her movements as if she were dancing at a ritual. She spun and stomped, lifting her hands to the sky and clapping out a beat. Calling on her *met tet* to take her.

"Are you okay?" Noah hesitated in the doorway, his arched brow and concerned gaze indicating he thought she'd clearly gone insane.

"Are you going to keep your promise? Do anything I ask?" Her rhythm increased with the vibrating energy pulsing through her. Baron Samedi's presence pressed harder on her shoulders, giving her one last chance to change her mind, but she was doing this. Fear was no longer an option, and the block she had created all those years ago dissolved with her determination.

"Yeah." Noah shuffled into the room. "What do you need?"

"Get ready to catch me." She took a deep breath and invited the loa inside her.

An electric shock ricocheted through her body, paralyzing her. She collapsed into Noah's arms, and he guided her to a chair.

"What's wrong? What's happening?" He straightened her head and situated her feet flat on the floor.

She tried to speak. To tell him her *met tet* had possessed her, but she had no control of her body. Instead, her eyes opened wide, and her lips curved into what felt like a Cheshire grin. Her body rose against her will, Baron Samedi in complete control, and she sauntered toward the altar.

Picking up the small bottle of rum, she uncapped it and tossed back the contents. The liquor warmed her throat, and she expected a light-headed sensation to form, but she felt no effects from the drink.

Her gaze locked on the top hat sitting atop the fabricated skull, and her hand reached toward it, her finger brushing the brim. All of her senses remained intact. She was like a puppet, the master residing in her own head.

Her hands trailed down her sides and up her stomach to cup her breasts. "Nice," her voice said aloud. "If I had access to a body like this, I'd never leave the bedroom." She glanced at James's ghost. "You're a lucky man," the Baron made her say with his Haitian accent.

She put on the hat and sunglasses and took a cigar from the mantel. "Tell your friends to stop. Whether he lives or dies is up to me."

"Uh, guys." Noah waved a hand, his brow creased in concern. "She said to stop."

"Bullshit." Luke continued the chest compressions.

"I said stop!" Her commanding voice rose above the noise, and Luke froze with his hands on James's chest. Though it was impossible to tell where her magic ended and Baron Samedi's began, that power had felt like her own. "Not bad," the Baron made her say, clearly impressed with her ability.

James's spirit floated in front of her. "Baron Samedi." He bowed his head and pressed his hands together in prayer. "Please don't take Odette. She deserves to live a full life."

"I gave her this life. Don't you think I know that, son?" He made her head turn. "Noah, go to the kitchen and get me a decent-sized bottle of rum. This flask ain't gonna do it. And I need a sprig of rosemary, some betel nut, anise seed, and henbane. And a cup of water."

Had she been in control of her body, her heart would

have been racing. Not only could Baron Samedi move and speak through her, but he had access to her knowledge, her memories too. And the combination of herbs he'd requested would be lethal for anyone to ingest.

"Yes, ma'am." Noah scurried to the kitchen.

"Bring his body in here by my altar." She stepped aside, and Luke and Cade obeyed, carrying James into the room and laying him on the floor.

Alexis followed, and the Baron sidled next to her. "Hey there, sweet thing."

"What the hell?" Alexis stared into her eyes, squinting her own as the realization hit. "Guys, I don't think Odette is here right now." She snapped her fingers in front of Odette's face, and Baron Samedi made her grin widen. "Who are you?"

"I'm Death, of course. Who did you expect?" Baron Samedi laughed and settled Odette's form on the floor next to James's body, James's spirit hovering by her side.

"Here's everything you asked for." Noah put the ingredients on the floor next to her.

James covered the herbs with his hands. "That combination will kill her. You can't drink that."

The Baron reached her hand through the spirit and picked up the henbane. "The woman wants to spend forever by your side, man. Stop complaining." Breaking the root apart, she dropped it into the cup of water. "Where's my rum?"

"It's here." Noah handed it to her. "I couldn't carry it all."

"When you're in the presence of a Ghede, boy, the rum always comes first." She unscrewed the cap and sucked down a third of the bottle. Surely now she'd feel the effects. If she'd been the one doing the swallowing, she'd have gagged. Thrown up all over the floor. Instead, she wiped her mouth and set the bottle down, feeling nothing but a tingle on her tongue. "That's more like it."

Closing her eyes, she took a deep breath, and the room vibrated with energy. The werewolves moved closer, encroaching on the sacred space Baron Samedi was creating, so she opened one eye and flicked a hand. "Go stand by the wall, all of you."

So much power filled her words not even the alpha argued. They all shuffled to the wall and stood obediently, their gazes trained on James's body lying on the floor.

She settled back into a trance, and her mouth began forming words she didn't understand. A chant in Haitian Creole flowed from her lips, but she didn't need to comprehend the syllables. The power building in her core was unmistakable.

Her body swaying from side to side, she rubbed her hands together, the friction building a heat almost unbearable on her skin. Pressing her hands to James's forehead, the ancient energy flowed through her arms and into his body, a connection forming between them as thick and strong as an iron cable running from her heart to his.

As the heat on her skin subsided, she crushed the remaining herbs and dropped them into the water before placing a piece of betel nut over both of James's eyes. Another Haitian prayer rolled off her tongue, more magic building in her core.

The calmness Baron Samedi exuded over her body was killing her. She needed her heart to race, her hands to tremble, her lungs to expel a scream. Anything to release the pressure inside her. If the Baron called on another ounce of magic, she would explode.

Reaching a steady hand to the cup, she picked it up, and James's spirit tried in vain to knock it from her grip.

Ghostly tears filled his eyes as he clutched his hands in front of his chest. "Please, Baron, I'm begging you. Spare her life."

A wry smile curved her lips, and she tossed the contents onto James's lifeless face. As the mixture splashed across his skin, a searing sensation ripped through her body, Baron Samedi taking his leave. Her stomach lurched as she collapsed onto her back, her vision tunneling until darkness consumed her.

CHAPTER NINETEEN

JAMES GASPED, HIS QUICK INHALE SUCKING THE Voodoo concoction into his nostrils. The mixture burned and rolled to the back of his throat, causing a coughing fit to wrack his chest. A commotion ensued around him, and the sound of shoes shuffling on the wood and his name being called repeatedly grated in his ears, making his head pound.

He rolled to his side and sputtered the last of the liquid from his orifices before opening his eyes. Odette lay next to him, her arm draped across her forehead, her eyes closed.

The pounding in his head subsided, and he registered the activity around him. Noah knelt by his side, resting his hand on his shoulder. "James? Are you okay? Is that…are you *you?*"

He blinked and turned his head toward his friend, squinting through his blurred vision. He was breathing, wasn't he? And awake. Why the hell were they so concerned with him when Odette lay unconscious on the floor?

Turning back to his fate-bound, he cupped her face in his hand, running his thumb across her soft cheek. Was she herself? *That* was the obvious question his friends should have been asking, and he'd tell them so if he could find his voice.

Odette stirred beneath his touch, nuzzling into his hand, a tiny smile playing on her lips. A very Odette-like smile. Cool relief flushed through his chest. Baron Samedi wouldn't nuzzle against him like this.

"James." Concern filled the alpha's voice, but James didn't miss the irritation edging his tone. Luke would want answers, though he'd probably figured most of it out by now.

He braced his forearm against the floor, propping himself up.

Luke rushed toward him. "Lie down for a while. You were dead for a good ten minutes."

"I'm fine." He pushed to sitting and rubbed a hand across his chest. He was better than fine. More life surged through his veins than he'd ever felt before. He held his hand up, and the collective gasp added to his own astonishment. He held the other hand up and turned them both over several times. He had all ten fingers. "How the hell?"

Odette really had made him whole, just like she'd promised.

A soft *mmm* emanated from her throat, and she rolled to her side, blinking her eyes open. With a small gasp, she sat up, clutching her head as she swayed. "James." She threw herself into his arms, climbing into his lap and burying her face in his neck.

Her magic danced across his skin, mingling with his with an intensity he'd never felt before. A shared connection, like she was actually a part of him now. He tightened his arms around her, soaking her in, the emotions compressing in his chest, expanding into an ache that consumed him. *Mine*, his wolf said with a penetrating fierceness. As if the man needed to be reminded.

He kissed her forehead and stroked her hair before glancing up at his alpha, silently telling him they were okay.

Luke nodded. "Cade, Alexis, take care of the body. Noah, clean up the mess and make note of what repairs are needed."

Noah clapped James on the shoulder as he rose to his feet. "I'm glad you're back, man."

"Me too." Cade nodded.

"I'd have been fine without you." Alexis grinned before heading into the foyer with Cade.

James pressed his lips to Odette's ear. "You scared me. I thought you were going to kill yourself."

Lifting her head, she brushed her lips to his. "I told Baron Samedi I'd pay any price to be with you. How that happened was up to him."

He pulled her close, nuzzling into her hair, the overwhelming feeling of sheer joy bringing tears to his eyes, tightening his throat. "And I asked him not to let you die."

"I guess he had no choice but to bring you back, then."

He tried to laugh, but it came out as a muffled sob. "We owe your *met tet* big time."

"We have the rest of our lives to pay him back, and I plan to enjoy every minute of it." She kissed him, and the magical connection flared, fire shooting through his veins.

He held her closer, sliding his fingers into her hair and

kissing her harder. He owed his life to this woman. She'd mended his soul, her love making him whole.

Pressing his forehead to hers, he held her face in his hands. "Thank you for saving my life...and for this." He held up his hand, wiggling his new finger.

"That was a gift from Baron Samedi. I didn't know he could do that." Taking his hand in hers, she trailed her lips from the base of his pinkie to the top, sucking the tip into her mouth. Her dark eyes bore into his soul, and an inferno ignited in his core.

He leaned in, taking her mouth with his again, unable to stop the possessive growl from rolling through his chest. *Mine. Forever.*

Luke cleared his voice, and James reluctantly broke the kiss to address his alpha. "I know you need answers." He glanced into his eyes and lowered his gaze, his silent admission that he'd done wrong by the pack, not telling them...or at least Luke...the truth about *L'Acallemon*.

"I expect you in my office tomorrow afternoon with a full report. You both deserve some rest after that ordeal. If you want to call it rest." A smile tugged at his lips, but he flattened it. "But I do have a rule about my crew sleeping with clients. You remember that, right?"

James fought a grin. "Sure do, boss. That's one rule I intend to follow."

Luke nodded. "I'll leave you to it then."

Odette stood, pulling James up with her. "Thank you for your help and for cooperating with Baron Samedi." She offered her hand to shake, and Luke accepted.

"You...*he* didn't give us much choice." Luke crossed his arms.

"I hope you know that I had no ill intent in any of this. We were only trying to stop the Rougarou."

The alpha narrowed his eyes at her and cut his gaze to James. "He trusts you. I trust his judgment. James, my office tomorrow at noon."

"Got it." James shook his hand. Luke knew better than anyone that when fate chose a werewolf's mate, there was no use fighting it. Fate would never match a were with anyone less than perfect for him.

The alpha sauntered through the foyer and out the front door, closing it behind him. Silence enveloped the home as James eyed the mess left behind. The dented, cracked drywall would have to be replaced, and the small table was toast. Dark-red blood stained the wood floor where the body had lain, and he bent to get a closer look. "I think we can sand this out. The repairs will add another three days onto the timeline, but we were ahead of schedule anyway."

"And the bedroom window?" Odette stood next to him, and he ran his hands up her shapely legs as he rose to his feet.

With his arms around her waist, he pressed a kiss to the curve where her neck met her shoulder. "We'll fix that too. Everything will be perfect," he whispered against her skin.

"Mmm… You are so good at scattering my thoughts and turning my knees to jelly." She pulled from his embrace and picked some dried herbs from his forehead. "But we need to get that window covered so no critters get in tonight."

He didn't hide the disappointment in his sigh. "Always the responsible one." She was right though, and the sooner they took care of the mess, the sooner he could take care of her.

She laughed. "One of us has to be. I'll set up a temporary protection spell, and you cover the window with plastic."

He let out another overdramatic sigh and slumped his shoulders, fighting a grin. "Yes, ma'am."

"And when you're done with that, you're going to make up for dying on me." She crossed her arms, lifting her chin as if daring him to challenge her order.

"How am I going to do that?" He placed his hands on her hips.

She gripped his wrists, pulling his arms together and pressing them into his chest. "However you see fit, as long as you make me scream your name."

Oh, he'd make her scream. Again and again. "Deal."

James cleaned up the glass and covered the window in fifteen minutes flat, thoughts of how he would make amends with Odette making his dick harder than a lead pipe. He adjusted his jeans and shuffled into the kitchen to find her leaning against the counter, sipping a glass of spiced rum.

He stopped in the entry, resting his hand against the jamb and admiring his fate-bound. Her dark jeans hugged her curvy hips, and the V-neck of her black shirt revealed enough of her delicate collarbone to make his mouth water in anticipation of exploring the rest of her soft, dark skin.

She smiled as he sauntered toward her, and she picked up another glass of rum. "Have a drink."

"I'd rather have you." Gripping her hip, he closed the distance between them. Her warm vanilla scent mixed with the spices of the rum, and he leaned in, gliding his tongue along her lip. She opened for him, deepening the kiss for a moment before pulling back and offering him the glass.

"You'll have me in time." She grinned. "We have plenty of that now."

"That we do." He took the glass and clinked it against hers before taking a long sip. "You didn't get enough of this stuff earlier? I think you downed half a fifth."

"Baron Samedi took it with him. This one." She gently rocked her glass. "Is for us." She drained the contents and set it on the counter. "The Baron also took what was left of Nicolas's spirit energy. Your soul is complete, and the ghost has crossed over. This is the first time we've been truly alone in this house."

"And all I can think about is making you scream my name, yet here you stand, cool as a popsicle." He sipped the rum and set his glass next to hers.

"Oh, I'm plenty hot, James. Don't worry about that. But I've been thinking."

The intensity in her gaze made his throat thicken, and he swallowed the dryness from his mouth. "I'm thinking about getting you naked."

She suppressed a chuckle. "Take off your shirt."

"With pleasure." Finally, he was going to get this woman into bed. He yanked his shirt over his head and went straight for the button on his jeans.

"Uh-uh." She shook her head. "Just the shirt for now." Biting her bottom lip, she swept her heated gaze down his chest, the gesture feeling so much like a caress his stomach tightened.

"Your turn." He motioned with his hands toward her shirt. Whatever game she had planned, he'd be happy to play as long as they both ended up naked in the end.

With a sly grin, she tugged her shirt off and dropped it on the counter. "My entire life has been a practice in self-control. While I fully intend to fulfill my promise to

Baron Samedi and live in his image, giving up my old ways isn't going to be easy."

He stepped toward her, but she put up a hand to stop him, and he froze. "I can help you with that."

"I don't think I need to completely give up my control issues, though." Her grin widened. "Self-control can be quite erotic."

He chuckled. "How so?"

"Put your hands behind your back." She unclasped her bra and let it fall to the floor. "No touching."

Though his fingers twitched with the need to feel her supple breasts, he did as he was told. She slinked toward him, stopping a scant inch away, so close her breath warmed his neck as she moved her lips along his skin, not touching, but leaving a trail of fire in her wake.

She stepped away, the intensity of the moment pulling his breath out in a rush. His skin turned to gooseflesh, and a shiver ran up his spine. "What kind of magic are you using on me?"

"None at all, love. This is the power of desire." Unbuttoning her pants, she worked them over her hips and slipped them off her ankles, a thin strip of black satin the only thing left covering her.

His heart thrummed, and he reached for her, but she raised her hands again. "I said no touching. Not yet. Take off your pants."

"Your self-control is admirable, but mine is lacking. I'm not sure how much more of this I can take." He toed off his shoes and removed his pants, kicking them aside.

She arched a brow. "You'll take however much I want to give you."

A growl rolled up from his chest. Damn, this woman was hot. He'd never been keen on taking orders from anyone but the alpha, but Odette had him wrapped around her finger. He'd move the Earth for this woman.

He took an involuntary step toward her, and she laughed. "Control yourself. Let the anticipation build, and the release will be that much sweeter."

Straightening, he fisted his hands at his sides to stop them from reaching for her again. If she kept this up, he'd be releasing in his boxer-briefs.

"Take off your underwear." She shimmied hers down her legs and stepped out of them, standing before him magnificently naked, her warm, soft skin beckoning him.

With a shuddering inhale, he removed the rest of his clothes, his dick springing free from its constraints. Her gaze locked on his cock, and she slipped the tip of her tongue out to moisten her lips.

That tiny flash of pink nearly crumbled him. His dick ached to fill her. His hands twitched to feel her. If any more blood rushed from his head to his groin, he'd pass out. He ground his teeth, forcing his growl into words. "I need you, Odette."

"I need you too, James." She closed the distance between them, her tight nipples almost brushing his chest as she hovered her mouth near his, still not touching, building the heat between them. "So bad."

Good God, he wanted to touch her. To bend her over the counter and sink his cock deep inside her. This little game of control had him hotter than hellfire, his core trembling with a need like nothing he'd felt before.

She hovered her lips above his skin, trailing down his neck, his chest, his stomach, her breath the only thing touching him. It was a painfully wonderful, erotic sensation, and as a bead of moisture gathered on the end of his cock, she paused and licked her lips.

"I'd like to taste." She glanced up at him with fire in her eyes. "Do you want me to taste it?"

He fought to find his voice. "Yes. God, yes. Please." He was breathless, and the woman hadn't even touched him yet.

She flicked out her tongue, licking his tip, the warm velvet sensation sending a shudder through his body. He held his breath, waiting for more, but she straightened, moving so close his dick rested against her stomach.

The sensation of her soft skin against his tightened his balls, and searing electricity shot through his veins. His hands trembled, so he clenched them into fists behind his back. Raw, primal need churned in his core, and his wolf howled in his head, begging him to take her.

"You're doing very well." Her lips tickled his ear. "Are you thoroughly turned on yet?"

"I'm a Roman candle with a very short fuse, sweetheart." Every nerve in his body was firing on overdrive. The heat from her skin against his felt as good as anything she could have done with her hands. Well, not quite *as* good, but pretty damn close.

She smiled. "So I've proved my point?"

"Clear as day."

She finally touched him. Her fingertips glided across his shoulders and down his arms like liquid fire. "All right, James. Make me scream."

He didn't give her a chance to change her mind. Pouncing like a predator, he wrapped her in a tight embrace and planted his mouth on hers. Her lips parted on a gasp as he gripped her ass and lifted her from the ground, setting her on the countertop.

She parted her legs, and he dove to her center, lapping at her clit and reveling in the sweet taste of her as she tangled her fingers in his hair. Sucking her sensitive nub into his mouth, he slid two fingers inside. Her wet warmth clenched around them, her lustful moan melting in his ears like salted chocolate.

The taste of her on his tongue made him shiver. He wanted to savor her. To take his time pleasuring her, but she'd awakened a passion inside him that he couldn't hold back any longer. They had the rest of their lives for savoring each other. Right now, he needed to be inside her.

Sliding her from the counter, he gently pushed her against the wall, covering her body with his, their magic entwining so he couldn't tell where hers ended and his began.

Mine. Possessiveness clenched in his chest, his wolf reminding him of his claim.

Grabbing her thigh, he lifted her leg to his hip and pressed against her opening. She gripped the back of his neck and held his gaze with fiery passion in her eyes. In one swift thrust, he filled her, and her gasp danced in his ears.

He lifted her other leg, wrapping it around his waist, and she leaned back against the wall for leverage, matching his thrusts as he slid in and out of her, maddening friction igniting every nerve in his body.

His climax coiled tight in his core, and he held her ass with one hand, stroking her clit with his thumb.

She clutched his shoulders, her nails digging into his skin as a beautiful, erotic moan flowed up from her chest. "Oh, James." She shuddered, her center contracting around him as he thrust faster and harder.

His release unfurled in his groin, and he leaned into her, his knees nearly buckling beneath him. His orgasm overtook him, slicing through his soul and mending the broken pieces, making him stronger than ever before. As his breathing slowed, he slipped out of her, lowering one of her legs to the floor.

"I'm not sure I can stand up after that." She laughed, clutching his shoulders with trembling arms. "Sweet Spirits, that was intense."

"I've got you, sweetheart." Slipping an arm behind her knees, he cradled her against his chest and carried her to the bedroom. He snuggled under the covers next to her, holding his fate-bound in his arms. "You weren't kidding about that control thing. That was the hottest sex in…the history of sex."

"Finding balance is important. I don't have to change who I am to embrace my wilder side." She rested her head on his shoulder and draped her leg across his waist.

"You don't need to change a thing. You're sheer perfection." His need satiated, he drifted in and out of sleep, comfortable, but unwilling to give in to slumber just yet. Spending every single day with this woman for the rest of his life wouldn't be enough, and closing his eyes seemed like a waste of the time they had left. Even if it was forever.

"James." She lifted her head to look at him. "You told Luke you intended to follow his rule about not sleeping with clients."

He brushed a curl from her forehead. "Yes, I did."

"You haven't broken that rule; you've shattered it to pieces. What will you tell him?" She rested a hand on his chest, and he covered it with his own.

"There's a caveat to that rule: don't sleep with a client, unless you plan on taking her as your mate."

Grinning, she propped her head on her hand. "I see.

Well, I wouldn't want you to get in trouble with your boss."

"I don't plan to." He returned her smile. "Odette, will you be my mate?"

"I always have been, James, and I always will be. In this life and every one that comes. Forever."

EPILOGUE

Odette signed off on the catering order and turned to scan the scene. Twinkling lights draping from massive oaks illuminated the park, and a jazz band occupied the stage, tuning their instruments in preparation for the party. The October air had an early fall bite, and she pulled her lavender shawl up around her shoulders to chase away the chill.

James stood in the back of the VIP tasting tent, nervously turning the bottles so all the labels faced forward. The pack had lent some of their members to help, and Amber, the owner of O'Malley's, slapped at James's hand and shooed him away.

After Odette's comment about liking his facial hair, James had let his beard grow in fully, giving her already-rough-around-the-edges werewolf a rugged, even more masculine look. He bent over to hide a power cord beneath a table, and she admired the view of his backside. She'd spent every day with the man for the last four months, and she still couldn't get enough of him.

She strode toward him and slipped a hand beneath the

back of his shirt. "They have placards. It's okay if the bottles are turned."

"I know." He grinned and pulled her to his side. "I'm just trying to make everything perfect for the first-annual Baron Samedi Festival."

"You can't call it annual unless it happens more than once, and this will only happen again if it's a success."

"It will be. You'll see."

Loosening the reins at the distillery had been the hardest part of her promise to the Baron. She'd found balance in every aspect of her life, James making sure she took a break to enjoy herself whenever she got too uptight. She went out with friends—his and hers—went dancing, communicated with the dead who approached her for help, and enjoyed life in general...something she hadn't done since she was a kid.

When she started playing music at the distillery, her employees had looked at her like she'd gone insane. When she had her intern plan the first company happy hour, they thought she'd been abducted and replaced with an alien replica.

The people around her were slowly starting to accept her new attitude toward life, and everyone from the distillery and the House of Voodoo had pitched in to make this tribute to Baron Samedi happen. If all went well, it would be an annual party to celebrate her *met tet* and all that he had done for her and James, and hopefully enlighten the attendees about the mystery of Voodoo in the process.

She took James's hand and guided him out of the tent. "Gates open in ten minutes."

"You've got this, sweetheart. I won't leave your side."

She leaned into him and took one last moment to

appreciate everyone's efforts. They had a children's section with inflatable bounce houses and an obstacle course. In addition to the VIP tasting tent, several booths with offerings of food and drinks were stationed around the festival grounds, and the Voodoo museum had an informative display set up across from the main stage.

Five vodouisants sat at tables beneath the trees, and Natasha waved her over. "Tyrell caught a stomach bug, so we're short one reader. Will five be enough?"

"If not, I can fill in as a medium. I'm sure there will be plenty of people who'd like to talk to lost loved ones." A familiar flutter beat in her stomach, but it died down as quickly as it had begun. Her powers weren't nearly as scary as they used to be.

Natasha shuffled her tarot cards. "Then who will run the show?"

"I'll take care of it," James said.

Natasha nodded. "You got yourself a good man right there."

"He's the best." She pressed a kiss to his cheek and waved as Noah approached.

"Hey, y'all. Sorry I'm late." Noah hugged Odette and shook James's hand. "Where do you need me?"

James glanced over his shoulder, a sly grin curving his lips. "I think Amber might need some help in the tasting tent."

"Dude." Noah's shoulders slumped, but his gaze drifted toward the tent as he shook his head. "I'd be better off selling tickets or something."

Odette cut her gaze between the two men. "What am I missing here?"

"He's had a thing for Amber since high school, but he's too chicken to do anything about it."

Noah's jaw tightened.

"She's nice." Odette followed his gaze toward the tent, where Amber stood, straightening her apron. "It doesn't hurt to talk to her, does it?"

"She's the alpha's sister." Noah shoved his hands in his pockets.

"So?" She looked at James for explanation.

"He's second-born, so he thinks he's not good enough to date someone with alpha blood."

She cocked her head. "Isn't the alpha's mate second-born? If she's good enough…"

"It's not the same." Noah pleaded with his gaze. "What else do you need help with?"

James slapped him on the shoulder. "Just the tasting tent. Hey, Amber?" He lifted a hand to get her attention. "Your help is here."

A genuine smile lit up her features, and something sparked in her bright-blue eyes. "Send him over."

"Ah, hell," Noah groaned.

"You'll survive." James gave him a push and laughed as Noah shuffled to the tent.

"That's the smile of a woman who is happy to see a man." She looked at James. "Can't he see that?"

"What we think about ourselves sometimes gets in the way of what we see right before our eyes."

She wrapped her arms around him. "I guess we know that better than anyone."

"We learned our lesson." He kissed her cheek. "He will too. Eventually."

ACKNOWLEDGMENTS

This book would not have been possible without the help of my friend James Corbyn. His Voodoo tour in New Orleans was the start of my research on the subject, and his guidance helped me understand the religion to the best of my ability. I hope I did it justice. Thanks, James.

I'd also like to thank my amazing friend and critique partner Kerri Keberly for reading every book in this series and helping me fill in the holes before sending it to my awesome editor, Victoria Miller. And Kaci Singer and my husband, Michel, for proofreading. These books wouldn't be what they are without their expertise. Thank you.

ABOUT THE AUTHOR

Carrie Pulkinen is a paranormal romance author who has always been fascinated with things that go bump in the night. Of course, when you grow up next door to a cemetery, the dead (and the undead) are hard to ignore. Pair that with her passion for writing and her love of a good happily-ever-after, and becoming a paranormal romance author seems like the only logical career choice.

Before she decided to turn her love of the written word into a career, Carrie spent the first part of her professional life as a high school journalism and yearbook teacher. She loves good chocolate and bad puns, and in her free time, she likes to read, drink wine, and travel with her family.

Connect with Carrie online:
www.CarriePulkinen.com

CPSIA information can be obtained
at www.ICGtesting.com
Printed in the USA
LVHW031555290519
619455LV00001B/24/P